OF DREAMS AND DESTINY

ALSO BY SANDHYA MENON

OF DREAMS
AND
DESTINY

A Rosetta Academy Novel

SANDHYA MENON

SIMON & SCHUSTER BFYR

NEW YORK   LONDON   TORONTO   SYDNEY   NEW DELHI

SIMON & SCHUSTER BFYR

An imprint of Simon & Schuster Children's Publishing Division
1230 Avenue of the Americas, New York, New York 10020

Text © 2023 by Sandhya Menon
Jacket illustration © 2023 by Anna Bucciarelli
Jacket design by Lizzy Bromley © 2023 by Simon & Schuster, Inc.

SIMON & SCHUSTER BOOKS FOR YOUNG READERS
and related marks are trademarks of Simon & Schuster, Inc.
For information about special discounts for bulk purchases, please contact Simon &
Schuster Special Sales at 1-866-506-1949 or business@simonandschuster.com.
The Simon & Schuster Speakers Bureau can bring authors to your live event.
For more information or to book an event, contact the Simon & Schuster Speakers Bureau
at 1-866-248-3049 or visit our website at www.simonspeakers.com.
Interior design by Tom Daly
The text for this book was set in Janson Text LT Std.
Manufactured in the United States of America
First Edition
2 4 6 8 10 9 7 5 3 1
CIP data for this book is available from the Library of Congress.
ISBN 9781534417601
ISBN 9781534417625 (ebook)

For Tiny, who asked for a DE book

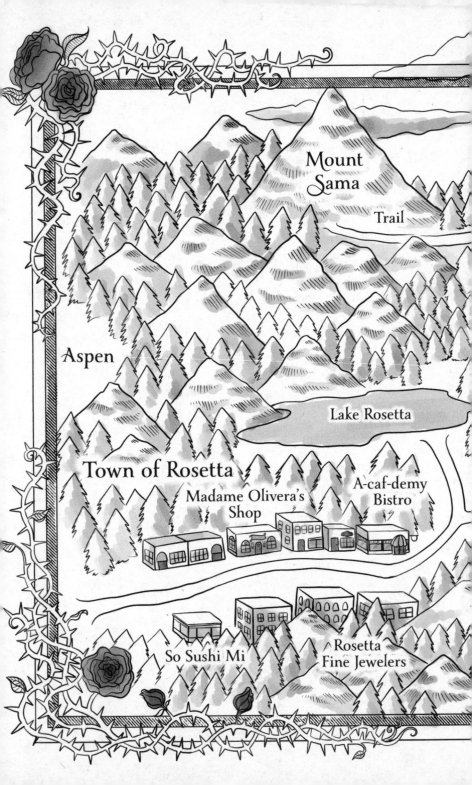

CHAPTER 1

Once upon a time, there was a princess who masqueraded as a whole person. But what people didn't know was that the princess was a doll made of pieces of sparkling glass. Some were shiny and sharp-edged enough to draw blood, others velveteen and rounded from years of being mishandled. Mostly, the princess was good at reflecting what everyone wanted to see: a vivacious, happy, charming girl fit to take over her parents' empire one day.

But for her eighteenth birthday, the princess, who'd never wanted for anything, got what she really *needed*—a fairy godmother. An otherworldly being, patient and kind, round-faced, with warm, twinkling eyes and a magic wand that spat stardust and magic wherever she pointed it. The fairy godmother took one look at the princess and knew just what she had to do: teach the princess to spin those broken pieces of glass into a strong, unbreakable heart that she could place back into her empty chest.

But could the princess do this without first pricking her finger and falling into a deep, everlasting sleep?

CHAPTER 2

DE

"Now, that's what I call a pile of magical bullshit." Daphne Elizabeth handed the self-help book disguised as a quirky coffee-table read back to Jaya, who tucked it away into her Rosetta Academy tote bag with a small smile. "Aren't we past the era of fairy godmothers and stardust? Why can't the princess just kick everyone's ass who wronged her and be done with it? Who says she needs to fix her heart anyway?"

Jaya raised a thick, manicured eyebrow at DE. "We could all use the occasional helping hand in the love department."

It was the last Saturday of spring break; classes would resume on Monday. DE had taken up Jaya's invitation for a girls' day out on the town, just walking around, eating gelato, and browsing Bookingham Palace, Jaya's favorite bookstore. It was a fine way to spend their last big break before graduation. DE glanced sidelong at Jaya, feeling a pang in her chest. In just under three months, they'd all be going their separate ways like points of light scattered to various corners of the world.

On impulse, she grabbed Jaya's mittened hand in hers. "You'll keep in touch, right? Even when you're wicked busy running your family's royal estate?"

Jaya's kind brown eyes bored into her. "Of course I will," she said in that regal British accent. "And you will too. After all, you get a four-year reprieve from running *your* family's hotel dynasty while you're away at Dartmouth." Jaya smiled. "Plenty of time for FaceTiming."

She said it with so much sincerity that DE nodded, pacified. "True, true." The sunlight was warm on her cropped red hair, and despite the chill still hanging in the air—Colorado wasn't quite done with winter's trappings yet—DE felt warmed through. At least her friendships were something she could count on. At least she still had that.

Kicking her boot through a giant snow pile, she said too casually, "And . . . what's the plan with you and Grey?"

Now Jaya's smile was bright enough to power the entire town of Rosetta. "We're still nailing down the specifics, but, um, I think we both want to take a gap year and travel. There are a few parts of rural Asia neither of us has seen, and we're desperate to do some charity work there."

"That's awesome." DE beamed at her friend's happiness, though her own heart felt small and remote in her chest. "I'm so happy you guys are so . . ." She whirled her own gloved hands around.

"So what?" Jaya pressed, frowning and tucking a dark curl behind an ear.

"You know. On the path toward 'first comes love, then comes marriage . . .' and all that stuff. Not to be too heteronormative about it. But it seems to be what you two want, so I'm happy for ya."

Jaya snuffed a laugh and elbowed DE. "Oh, stop it. We're light-years away from that. Right now we're just enjoying this . . . this season. Being together."

"Mm-hmm."

They crunched along the thin snow for a little bit, the occasional car or small SUV trundling by on the road beside them. Rosetta was still very much an old town; if the streets weren't exactly cobblestoned, you could *imagine* a time when they were. The storefronts had all been cultivated to maintain that old-timey look too, with faux gas lanterns and ornate scrollwork adorning most of them. They passed one called Casa del Tesoro, which was filled with what looked like antiques and high-fashion clothing, but it seemed to be permanently shuttered.

"You know that new boy . . . Alexander Murthy? I think he goes by Xander. I've talked to him a bit. He seems quite nice. Pleasant. And he's handsome, too." Jaya studiously rummaged in her tote bag as she said all this, as if it was just a casual nothing comment.

"Good for him," DE said quietly, feeling a ripple of defensiveness. She readjusted her favorite scarf—deep purple, with tiny silver moons embroidered on it—smoothing down each individual fringe.

Jaya looked up at her. At five foot four, she was a mere shrimp to DE's six-foot height. Sometimes DE wanted to pat the top of her head, but something told her this would be ill-advised.

"Maybe we could invite him to sit with us at lunch tomorrow," Jaya said. "He seems to be a bit of a loner, but maybe that's just because he hasn't been asked. It must be difficult, moving to a new school a few months before graduation, when friendships are already established."

DE looked Jaya right in the eye as they turned the corner onto a different tree-lined avenue. A couple of younger people from Rosetta Academy passed them, and both Jaya and DE smiled (well, Jaya smiled, DE tipped her chin). "What are you trying to do?"

Jaya held up her hands. "Nothing! I'm just saying I know what it's like to be the new kid, and it's never any fun."

"I'm sure Xander can make his own friends without you mother-henning him to death," DE said before she could put the brakes on her mouth. Seeing the brief flash of hurt on Jaya's face, she slung her arm around her friend's slender shoulders. "I'm sorry. I'm an ass." She sighed, watching her breath curl out of her in a white mist. "I'm just . . . really done with boys. You know?" Even saying it made her feel small, like she'd been weak enough to let Alaric suck the life out of her. Which wasn't the healthiest way to be thinking, she was pretty sure. And yet, there it was.

Jaya, oblivious to DE's spiraling thought process, nodded and squeezed her hand. "I know. But it's been a few months now since Alaric and . . . well, everything. Maybe it's time to get back on the horse? Or at least go near a stall?"

"You know the defining feature of horse stalls? They stink of horse shit." DE took her arm from around Jaya's shoulders. "No thanks."

"You're so resistant," Jaya mused, half to herself. "You remind me so much of Grey when we first met." She stopped and took a deep breath, turning to DE, her eyes bright. "But that's all right, because I have something planned that should help."

DE heard faint alarm bells. "Uh-oh. It's never good when you smile like that."

Jaya frowned. "Like what?"

"Like a deranged little helpful psychopath."

"This is going to be good. I promise." Without another word, she took DE's hand and ushered her across the slick road, the sunlight winking on crusts of ice and turning them into diamonds.

"Where are we *going*?" DE asked, focusing mainly on not losing her footing. If she fell, she'd definitely take Jaya down with her and then they'd both be run over by someone's Range Rover, and Grey would never forgive DE.

Coming to an abrupt stop in front of a store, Jaya raised her arms toward the sign. "Ta-da! The grand finale to our day out."

DE squinted in the sunlight as she looked up at whatever her friend was gesturing to. This was another one of those storefronts that had been made to look antiquated and charmingly ancient. The brick front had mottled with time, and two gas lanterns flanking its doors blazed invitingly against the frozen steel-gray sky. The sign was ornate and gold and proclaimed that this was the domicile of one MADAME OLIVERA, PSYCHIC AND CLAIRVOYANT.

DE's mouth in a flat line now, she turned abruptly to Jaya. "What—and I mean this in the politest way befitting a princess's sensitive ears—the fuck?"

"Come on!" Jaya squeezed her elbow, smiling beatifically like only she could. "It'll be fun. I know it sounds ridiculous, but I took Grey here once a long time ago and it was actually really helpful. The woman said some rather insightful things."

DE narrowed her green eyes. "You're right. . . . That does sound ridiculous."

"What do you have to lose?" Jaya shrugged as she adjusted the tote bag on her shoulder.

DE began counting on her gloved fingers. "Um, let's see: my dignity as a person, whatever money this person's going to charge, the ability to look myself in the eye in the mirror, the knowledge that I am a self-respecting member of society—"

"I've seen your Ouija board," Jaya cut in, quirking one corner of her mouth. "Don't tell me you don't believe at least a little in the occult."

"That Ouija board's a joke!" DE said unconvincingly. "Okay, it's mostly a joke. Okay, I've been hoping to make contact with my Nan. But seriously—this?" She threw a hand out at the psychic's storefront. "Really?"

As if on command, the front door popped open a few inches, just enough so the bell above the door chimed and a waft of hazy, cedarwood-scented incense wrapped its tendrils languidly around the two girls. They waited, but no one stepped out to greet them. It was like the door, hearing their conversation, had opened on its own.

DE and Jaya stared at each other, neither of them speaking. "C-coincidence," DE said finally, her throat scratchy.

Jaya opened her mouth to respond but was interrupted by the jangling of her cell phone from within her tote. Reaching inside, she checked the screen. "Oh no; it's Rahul. Grey needs me."

"What? Right now?"

"Yes." Jaya looked up at DE. "Apparently, he was hiking Mt. Sama and fell and cracked his knee on a rock. Rahul says it's not dire, but you know how Grey is. He's refusing to go to the infirmary. I should go convince him." She looked slowly from the ajar front door back to DE. "But you should go in. By yourself."

DE rolled her eyes. "No way. I'm coming with."

Jaya shook her head. "No, I'm serious, Daphne Elizabeth. I truly feel this is a sign. Maybe there's something here for you. Do this as a favor to me, if you won't do it for yourself."

DE blew out a gusty breath and regarded the weird front door. Had a breeze pushed it open? The gold lettering on the glass glinted in the waning sunlight, inviting her in. "Oh, fine," she said finally, a little intrigued in spite of herself. Jaya was right; she *did* have a soft spot for the occult.

Jaya squealed and hugged her. "I expect a full rundown later."

"Yeah, yeah." DE couldn't help a fond smile. "Now go kiss Grey's boo-boo all better."

Jaya giggled. "All right. You'll be okay getting back?"

"Yeah, I'll probably just walk. Or if it gets too cold, I can always text the school's car service."

With a final lifted hand in farewell, Jaya crossed the street and was gone. DE turned back to the agape door.

"Okay, Madame Olivera," she breathed quietly, stuffing her hands into her coat pockets. "Let's see what you've got."

CHAPTER 3

DE

The main room flickered with blue shadows, a small crystal chandelier overhead, and a few LED candles on a wooden shelf providing the only real illumination. A waterfall incense holder sent undulating waves of bluish-white smoke into the air, which she watched for a moment, mesmerized. There was a series of small rectangular windows high up on the tapestry-covered wall, but they were facing away from the sun and barely let in any daylight, as if they were blocked by unseen trees. There was a faded gold couch and a heavy wooden coffee table, but, as far as DE could see, no crystal balls, taxidermied ravens, or cat skulls. She found herself just slightly disappointed.

A silver beaded curtain in the corner parted slightly. "Yes?" a deep female voice called.

DE turned and squinted, trying to see better, but it was impossible. The incense had filled the space with a smoky haze, and the room beyond the beaded curtain seemed even darker than this one. "Um, hi. Hello. I'm here for . . . Madame Olivera?" She felt like a jackass just saying that obviously fake name.

"Ah, an inquisitive mind, a seeker of knowledge. How can I be of assistance?"

DE couldn't be sure, but she thought she saw two gleaming eyes judging, weighing, studying her through the beaded curtain. She took a step closer. "So, I hear that you're . . . a psychic?"

A flash of teeth. "I suppose that depends on who you ask. But if it's answers you're looking for, I think I could help."

Well, if she's not a psychic, she should be, DE thought. The roundabout answers, responses that could be taken in more than one way—she had the technique down, at least.

If DE went back empty-handed, she knew Jaya would be disappointed. Plus, it was a way to kill an hour. She shrugged. "Okay."

The curtain parted some more. "This way."

After just a moment's hesitation on the threshold, DE stepped over.

Madame Olivera's interior "lair" wasn't even as well-lit as the main room outside. *Jesus*, DE grumbled to herself. She was all for mood lighting and dramatic flair, but wasn't this a bit much?

The woman, who was leading the way to what looked like a small cluster of wicker furniture, turned and threw one arm out. It was covered with bracelets and bangles that clinked mutedly. Her face was heavily shadowed, and now DE realized it was because she was wearing a hat with a draping veil. DE couldn't even tell what ethnicity or age she was. She kinda wanted to ask where the woman had gotten the hat—it was *quite* the vibe—but decided against it.

"We shall begin momentarily," Madame Olivera intoned. "Sit where you please."

Fake voice: check. The woman had deepened her voice for sure and was pronouncing each consonant carefully, as if trying to disguise her real accent. DE chose a small wicker armchair with a hard-to-see floral pattern on the cushion.

"What's your name? Like, your *real* name? Madame Olivera's a stage name, right?" DE asked suddenly as Madame Olivera settled on the love seat across from her. Between them was a small wicker table with a glass top, the kind that you usually saw in old condos in beach towns. She wasn't sure why exactly she'd asked that, only that she was feeling increasingly out of control in this weird room, and Daphne Elizabeth McKinley hated feeling out of control.

The question gave the psychic pause. She looked at DE for a long minute, as if she'd never been asked that before. DE only had an impression of shrewd and calculating eyes, watching her from behind the thick veil. The fact that she couldn't see this woman while the woman could see her—well, as much as was possible in this dark cave of a room, anyway—was more than a little unnerving. "Is it important that you know my name?"

DE shrugged and looked around, making note of the shelf in the corner that glinted dimly with apothecary bottles, a huge rough crystal—maybe amethyst—and what looked like varying sizes of sticks and twigs from the forest.

"I don't know. I've never been to a psychic before." DE turned back to face the woman, infusing her voice with a confidence she didn't quite feel in the moment. "But I think I can make an educated guess about how this is supposed to go. You help me feel comfortable and like you have all the answers, then I ask you my question and you make me feel better about all my regrettable life choices. Right?"

A suggestion of white teeth from behind the veil. The woman was smiling at her. "You seem to have a very good idea of how this is all going to work."

DE snorted and leaned back in her chair, which creaked softly. "No disrespect to you, but I know this is all an assembly line. It's like any other business: get the customer in, give them what they need, get paid, get them out. And on to the next one and the next one. Repeat customers are, of course, gold, so you always want to give people good news."

Madame Olivera (DE guessed she wasn't going to reveal her real name, after all) cocked her veiled head, her voice genuinely curious. "Then why are you here?"

DE waved a hand toward the door. "Oh, my friend. Jaya. She saw you before, and she's desperate to help me."

Madame Olivera waited, and DE squirmed in the silence. "Do you need help?" There was no judgment in the woman's voice, still only curiosity.

DE ran her finger over the glossy wicker on the arm of her chair, her eyes on her lap. "My friends definitely think I do. And I guess any shrink would tell you that too. But I think . . . it's complicated. Sometimes when you get hurt, you should rally and fight back and all that shit. But other times, you should take it as a warning, you know? You should take it as a sign from the universe that you need to sit the hell down and keep to yourself."

DE looked up, expecting Madame Olivera to express confusion, or maybe even tell her that she was right, she definitely needed help, and oh, by the way, here was the number to a really good therapist. But the psychic just continued to look at her, the veil obscuring her face, just a hint of glittering (blue? Black?) eyes visible through the diaphanous fabric.

"And does keeping to yourself make you happy?"

DE considered the question, her chin in her hand, her legs crossed. "Dunno," she said finally. "I can't remember happiness anymore, to be honest. It feels like a song I heard a long time ago and then forgot." To her horror, she felt tears spring to her eyes, hot and unforgiving. "I'm sorry." Standing so suddenly the chair scraped backward, DE reached into her pocket. "I'll still pay you for your time. But I shouldn't have come in here." *And least of all unloaded my shit onto you, a literal stranger,* she added mentally.

"Please, stay." Madame Olivera waved away DE's money, but DE put it down on the table between them anyway. "We have much to talk about."

"Yeah, I don't think so. I mean, I appreciate you playing therapist or whatever, but—"

"You have to listen." The woman's cool, pale hand shot out and grabbed DE's wrist, bangles jangling. The movement was so quick, a lightning strike, really. DE hadn't even seen her move. And once she registered what was happening, she was too shocked to pull away. She could feel the pressing intensity of the woman's veiled gaze. "There's a storm coming, Daphne Elizabeth. Souls will slumber in the perpetual twilight . . . and one will perish. You must remember *you* have the key to vanquish the storm. Look into the past—and your heart—for the answers. Take down the walls you've built up, and you can save yourself."

DE stared at Madame Olivera, at her hand clasped so tightly around DE's wrist that the skin there was turning red. She tried to remember if she'd mentioned her own name and couldn't. "Um . . . yeah . . . I'm pretty sure any major storm like that would be reported on in the news, but . . . yeah. Thanks. For the warning." The last thing she wanted to do was set this woman off even more when she was clearly going through something. The door was just a few feet away; freedom would be hers if she could just play this right and get the hell out.

Madame Olivera paused, as if assessing DE's expression. Then she loosened her hand and let it drop. "Keep it," she said, to DE's confusion.

But then she realized the psychic had put something in her hand—a small square of silky-thin paper, insubstantial as smoke. DE slipped it into her pants pocket without looking at it and forced a smile. "Thanks, Mad—uh . . . this has been great. Really." Then, raising one hand, she backed out of the room and, when she got to the main area, turned and ran to the door.

She didn't stop running until she got to the sloping hill that would take her back to Rosetta Academy.

Jaya Rao was in *so* much trouble.

CHAPTER 4

DE

The senior common room was a hive of activity when DE got there. She lingered in the doorway for a minute, watching. Grey was sitting in a green velvet wingback chair in front of the gigantic fireplace, his enormous foot propped up on a matching footstool. His pants leg had been pulled up above the knee. Jaya knelt beside him with some gauze, while Rahul and Caterina sat observing in a nearby armchair, Caterina perched gracefully on Rahul's lap. That was still taking some getting used to—the unlikeliest couple in the entire school having fallen ass-over-forehead in love—but it was sweet in its own implausible way.

Jaya tutted over Grey's knee, pulling DE's attention back to the two of them. DE could tell that while he was definitely enjoying Jaya's ministrations, Grey was also growing more impatient by the minute.

"I'm fine, honestly," he insisted with the air of someone who'd said it sixteen times already, his big frame half squirming in the chair. "Seriously, Jaya, you don't have to do all that. Just come sit with me."

"This is a very deep cut!" Jaya protested, giving him a severe look. "You should be in the infirmary, getting stitches!"

"He *was* in the infirmary," Rahul put in, "but then he left. He told Nurse Gregory he only wanted gauze and some Neosporin. Against medical advice, naturally."

Grey gave him a look. "Thanks a lot for that, bro."

"Jaya deserves to have all the information, as she will most likely be your primary caretaker in the event that you develop tetanus."

Jaya looked horrified. "Tetanus?"

Rahul nodded once. "Yes. Most people believe the only way to contract tetanus is from a rusty object such as a nail, but that's factually inaccurate. Tetanus is caused by a bacteria, which resides in dirt, soil, and manure. Since Grey cut himself on a rock, which presumably had some soil—"

"Okay, my love," Caterina cut in, in the gentlest voice DE had ever heard her use. She kissed the side of Rahul's head. "I think we all get the picture. Let's not give Jaya a heart attack, hmm?"

Rahul sat back, but he didn't look embarrassed. In fact, he was playing contentedly with the ends of Caterina's hair, lost in some kind of love bubble. DE's heart ached while her stomach wanted to regurgitate breakfast.

"Hey, guys." She stepped fully into the common room and walked up to the group, flopping down on an empty love seat nearby. Nodding at Grey's bloodied leg, she added, "Let me guess: zombies?"

Grey shook his head sadly, his shaggy hair flopping around his forehead. "They just can't get enough of my sweet, tender flesh."

Sighing, Jaya sat gingerly next to Grey on the arm of the wingback chair. "I give up. You're hopeless."

"Hopelessly in love," Grey added, leaning his head against her, cinching her waist in with one arm.

DE groaned. "I can't take all this PDA. Please, have mercy upon my mortal soul."

Jaya perked up and looked at her. "Hey, you're back awfully quickly. What did Madame Olivera say?"

Grey gave DE a half smile. "You went to see Madame Olivera? Did you tell her that her favorite dashing scoundrel Grey Emerson says what's good?"

DE rolled her eyes. "Yeah, I did see her. And I have to say, I think a better stage name for her would be Madame Eats Lead Paint in Her Spare Time."

Caterina stifled a laugh, but Jaya frowned. "What?"

DE leaned her head back and waved a hand. "Yeah, the woman was totally weird. First she tried to play therapist, and then she told me I had to open my heart or a hurricane would come and obliterate me or something? I don't know. At that point I was just biding my time and waiting to get the hell out of there. I'm guessing it was the same kind of generic thing any psychic would tell anyone, but with a little added sprinkling of kookiness just for me."

"Well, that sucks! Maybe she was having an off day or something," Grey suggested. "She was pretty good when we went to see her, wasn't she?" He was looking at Jaya for confirmation, but Jaya was lost in thought, her pointy finger tapping her equally pointy chin.

"But she told you to open your heart?" she asked, lifting her eyes to DE.

DE nodded. "Something like that, I'm pretty sure." There was a momentary silence, broken only by the sudden popping of wood in the giant fireplace.

Jaya and Grey looked expectantly at her, their eyebrows

raised. DE's eyes shifted to Rahul and Caterina, who had identical expressions on their faces. She threw up her hands. "What?"

"No, it's just that . . ." Jaya scratched at the velvet fabric of the armchair with a fingernail before lifting her dark eyes to DE's again. "Don't you think she may have a point?"

DE sighed. "Not this again. I already told you guys, I'm—"

"Not ready to date," all four of them chorused back at her.

DE sat back and crossed her arms. "Well, at least we're all on the same page."

Grey shifted his bad leg on the footstool and winced. "Look, DE, I know how much it sucks to open yourself up, okay? Believe me, I *know*. It's terrifying and difficult and it sucks. But I'm telling you, it's worth it." Here, he took Jaya's hand and squeezed gently. "*So* worth it when you find the right person."

DE looked past him and Jaya at the mountains outside, showcased magnificently by the floor-to-ceiling windows in the common room. It was only four o'clock, but already the sun was setting. The peaks were muffled with orange Creamsicle–colored snow, and DE remembered how when she was little, she used to imagine the mountains were scoops of ice cream towering into the sky. She looked back at Grey. "That was a fantasy I believed in too, not that long ago. But just because it happened for you guys doesn't mean it's going to happen for me."

"Why not?" Caterina asked, her voice imperious but simultaneously kind somehow—or what passed for "kind" in Caterina Land, anyhow. DE was still a little shocked that they were on speaking terms, to be honest, after the whole Alaric debacle. "Are you going to let a boy like *Alaric* dissuade you from what your heart wants?" The way she said "Alaric," she may as well have actually said "a hissing cockroach sandwich."

"There are many boys who are nothing like Alaric," Jaya put in. "For instance, that new student I was talking to you about. Xander. He's really cute *and* he seems really nice."

Rahul added matter-of-factly, "There are also unsubstantiated rumors that he's from a mob family. I'm checking my sources to see if there's any merit to them."

Grey raised his eyebrows. "And that he's a deepfake AI, who is *actually* the Russian president's righthand woman."

Jaya rolled her eyes. "People are just exaggerating!" She paused. "Anyway, just because his *family's* involved in that kind of thing doesn't mean that he is . . . necessarily."

They studied each other as DE tried to process this logic. Then, sighing, she shook her head. "That's irrelevant anyway. It's not even just about Alaric or finding a new guy. It's me. I'm . . ." She stopped. She'd almost slipped up and said "broken." It's what she really thought, but DE knew if she voiced the thought out loud, her friends would be all over her, protesting loudly. And right now, she didn't have the energy for that. ". . . lost."

"Lost people can be found," Grey said, his blue eyes meeting and holding hers. "Maybe you just need a compass. Don't write yourself off yet."

DE smiled a little. "I appreciate you guys more than you know. But I'm ready to change the subject. So. Where's Leo?"

Rahul pushed his glasses up on his nose. "Off with Will, as usual. I think he said something about going to eat dinner at that new Indian fusion place in Denver."

Their friend group had been rocked when, just a few weeks ago, Leo had announced that he and Samantha Wickers had broken up. DE thought that maybe she, Jaya, and the rest had taken it harder even than Leo and Samantha, who had parted pretty amicably. But their devastation had been tempered when he'd begun dating Will, a senior they all loved. And so far, they had to admit, Leo and Will made a cuter couple than Leo and Samantha had, which was saying a lot.

DE was happy for Leo. She really was. Just like she was happy for Rahul and Caterina, and Grey and Jaya. But there was a tiny twisting tendril in her heart, like a small corkscrew that was winding tighter and tighter, that asked if maybe there wasn't something to what her friends were saying. *Should* she open her heart again to the possibility of love? If she truly was happier without it, then why did she feel this lingering sadness, like a perpetual cold blanket around her?

Shaking her head to herself, she stood. "Welp, I'm gonna go check in at the mail room. They said I had a parcel or something. Probably the 1940s peacoat I ordered from that Parisian boutique, Sale la Vie."

Jaya giggled. "I *do* love a good, punny store name. Okay." She hopped off the armchair and gave her a hug. "Text me if you want to get dinner later."

DE pasted on a smile. "I will." Waving to the rest of her friends, she walked out of the common room. They watched her go in silence, and she had the awful feeling that they'd talk about her when she was gone. Nothing mean, obviously, but she didn't really like the thought of being the subject of worry and concern, either. Was she really *that* pathetic now, the one in the friend group everyone saw slithering down a death spiral?

CHAPTER 5

DE

DE pushed the thought out of her mind as she turned down the long, sconce-lit hallway that would take her to the mail room. Daphne Elizabeth McKinley was many things, but pathetic wasn't one of them. She smoothed her black lace top down as she walked. She'd gotten it made specially out of what was supposed to be high-end Halloween-themed fabric—the delicate lace was shaped into spiders and spiderwebs—because she'd immediately seen the possibilities. She'd paired it with a forest-green bralette underneath and high-waisted pants in the same green. DE knew she looked good, and the appreciative looks and smiles she was getting from the other students she passed in the hallway confirmed it. She may not have a boyfriend, but so what? At least she'd always have fashion.

Feeling pretty good about herself, DE turned the corner—and stopped short when she almost ran headfirst into someone just as tall as she was. "Oops, sorry—" she began, her words withering on her lips the minute she saw who she was talking to.

Alaric Konig.

He stood there, his blond hair higher and thicker than she

swore it had been before spring break. She'd avoided him pretty successfully so far this semester, but now that he was this close and she could smell his custom cologne and see the flecks of gold in his blue eyes, she felt her stomach twisting on itself painfully.

For one horrifying moment, DE thought she'd throw up on his polished leather shoes. But the moment passed, and she braced herself subtly against the dark wood–paneled walls. "H-hey, Alaric." She hated the slight wobble in her voice. It gave away the fact that she wasn't 100 percent over their breakup, but there it was all the same.

Smiling wolfishly, Alaric slipped his phone into his pocket, his manicured fingernails glossy and perfect. He always moved with so much liquid grace, it was like watching a magician perform a trick when he did even the most mundane tasks. "Well, hey there."

What she *wanted* to say was: *Eat a bag of cow udders and die, Konig.* What she *said* was: "How, um, how was your break?" The minute the question was out of her mouth, DE wanted to stuff it back in. Why had she asked that? She didn't want to make *conversation* with him. What she wanted to do was pretend he didn't exist and move coolly down the hallway, the way Caterina would. She thought about the way Caterina had said Alaric's name earlier, in the common room, and tried to channel that disdainful energy. Adjusting her expression, she waited for his answer.

"Mm, it was good, except for one thing." Alaric moved closer to her, so DE was pressed flat against the wall. His blue eyes darkened.

DE swallowed, the disdainful energy gone, imploding in a sad *whoomph*. She'd never been good at playing it cool with Alaric. "What was that?"

Moving a finger down the side of DE's neck, Alaric murmured into her ear, "I was lonely."

Goose bumps sprouted along DE's pale skin, but she couldn't tell if they were *I want more* goose bumps or *Get the hell away from me* goose bumps. And therein lay the rub with Alaric. She never knew which way her heart was being pulled; she could never quite find her footing. "What about Lizl Falk?" she found herself asking. Alaric's supermodel girlfriend had had all of Rosetta Academy talking just weeks ago.

Alaric made a scoffing sound. "Gone. It was never with her like it was with us." His eyes gleamed, hard as sapphires in the sconces' amber light. "Do you think about me, Daphne Elizabeth? Do you wonder what it'd be like to be together again?"

Together again? DE stared at Alaric's Renaissance-era-sculpture face, so perfectly angular, so well groomed. Was he serious? He wanted to go out again? As if she'd *ever ever ever* entertain that idea. The previous piece of advice she'd wanted to give him sprang to mind again: *Eat a bag of cow udders and die, Konig.* But again, her traitor mouth thwarted her excellent repartee. "I . . . ," she began, and then stopped, feeling like her tongue had swelled to eighteen times its usual size.

He smiled at her hesitation. Sliding his hands into the back pockets of her pants and cinching her close to him, he said, "I rather enjoyed sneaking around, grabbing bites of the forbidden fruit, didn't you? Perhaps we could do that again. Once I'm dating someone else."

DE felt her heart take the express elevator down to the pit of her stomach. He wanted her to be his sidepiece again. Alaric didn't want to *go out* with her, he wanted to *hide* her. He wanted to feel like the badass playboy, the one the girls couldn't get enough of. This wasn't about her at all; it was about his insatiable, monstrous ego. She was so *stupid* for even considering it could be anything else.

Putting her hands between them, she pushed on his chest until he pulled his hands out of her pockets and stepped back. DE smoothed down her short red hair. "Get the hell away from me."

Alaric's face hardened. "What's your problem?"

A disbelieving laugh shot out of DE. "What's *my* problem? Buddy, I'm not the one asking people to be my dirty secret. I can't believe I ever went out with you in the first place."

Alaric grinned, an ugly, twisted thing. "At least I'm not in denial. You were never anything *but* a dirty secret. You're not the kind of girl who guys date in the open, Daphne Elizabeth. You're the contingency plan."

And there it was. In just a few sentences, Alaric had laid bare DE's biggest fear, that most shameful, horrifying thought that kept her up in the blue hours of night. She was meant to be the plan B. She was the backup, never the main girl. She wasn't meant to be the heroine of the fairy tale. Even her own family treated her like an invisible nobody, and now here was Alaric, pretty much confirming it all.

Her eyes burning, DE blinked fast and looked away. "Fuck you." She said it so quietly, she wasn't sure Alaric even heard.

He laughed to himself and, without another word, sauntered away.

DE sank back against the wall, gazing down at her feet in an effort to compose herself as other students occasionally walked by, giving her curious looks. Tears dripped onto her black boots and slid sadly onto the wooden floor, where they lay glimmering like diamonds. In spite of her best intentions, her mind played back Alaric's words: *You're the contingency plan.*

And that was why it was ridiculous to even consider what her friends wanted her to do, what she herself sometimes thought about doing: opening her heart to love again. This was what was waiting for her on the other side. Guys like Alaric, guys who'd tell her she wasn't the kind of girl they could date in the open. Not the kind of girl they could be proud to be seen with. Not the right kind of girl in any way.

DE squeezed her eyes shut and took a deep breath. *Enough. Push it away and get to the mail room.* When she opened her eyes again, something on the floor by her feet caught her eye, white against the gleaming dark wood. It was a small square piece of paper, the one Madame Olivera had pressed into her palm, she realized. She'd totally forgotten she'd stuck it into her pants pocket. Alaric must've pulled it free when he took his hands out.

Bending, DE picked up the flimsy square. Embossed on it was an intricate design of a snowflake, rendered in silver foil. Each line of the snowflake was made of thorny vines, she realized as she looked closer. And the space in the center of the snowflake was shaped like a key. She flipped the paper over. In silver script were the words: *The blood of lost souls wakes the storm. You have the key to vanquish it. Open your heart. I will guide you.*

Yeah, because opening her heart had worked out so well for her in the past. Madame Olivera the "psychic" probably had these made up in batches of five hundred, which she bought online at VistaPrint for twenty bucks a pop. Crumpling the paper in her fist, DE strode to the end of the hallway, where there was a picture window and, in front of it, a large trash can disguised as the statue of a gargoyle (at Rosetta, trash cans were never allowed to just be trash cans).

Looking out at the pine trees silhouetted in the dusk, DE took a deep breath and tossed the paper into the gargoyle's open, waiting mouth. "There," she muttered, trying to tap into a sense of closure she was sure must exist somewhere deep within her soul. "That's what I think of your advice."

She'd barely finished her thought when a sudden, screaming wind ripped through the ancient trees, bending them like a handful of twigs. It howled and shrieked like a beast in agony, rattling the glass of the picture window as if some great invisible wolf had grabbed it between its powerful jaws and shaken mercilessly. DE took a step back, her heart flying into her throat, but even as her foot came down, the wind died out as if it had never been there in the first place. The pine trees were calm once again, still and tall and peaceful. The window glass settled into place.

DE blinked. "What the *hell* was that?" she whispered, half expecting the wind to begin howling again in response. But, of course, it didn't. Just a weird coincidence. That was all.

DE turned on her heel and headed down the stairway to her right. If she wasn't careful, she wouldn't make it to graduation with her sanity intact.

CHAPTER 6

DE

Late that night, close to one a.m., DE wound her way up the north wing of the main campus building, her soft-soled shoes whispering on the stone. Snuggling into her fluffy blanket hoodie, she kept to the dusty side stairways that were in disuse because the newer, main stairway was grander and better lit. But the side stairways served her purpose well—tonight she wanted to merge with the shadows and be invisible. In her hand she held her small journal, and tucked away in her jeans pocket was a key she'd had made so long ago, she couldn't really remember when she'd done it.

Panting slightly with the exertion of the climb, DE found herself at the highest floor. She smiled up at the ceiling. Nestled there was a trapdoor to the old attic, chained and padlocked against wandering, wayward pupils. But, of course, they hadn't counted on DE, her key, and her almost preternatural sense of Rosetta Academy's hidden nooks and crannies. It was kind of sad, but she knew this school better than she knew any of her family's homes because she'd spent so much more time here. Summers her family couldn't be bothered to have her meet them, holidays when they were too busy to pick her up—she'd spent all of them locked up at Rosetta Academy with nothing better to do than explore the buildings and the grounds. And it had served her well.

Now, using an old stick she kept in the corner of the landing, DE pulled the padlock down far enough that she could use her key to unlock it. Then she pulled on the little ring handle until the stairs lowered. She'd greased the hinges a while ago, and they were virtually silent as they wound their way down to her, ready for her ascent.

She climbed quickly and pulled the stairs up after her. Then, standing, she pulled on the chain that would light up her corner of the attic. When she'd first found this place years ago, she'd been happily surprised that the power was still hooked up. It was just a matter of bringing a light bulb and screwing it in. Et voilà, a nice, private, usable space nobody knew about but her.

The attic itself was massive and cold, sprawling in all directions into darkness, stacked with boxes and trunks and papers that were much, much older than she was. DE had explored it all when she'd first found this place, back when she'd chosen prime real estate by the small, diamond-shaped, dusty window for herself. It faced the dense woods surrounding campus, so she knew she wasn't in danger of anyone seeing the light and spotting her presence.

Pulling her coat tighter around her, she made her way to the trunk she'd pushed up against the wall under the window many eons ago, the wood floors creaking and sighing under her weight. The ad hoc window seat was the perfect place to perch and think. She peeked out the window like she always did when she first sat down; the woods were quiet and completely still, the blue pines bathed in liquid silver moonlight.

Sighing in satisfaction, DE opened her journal and clicked open the pen tucked inside. She'd first begun journaling when Alaric had broken up with her, and she wasn't exactly proud of the practice. There was nothing wrong with journaling per se; it was just that it didn't really jibe with her vision of herself. But then again, neither did being the contingency plan or the dirty secret on the side. Alaric had changed a lot of things about her, whether she liked to admit it or not.

Tapping her pen against the page for a moment, DE began to write.

People say I need to pick up the pieces, but what if there aren't enough pieces left? I'm afraid I'm broken, beyond repair. Grey says maybe I just need a compass to find my way again, but to use a compass, you have to at least be in the vicinity of where you need to be. I'm on another fucking planet. I'm not even sure who I am anymore. DE, the fun-loving, spontaneous freak, always up for anything—does she even exist anymore? Or is she just a shadow slipping farther away with every moment, disintegrating into the night?

DE stopped and studied her page, head cocked to one side, mouth quirked in dissatisfaction. Ugh, too dramatic? Yep, definitely too dramatic.

She was just reaching up to rip the page out when the attic window's diamond-glass pane began to rattle. Alarmed, she looked up to see that the forest, which just moments ago had been totally silent, was now a frenzy of activity. The trees were shaking in fear as a predatory wind whipped through them, hell-bent on ripping them apart. DE jumped back as a fistful of hail hit the window, pinging loudly, eager to get in.

"Shit," she whispered, her green eyes wide.

And that's when the lights went out, plunging her into a

darkness so complete, she was afraid she'd lose herself.

"Double shit," she muttered, looking around as if her eyes might be able to adjust somehow to this inky nothingness. They didn't, naturally. The only thing happening was her heart rate spiking.

For a few moments, DE focused on breathing in and out, trying to calm herself down. Maybe the lights would come back on. Maybe this was just a temporary malfunction. But the moments passed into minutes and nothing happened. The power stayed firmly and stubbornly out.

"Okayyyy." DE swung her feet off the trunk–window seat, breathing a sigh of relief when they hit the solid wood floor. It was easy to feel like she was suspended in a bubble of pitch-black, but no, there was a floor here. She was fine. "I'm just going to have to find my way in the darkness. No big deal. I've been here a hundred times. I can do this. You can *do* this, McKinley." She wasn't *totally* sure that was accurate, but she needed this pep talk. And more than that, she needed to get out of the attic and back to her dorm room, which she was sure would have the benefit of Rosetta Academy's generators.

As she gingerly made her way step-by-step toward the approximate location of the trapdoor, DE cursed herself for not bringing her phone with her. She could've really used a flashlight. But at the time, she hadn't wanted to be disturbed. She'd wanted a half hour of peace and quiet by herself, without the world intruding. She was an idiot.

A couple of more feet and DE tapped around with her foot. The trapdoor should be where she was standing, but she couldn't feel anything. Oh god. What if she was totally disoriented and in a completely different part of the attic than she'd thought?

What if she'd gone deeper and deeper in? What if there were *rats*? Would rats even be *allowed* on Rosetta Academy grounds? *Focus, McKinley.*

She was turning around in a desperate circle, trying to feel *any*thing with her foot, when it caught on what must've been the trapdoor's O-ring handle. In the dark, DE grew even more disoriented when she tried to free her trapped foot, and without warning, she found herself tipping over, having lost her center of gravity completely.

With a shriek, she landed, her tailbone cracking on the wooden floor, her breath whooshing out of her. "Ow, fucking hell!" She sat there for a minute, breathing hard, trying not to freak out. "This is fine. Everything's fine."

Then she heard the sneaky creak of the wooden floorboard next to her and the unmistakable sound of a human footstep. She wasn't alone in the attic.

DE was opening her mouth to scream when a big, warm hand grasped her upper arm.

CHAPTER 7

XANDER

He could *feel* the scream building up in her, like helium blowing up a balloon to bursting.

"Shh," he said, squatting down beside the girl. He couldn't see, obviously, but he could feel her warmth, the shape of her on the floor. And, of course, he'd heard her hit it not too long ago. "It's okay. I'm just trying to help you up."

She wrenched her arm away from his grasp and flailed. It turned out to be a good strategy, though, because she ended up pushing his chest, which upset his balance. He had to give it to her; she was strong. Amid the sounds of her scrambling up, she asked, "Who the *fuck* are you? And what the *fuck* are you doing in my attic?"

Her voice came from above him, so she must be standing now. Xander rose from the balls of his feet too. "*Your* attic?" He couldn't keep the laugh out of his voice. "Sorry, I didn't see that on the lease agreement I signed."

"Ha ha ha. Were you spying on me the whole time, you psychopath? I'm going to tell the administration. You're so dead."

He held up his hands, though he knew she couldn't see him.

"Hey, no, I wasn't spying on you. I was already here when you came in, and, um, I didn't want to leave or make it awkward. So I just stayed in my corner and did my thing." He gestured toward his corner, which was about as far away from her window seat as it could be, but obviously, she couldn't see that either. "I figured you'd leave at some point and be none the wiser."

He could hear her blowing out a breath, and he knew she was wondering whether to believe him. "Do you have your phone?" she asked finally.

"Yeah, here. I turned it off because I just wanted some peace and quiet up here."

He heard the girl let out a breath at that and mumble something about what *sounded* like "two idiots in the attic," but he couldn't be sure.

Xander pulled his phone from his pocket and turned on the flashlight. The girl blinked. She was tall, almost as tall as him, and had hair that matched his favorite red maple tree back home. It was hard to see her face fully because of the harsh shadows the flashlight threw out; plus, he looked away quickly because he didn't want to seem like a creep. Well, any more of a creep than he already must seem.

He heard her sigh in relief. "Finally. Some light."

Xander swung the flashlight to the trapdoor. "Look, you found the trapdoor with your foot. I'll see if I can get it open." He was moving carefully in the direction of the trapdoor when the single light bulb flickered back on.

Xander turned his phone's flashlight off and then swung around to look at the girl he'd been speaking to. His breath caught in his throat.

She was statuesque, at least six feet tall, with short hair the color of a thousand saturated autumns—he'd been right about that much. But he hadn't been able to see her eyes very well with the flashlight . . . and oh, her eyes. They were a light green, filled with a wildness that reminded him of a panther he'd seen once, pacing its cage, aching to get out.

He wondered what kept this girl caged.

Then he shook his head. *You shouldn't be wondering that,* he reminded himself. *You're here for a particular reason, and that reason does not include girls, not even ones with untamed green eyes.*

The girl, who'd been studying him with the same intensity he'd been studying her, shook her head and looked away. Even in the shadows cast by the single light bulb overhead, she was breathtaking. But he got the feeling she didn't know it.

"You're the new student," she said, her voice quiet. She appeared to have relaxed, as if she could sense that he wasn't a murderous killer skulking in the attic, waiting for easy prey.

"Xander Murthy," he confirmed, holding out a hand, absurdly enough. As if they were meeting in a formal dining room instead of in a dusty attic in the middle of a power outage.

She moved forward a few steps and grasped his hand. Her own felt featherlight and cool, like her pale skin was made of glass. "Daphne Elizabeth McKinley. But they call me DE."

"DE," Xander replied, feeling the letters in his mouth, grasped between his teeth. "It's nice to meet you."

"Xander Murthy." She narrowed her eyes and crossed her arms. "I've heard things about you."

He couldn't help a smile at that. It was a weird thing to say to a stranger, and he liked that. "Oh? Like what?"

"You're a lethally trained government assassin sent to execute one of the politicians' kids. That's why you've transferred here so late in the year, right before graduation."

Xander snorted and stuck his hands in his jeans pockets. "Really."

"Or that your family has some very intricate connections to the mob."

Xander raised his eyebrows. "The *mob*? Impressive."

"Or that you're a highly paid adult escort masquerading as a student." A faint smile flickered at her pink lips. "But you're not *quite* pretty enough for that one, I think."

Xander couldn't help the laugh that escaped him. "Okay, that one's my favorite, hands down."

DE pushed the toe of her shoe into the dusty wood floor, and he could feel the question between them: *So what* are *you doing here?* But that was a question he couldn't answer.

Trying to divert her attention away from that topic, Xander asked, "So how'd you even get in here?"

The corner of DE's mouth quirked and he watched in fascination. "I made a key."

The fascination turned quickly to admiration, not that he was letting her see all of that yet, not when she might still think he was a trained assassin, for fuck's sake. "A key. That's um . . . wow."

She sighed. "Yeah. I've been stuck at this school since kindergarten. You have to find ways to amuse yourself, you know?"

Xander studied her. "And ways to get away."

She met his eye and didn't say anything for a moment. "Yep."

Another moment of silence. It was like each of them had more to say but not the words to say them. So Xander turned and opened the trapdoor, letting in a gust of warm air from the heated school building. "Guess I'll leave you to *your* attic," he said, winking at DE. "Have a good night."

"Oh." She blinked at him. "Um. You too."

She raised a hand as he disappeared down the stairs. He had to try with all his might not to look back up at her once he reached the bottom.

CHAPTER 8

DE

The sky was a frigid steel cage Monday morning, the first day of classes after spring break. DE pulled her thick cashmere scarf higher around her chin as she walked to her first class alone, feeling the bite of snow and ice in the air. "It's the end of March," she grumbled, hands grasped tightly around her steaming to-go cup of cappuccino. "It's *spring*."

It didn't help her mood that for the fourth quarter, she'd been forced to enroll in a freshman class: The Rise of Elite Academia in 19th-Century America: A History of Rosetta Academy. She was supposed to have taken it as a freshman but had never gotten around to it. Honestly, she'd been hoping the administration would sort of forget about the fact that she'd never taken it, but of course they hadn't. The Rosetta Academy administration didn't forget anything. Now she was going to be the only senior in a shining sea of baby-faced freshmen. The thought made her want to fling her coffee into the stupid, icy face of this stupid, icy day.

But thinking about the weather had her thinking about the power outage late last night, and, by extension, about the very mysterious Xander. It was a little creepy at first that he'd just . . .

been there, but she got his explanation. She believed it. He'd just had the same idea as her, although she hadn't thought to ask him how he'd been able to get into the attic. The trapdoor had been padlocked.

She thought about him standing there, skin the color of dark, polished wood, his chocolate-brown hair flopping onto his forehead, his frame slender but strongly built. He had eyes the exact hue of the sand dunes she'd visited in Dubai last year, and his laugh had rumbled deep in her chest.

DE shook her head and took a sip of coffee. It didn't matter about his eyes or his laugh or his hair. Xander was a boy, and he was off-limits. She'd done an actual reverse love spell during spring break to make sure no guy would be able to steal her heart away again, she reminded herself sternly. Who cared why Xander Murthy was here at RA this late in the year? It wasn't her problem.

DE walked into her classroom, sighing inwardly as she saw all the fifteen-year-olds with their perfectly pressed uniforms and composition notebooks already lined up on their desks. Ah, to be that young and hopeful for her high school career again. Now the only thing DE wanted was to put Rosetta Academy and every negative association she had with it out of her mind and move on to the next phase of her life. College. Dartmouth. It was something different, and so she'd grasp it with both hands and a sense of hope she never felt anymore. It was at least four years—more if she went to grad school—of freedom from her family, their hotel dynasty, and responsibilities in the real world. (Because yes, she was invisible to them now, but it had never been in question that once she was done with school, she'd take over the day-to-day functioning of McKinley Hotels so her parents could retire.

The "perks" of being an only child.) And BTW, she definitely planned to extend her no-boys rule to college life. She didn't care how unrealistic Jaya thought that was. Jaya wasn't in her head or her heart.

Unwinding her scarf and stuffing it into her backpack, DE took off her coat and took a seat at the very back of the class. Her desk wobbled, but she didn't give a crap. Invisibility presided over comfort.

"Dude, I'm telling you, they're predicting one-hundred-mile-per-hour winds. It's gonna be lit."

"A hundred miles per hour? No way. That's ridiculous."

DE turned to watch two boys arguing by the window.

"I'm telling you, man," the first boy countered. "This is going to be big."

"Then why haven't I heard about it?" the second boy said. "There was nothing on my news app."

The first boy pointed at the sky. "Just look at that cloud cover. And the hail last night? The major weather channels haven't started reporting on it yet, but they will."

"I *love* that coat."

DE turned at the voice in front of her to see an Asian girl, with black hair in two glossy French braids, turned around in her seat. Her brown eyes were wide as she took in DE's new fuchsia coat, which she'd draped over her desk when she sat down.

"Oh, thanks," DE said, smiling. "I got it from this Parisian boutique I love. I had them add the tulle to the bottom and the brocade buttons." She gestured to the additions.

"Wow," the girl breathed, running her hand around the gold-and-emerald brocade. "It's *stunning*." Then, looking at DE shyly, she added, "You're Daphne Elizabeth, right?"

DE sat back. "I am! Have we met?"

The girl shook her head, her braids bouncing. "Oh, no. I'm just—I'm a huge fan."

DE frowned, sure she'd missed something. "Of . . . ?"

"You," the girl replied, her cheeks getting pink. "That probably sounds super weird, but you're, like, a legend in our grade when it comes to your fashion choices. At least among my friends and me."

"Really?" DE laughed. "That's awesome."

"Totally. I'm Anna, by the way."

"Nice to meet you, Anna." DE grinned. Maybe this class wouldn't totally suck. She had a *fan*.

"I'm really interested in fashion too. I want to be a fashion designer." Anna reached into her purple backpack and pulled out a makeup pouch. It was made of a colorful fabric that DE immediately loved, with tropical birds in every color printed all over it. The zipper pull was a tiny flamingo.

DE leaned forward. "I love that fabric! And the flamingo!"

Anna flushed. "Oh my god, really? I designed this and had it made. I painted all the birds in watercolor first, and the company had it printed onto fabric."

DE ran her hands over the pouch, taking in the iridescent parrots, the magical blue peacocks. "That's amazing." She met Anna's eye. "You're wicked talented. I have no doubt you're gonna be big. And then I'm gonna buy all my stuff from you."

Anna waved her hands over her cheeks. "That means so much to me, coming from you. Thank you."

"Of course." DE took a sip of her coffee. And then nearly spit it out when she saw who was entering the class.

Xander walked in, caught her eye, and then walked confidently down the aisle, his posture perfect in a way that DE's never was, and a small half smile on his handsome face. "Fancy seeing you in here." He sat in the seat next to her, and DE felt her insides thrill, in spite of her best intentions. She reminded herself, *yet again*, of the reverse love spell.

"Seems you're everywhere I go," DE muttered, taking another sip of her coffee, mostly just to have something to do. She found that she couldn't quite look at him in the bright light of day.

"Seems like." Xander tipped his chin toward Anna, who was watching this exchange, agog. "Hey."

"Hey." She giggled and then raised her eyebrows at DE, who rolled her eyes over her cup at the younger girl. Grinning, Anna turned around and began talking to someone else, another freshman girl who'd just sat down in front of her.

"So." Xander tipped his chair back. His tie was loose, DE noticed, and the sleeves of his uniform shirt had been rolled up to the elbows. He had nice forearms, brown and downy with hair. "Why are you in here? Shouldn't you have taken this class already?"

"Yeah, well, I slacked off, and now it's come back to bite me in the ass."

Xander laughed. "Well, I'm glad you slacked off . . ."

DE jerked her gaze toward him. Was he flirting with her? Clearing her throat, she looked away.

". . . because now I won't be the only weird old person in here," he finished.

Oh. So definitely not flirting. She cut her eyes at him. "Speak for yourself. I'm not a weird old person. I'm cool and hip *and* I have a fan." She gestured at Anna. "Apparently."

"A fan?" Xander looked faux impressed. "Wow. Didn't know

you were famous when I ran into you flat on your ass last night."

"In some circles," DE retorted, her nose in the air. Then, narrowing her eyes, she added, "How did you get into the attic, anyway? The trapdoor was locked."

"I have my ways," Xander replied, examining his short fingernails. DE couldn't help but notice that they were about as different from Alaric's as you could get—not glossy, not filed or shaped in any way, but still neat and square. An assassin's fingernails, perhaps.

"Seriously." She half turned in her chair.

He held her gaze for a moment. "Rosetta Academy is full of secrets," he said finally, looking away. "Maybe I'll show you sometime."

CHAPTER 9

DE

What did *that* mean? DE was studying him for a moment, opening her mouth to ask what he was talking about, when the lights in the room flickered like they might go out. Outside, the wind beat on the windows and howled like a person possessed.

"Ooooh," the freshman students chorused, looking around in excitement.

DE sat back, unimpressed. She'd been in the creepy attic in a blackout. This was nothing. She tossed a sideways glance at Xander and could tell he was thinking the same thing.

A moment later, a woman swept in and walked to the teacher's desk. DE had heard they'd hired someone new for the quarter to teach this class, but until now she hadn't really thought about who that might be. This woman was tall—taller even than DE— and pale. She wore a maxi dress with long sleeves and a black velvet skirt, her silver hair in an old-fashioned updo, as if she thought she was in a Victorian novel.

Everyone was quiet as she set her books down on the table and then turned to face them, her eyes dark and inscrutable. It occurred to DE that she was one of those people who could be any age from forty-five to seventy or even older.

Her skin looked tissue-thin and almost translucent; her fingers, long and skinny and tapered, reminded DE of the barren winter branches of the aspen trees that scraped the Colorado sky. The teacher took the time to look at every one of the students in class, and when her eyes came to rest on DE, DE felt her heart thump in her chest and her mouth go dry for reasons she couldn't name. But then the teacher's eyes moved on, and DE let out a shuddering, quiet breath.

Finally, after what seemed like an eternity of silence, the teacher spoke. "Good morning. My name is Bianca Blackmoor." Her voice was deep and mellifluous, like an old woodwind instrument. Her accent wasn't American, but what it *was*, DE couldn't have said. It seemed a blending of all accents everywhere, though, obviously, that was impossible. "You may call me Ms. Blackmoor. I am here to teach you about the history of Rosetta Academy." She smiled thinly. "But first, I'd like to know what *you* know of its history. Can anyone tell me the story of the Academy's founding?"

Yawn. DE struggled to not put her head down on her arms and take a nap. This story had been drilled into every Rosetta Academy student's head since kindergarten. Boring rich old white dude built the school for other boring rich old white dudes' sons in the 1800s. There. She'd summed it up in one sentence. But DE didn't think Ms. Blackmoor would appreciate her take on the Academy's "illustrious" (adjective lifted straight from the school's glossy marketing brochure) history.

A slight blond boy at the front of the class raised his hand, and Ms. Blackmoor called on him. He tapped the eraser of his pencil against his desk as he answered. "Tobias Huntley II, one of the great American oil magnates of the nineteenth century, opened the school in 1872. He was from Colorado, and although he'd been educated in the best boarding schools in Europe, he wanted a place closer to home, where his own son, Tobias Huntley III, could be educated just as finely as he was all those years ago. He chose the town of Rosetta because it was close enough to the mountains so his son would have plenty of exposure to skiing and other winter sports, which he thought was essential for a man of the world, but also secluded enough that his son could earn his education while keeping the bustling world at a remove."

DE smirked to herself. The boy's explanation had also come right from the marketing brochure that prospective students and their powerful parents saw. It was a nice, genteel origin story. But she could read between the lines: "keeping the bustling world at a remove" just meant old man Huntley thought his son was too good to be mixing with the riffraff of American society and wanted to gate him off in the mountains along with other sons of tycoons and magnates, while also, of course, pocketing their money as a nice side income.

She took a sip of her coffee in an effort to jolt her brain awake for the rest of the class. She was expecting Ms. Blackmoor to award the boy a verbal gold star for answering so quickly and seamlessly, but instead, the woman was staring down at him, her dark eyes glittering. There was a hint of a smile at her lips, and her fingers fluttered lightly against the front of her velvet dress. "Really?" Ms. Blackmoor said, her voice low like a cat's purr. "Is *that* what you think?"

The blond freshman boy blinked up at her, his pencil coming to a standstill. There was an interested rustle in the class. DE glanced at Xander, who was now sitting up, watching Ms. Blackmoor with curiosity.

Ms. Blackmoor looked around at the class. "Many of you have been taught a history of Rosetta Academy that's really like a room with the shades drawn. You can see broad shapes and the general layout of the room, but the details are lost. And the details, my dears, are usually what make up the soul of the thing."

"What are you saying?" the blond boy asked. "That that's *not* how Rosetta Academy came to be founded?"

"I'm saying," Ms. Blackmoor said, smiling down at him, "that you don't have the full picture. And that's what I intend to do in this class. Paint you the full-color image you're all entitled to." She paced to the large bank of windows on the right side of the room and stood looking out for a moment, silhouetted against the gray light of the cold day, dark and still, before she turned around again. "Tobias Huntley II *did* found the Academy in 1872. And it's true he did it for his son. But what none of you know is that the younger Huntley, who cut a large and imposing figure even as a teenager, had some rather nasty proclivities." Ms. Blackmoor walked to the front of the room, her low heels producing a mesmerizing *click-clack-click* to underscore her story. "He was known in some whispered circles as the Huntley Hunter—a name that, while it lacked imagination, was not inaccurate. Tobias Huntley III lived on his family's estate in Boulder for much of his youth, and while he was there, a number of young women in his vicinity went missing, year after year. They were mostly daughters of groundskeepers and maids and chauffeurs, the working class who relied on the Huntleys for their livelihoods, people who wouldn't dare point a finger at the young and powerful Master Huntley.

"But even all the money in the world can't keep the rumors

at bay forever. When Huntley's governess went missing, tongues began to wag. People began to demand answers. What was happening to the young women who got sucked into the Huntleys' gravitational pull? At this time, Tobias Huntley III was only fifteen years old."

CHAPTER 10

DE

"Jesus." DE felt goose bumps ripple up her arms. Xander caught her eye and raised his eyebrows, looking a bit wan himself. In front of her, Anna, DE's "fan," shivered lightly and rubbed her arms.

Ms. Blackmoor smiled grimly, as if she'd heard DE's muttered exclamation.

"But what does that have to do with why Tobias Huntley II founded Rosetta Academy?" a Black girl with thick locs in the third row asked. "Just to stow him away? He could've sent him anywhere, if that were the case; he didn't have to build a whole school."

"An astute observation," Ms. Blackmoor replied, turning to face the girl. "You're right. If his motivation were just to send his son away from the public conjecturing, he could've sent Tobias anywhere. But sources close to the family say the older Huntley suspected the rumors were true and wanted his son somewhere he would be able to keep watch without explaining himself. Hence, building his own school."

"This is all very illuminating . . . and slightly disturbing, but

I don't think any of us will be writing home to our parents to correct their notions of Rosetta Academy," DE quipped from her seat, and there was a ripple of laughter around the room.

Ms. Blackmoor shifted her gaze to DE, smiling slightly. "No, I'd think not. The reason I chose to share that story with all of you is that every institution, no matter how purportedly hallowed, carries its twisted and gnarled scars. Rosetta Academy is no different; she claims and keeps her secrets. This Academy has birthed many distinguished alumni, people who've changed the world for good. That's commendable and deserves praise and attention. But Rosetta's blackest corners must be peered into too, especially because she nurtures her secrets so closely. None of us should forget where we've come from, lest we tumble down those dark tunnels we've already traversed."

DE opened her mouth to respond, though she had no idea what she was about to say. She didn't get the chance to find out.

An inoffensive, tinkling chime from the hidden speakers around the room let the students and Ms. Blackmoor know an announcement was incoming. A moment later, the principal, Dr. Waverly, spoke. Her authoritative voice boomed into the classroom.

"Pupils and educators, please make your way to Huntley Hall at this time for an important and urgent announcement. Pupils and educators, Huntley Hall, please."

Anna turned to look at DE as she and the rest of the class began to get out of their seats. "What do you think that's about?"

DE frowned as she wound her scarf back around her neck, shrugged into her coat, and spoke to Anna as well as Xander, who was listening, interested. "I don't know. The last time they interrupted class so abruptly was seven years ago, and that was to let us know the assistant principal had died in a snowboarding accident."

She couldn't shake the sense of foreboding that cloaked her as she followed the rest of the students out of the classroom, Xander on her heels, and into the gusty morning outside. There was the wet taste of snow on the wind, and the frigid air bit at DE's nose and scraped her throat raw. Huntley Hall was only a short walk across the green, but she suddenly found herself not wanting to go.

CHAPTER 11

DE

Like the rest of Rosetta Academy, Huntley Hall had been constructed (by the apparently murderous Huntley family) in the Victorian Gothic architectural style common to the latter half of the nineteenth century. The two-story building's pale stone was as heavy and imposing as an emperor's crown, the wickedly pointed arches piercing a stoic ash sky. The window and door frames were carved with an intricate hand, the ancient stonework as finely fitted as lace on the most exquisite bridal veil.

A staff member was holding the main doors open for students, and DE allowed herself to be carried in on the swell of noisily chattering students without allowing that sense of foreboding to make her stumble. She'd lost Xander somewhere in the crowd, but she was sure he'd find his way. It was all going to be fine. Whatever this announcement was, it would be taken care of by the Rosetta admin, and DE would get on with her life.

She followed the throng down the carpeted hallway and through another set of double doors marked HALL 1. As ornate and old-fashioned as Huntley Hall looked on the outside, it had been fitted with every sleek technological advancement on the inside. Hall 1, for instance, could easily seat all twelve hundred Rosetta Academy high school students, plus the thirty or so teachers and staff.

It was a cavernous space, with wool-lined, soundproof chambers and a custom design that enhanced acoustic performances for the many musical concerts the school hosted. (The New York Philharmonic and the Orchestra of the Age of Enlightenment had played here more than once in the time DE had been a student. And the pop singer Peyton Platinum, whose songs constantly topped the charts and who was a personal friend of one of the students' parents, had given a performance two years ago). There was a three-stop orchestra pit that could be raised and lowered to five different levels and intelligent lighting that would change and adapt to whatever kind of musical performance was being given. But when there were no musical performances, the lower parterre could be used for a lecture space, which is what was happening now.

Dr. Waverly, wearing a light-yellow Chanel pantsuit, stood patiently waiting for students to file in and take their seats. The students at Rosetta never waited on staff at events like this; if anything, it was the other way around. DE sat toward the back of the room. Maybe Jaya and the others would be in soon and she'd be able to flag them down.

"This seat taken?"

DE glanced up to see Xander, his dark hair mussed from the windy day, pointing to the empty seat next to her. He'd turned up just like she'd known he would. She sat up straighter for some reason and cleared her throat. "Ah, nope."

"Excellent; just as I'd hoped." He sat with a big whoosh, shaking her seat too. A smell of something warm and sweet and intoxicating, like Irish creme liqueur, wafted over to her, and she tightened her hands around the armrests of her seat.

I am not *smelling him*, she told herself severely. *I am merely breathing in. I'm a human. I have to* breathe.

"Does Dr. W call a lot of these?" Xander asked, looking down at the principal on the parterre.

"Nope." *Come on, use some different words, Daphne Elizabeth. More than one syllable would be good.* "She must have something pretty important to say. Probably about graduation or something."

"But then wouldn't she just have called the seniors instead of the entire high school?"

"Yep." DE felt her face flush. "Um, good point." Why hadn't she thought of that? Well, if she were being honest with herself, she knew why. It had something to do with the warm, nice-smelling boy sitting inches away from her. Totally stupid and shallow.

Suddenly Xander leaned in close to her, his eyes twinkling. "Maybe," he said in a voice so deep, DE felt it low in her belly, "she wants to confess about the bloody past of Rosetta Academy."

It was a silly, cheesy line; the kind of thing you said to someone you barely knew to break the ice while you waited for something else to happen. DE knew that. And yet, she froze. She could feel herself freezing—could feel the blood turning slushy and then stopping in her veins, could feel her heart slowing down, could feel her eyes wide and refusing to blink, could feel the air slow down and stop whooshing from her lungs. But she couldn't help herself. While she stared into Xander's sand-colored eyes, the entire world seemed to freeze right along with her. One half of her brain told her she was a total idiot and reminded her about the reverse! love! spell!; the other half was mesmerized.

Finally, what felt like hours later and with monumental effort, she forced herself to blink and look away. And, unfortunately, happened to look right at the clot of her friends—Jaya, Grey, Rahul, Caterina, Leo, and Will—who were standing a few rows down and grinning at her and Xander. Finally, Jaya waved at them before whispering something to the rest of the group, who promptly sat where they were instead of making their way up to DE. Leo darted a quick glance at her over his shoulder and then turned back around again to murmur something in Will's ear.

She waved her hands in frustration to get their attention again, but they weren't looking anymore. They should be sitting up here with her. Sighing, she sat back and crossed her arms. Great. Now she was going to get an earful at lunch about sitting with *Xander, the new, cute boy*.

"Are those your friends?" Xander, completely oblivious to the existential turmoil that had been raging within DE, asked. He popped a piece of gum into his mouth and offered her a stick.

She shook her head at the gum. Just having him near her, talking into her ear, had sent her into a tailspin. Who knew what consuming the gum that had been resting in his chest pocket, against his heart, would do? Gum could be dangerous. Gum could be deadly. "Yeah. I guess they didn't see me here." A blatant lie, but Xander didn't argue.

"Welcome, students," Dr. Waverly began from the front of the room. The thoughtfully designed acoustics of the hall allowed her to speak without the need for a microphone. "Thank you for arriving so promptly and listening so carefully to what I have to say to you this morning." She stared pointedly at a group of unruly sophomores in the fifth row until they got the message and quieted down.

"Rosetta Academy received a special weather report early this morning," Dr. Waverly continued, her manicured hands clasped neatly in front of her. The muted spotlights turned her gray hair a glossy steel. "A historically large storm front is moving toward us at an unprecedented rate. The meteorologists are predicting up to six feet of snow in the next seventy-two hours. Drifts could reach up to twenty-four feet, and winds are expected to reach a hundred miles per hour."

There was a ripple throughout the hall as students began to chatter with each other. Beside her, Xander blew out a breath. DE chewed on her lower lip, tasting vanilla lip gloss. That sounded like a hell of a storm. Something niggled in the back of DE's mind, but before she could grasp it, it was gone.

"Luckily," Dr. Waverly went on, raising her voice so she could be heard above the din, "the younger students have finished out their term already, in accordance with Rosetta tradition, so we won't have to worry about them. But you, in high school, will have to endure the storm with the staff and teachers on campus, I'm afraid. Your parents are in the process of being notified, but unfortunately, it's too late to have them collect you or for you to fly home as we're already seeing high winds and low-pressure areas too dangerous for pilots to maneuver. With our commanding position so high in the Rockies, we have been especially adversely affected.

"However, I would like to assure all of you that every precaution is being taken to keep you safe and to keep the Academy insulated from the most deleterious effects of the storm. We were fortunate enough to be able to secure deliveries for even more emergency supplies and rations today, thus ensuring that we will be self-sufficient for up to a month if need be. Naturally, we don't forecast the roads being disrupted for nearly that long.

"That being said, school is canceled for the rest of today so staff and educators can prepare for the storm. We will make decisions about the rest of the week as we see what each day brings."

There was another renewed swell of chatter and excited conversation as everyone processed this new information. An impromptu day off was as rare for Rosetta Academy students as it was for the president of the United States. (Of which the Academy had graduated three so far.)

"Before I dismiss this meeting," Dr. Waverly called, "are there any questions or concerns I can address for you?"

There were a few questions about whether students were allowed to go into town—the answer to that was no—and whether someone could have their private jet pick them up "really quick"—also no. Then Xander surprised DE by raising his hand.

"Yes, Mr. Murthy." Dr. Waverly smiled at him.

"This storm sounds like it has the potential to be extremely dangerous," he said, his thick eyebrows knitted together. "Does Rosetta Academy have any experience dealing with a storm like this in its history?"

A flash of something passed over Dr. Waverly's face, but it was gone before DE could put a name to it. The principal's mouth relaxed into another smile. "Close enough for you to not have to worry, Mr. Murthy. I assure you, our administrators and staff have been trained for every weather eventuality possible. We will get through this together, in one piece, unharmed."

DE glanced at Xander. He sat back in his seat as if assuaged, but the muscle in his jaw was as clenched tight as a fist.

CHAPTER 12

XANDER

What were the chances? Xander didn't consider himself a superstitious guy, but hell if this wasn't making him a little bit nervous.

As soon as Waverly dismissed the students, he got up and began to make his way to the front of the hall. He had things to do, now that they had the day off. He had more time than he'd imagined he would, which was good. It was really good.

"Xander, right?"

He turned toward the refined, British-accented female voice to see an Indian girl with long black hair looking at him from her seat. He recognized her from earlier; she had been the one who'd waved at DE. The rest of DE's friends were seated next to her, and all of them were goggling at him as if he were a special exhibit at the Denver Zoo.

"Um, yeah." He stepped out of the line of students pushing forward to the exits. "Hey."

The girl stood up. "Hello. My name is Jaya Rao. I'm a friend of Daphne Elizabeth's." She gestured behind her to the rest of the group. "This is Grey, and then we have Rahul and Caterina, and Leo and Will. We were just talking about lunch, actually.

The dining hall's rustling up some broccoli potato soup, which is honestly some of the best I've ever had. It's marvelous on a cold day like this." She smiled warmly. "Would you like to sit with us?"

"What in the what is going on?"

DE had walked up and was standing beside Xander now, also out of the flow of students. Her hands were on her hips, and her green eyes were narrowed.

"We were just inviting Xander to lunch!" Jaya responded brightly, absolutely not catching on to the vibe that DE was putting out.

"I'm sure Xander has lots of places he'd rather be than eating broccoli potato soup with us." DE's smile was pasted on, but Xander couldn't help noticing the pink flush that was traveling from her neck to her cheeks and her forehead.

Xander studied her for another moment before realizing everyone was waiting on him for an answer. "You know," he said slowly, turning back to Jaya. "I'd love to have lunch with you all. Broccoli potato soup sounds especially good on a day like today." He gave DE a big grin, which she returned with a scowl.

This was going to be fun.

DE

Of course her harebrained friends engineered it so DE was sitting next to Xander. In fact, she was squeezed in so close to him at the dining table that their elbows kept touching. DE was too tall to compress into herself to prevent this from happening, but also, she didn't find the warm weight of his arm pressing into hers *entirely* unpleasant.

She glowered at Jaya over her soup, hoping her annoyance gave Jaya a few electric prods in her brain. But Jaya laughed merrily at something Xander was saying, completely oblivious. "Well, I feel for you, I really do. I came in junior year, so, you know, I didn't grow up here on campus like the natives." She waved her hand at the rest of the people at the table.

"How long have you been at Rosetta Academy?" Xander asked, turning to DE.

Everyone else at the table stared at the two of them, like this was the most riveting soap opera they'd ever seen. Could they be more obvious about their intentions for Xander? Jay-zus.

DE cleared her throat and hoped she didn't have broccoli stuck in her teeth. "Um, since I was in kindergarten. I'm a lifer."

Xander snorted. "A lifer. You should put that on a T-shirt."

Her friends guffawed with laughter, as if they'd never heard anything funnier, even though Jaya had literally just called them "natives." Xander looked a little surprised and more than a little confused, while DE narrowed her eyes at them, hoping to telescope the thought: *Continue this and I* will *kill you all.*

When everyone had calmed the eff down, Will asked, "What do you think of the Academy so far?" Will, unlike the others, wasn't goggling at Xander like he was the great messiah they'd all been waiting for. Leo, seated next to him, was staring so hard, his spoonful of soup was suspended in the air, his mouth slightly open. For fuck's sake.

DE smiled gratefully at Will, and he winked conspiratorially back. At least there was one person here who hadn't totally lost their marbles.

Xander glanced around at the airy senior dining hall before replying. DE saw him take in the granite counters, behind which staff bustled, eager to provide the waiting uber-wealthy children with their nutritious, delicious, chef-prepared meals. He gazed upward at the soaring ceilings, with their modern lighting. At the floor-to-ceiling windows, which looked out on rolling hills, the Rosetta Academy garden, and the expansive sky that was currently a foreboding steel gray.

"It puts up a good front," he said finally, gazing into his bowl of soup thoughtfully. "A very good front." Then, looking up at everyone, he smiled. "It's beautiful."

Leo began telling a story about the original architect of the main building, but DE studied Xander. What did he mean by "It puts up a good front"? He'd tried to cover it up by saying the school was beautiful right after, but DE's Spidey-sense was tingling. She got the feeling he knew more about Rosetta Academy than he was saying, but that didn't make sense, did it? The dude had literally *just* transferred here. What could he know that she didn't, having spent most of her life at the school?

Grey, who'd been quietly and efficiently tucking into his second bowl of soup this whole time, looked up. "So why'd you transfer so late into senior year?"

Xander took his time answering, wiping his mouth carefully with a pressed and monogrammed Rosetta Academy napkin first. "Ah, family thing."

They waited, but there was nothing more forthcoming. The guy was a wall.

DE noticed Rahul and Grey exchanging a look, and then Rahul asked, "How'd you and DE meet?" DE gave him a sharp look, but he shrugged. "When Jaya brought Xander up the other day in the common room, you didn't seem to know who he—"

"Ha ha ha!" DE interrupted loudly, her eyes flashing a death glare at Rahul while her mouth curved up into a dazzling smile. "Let's give Xander a break, you guys. I'm sure he doesn't feel like playing twenty questions right now!"

"Not at all," Xander replied. If he thought her interjection or what Rahul had begun to say was weird, he didn't let on. "To answer your question, Rahul, DE and I met at an . . . exclusive club. It's full of *high* flyers. Although some, like DE, are pretty *down-to-earth*." He flashed a grin at DE, and she narrowed her eyes at him.

Oh, har de har har. He was talking about meeting in the attic, and her unfortunate fall when she'd tripped. Jerk.

Still, somehow, at the memory of seeing him for the first time in the dim light of the attic, she found that she suddenly couldn't make eye contact with anyone.

"Right . . ." Jaya looked back and forth between them, but DE kept her eyes resolutely on her soup, as if it were a life-or-death situation that demanded she shovel the stuff into her mouth at a record-breaking pace.

Jaya, who had a strange ability to read her mind, gave DE a sympathetic smile (DE saw it in her peripheral vision in spite of her total focus on her soup) and then smoothly changed the subject. Thank god for her princess training. "Are you guys worried about this storm?" she asked, her eyes drifting to the windows. Right on cue, a squall shook the glass in their panes, the snow tap-tapping to find its way in.

"Not in the least," Caterina replied in her usual imperious way, although there was a softness about her nowadays that she couldn't ever fully put away. "I spoke to my father this morning, and he said it shouldn't be as bad as they're forecasting. The roads should be cleared soon, and we'll be back to regular programming before long."

Rahul nodded. "I concur. Colorado storms can be unpredict-able, but they usually die down before they ever get to a point of meteorological concern. I think Dr. Waverly is simply exercising an abundance of caution for liability purposes."

DE felt a prodding discomfort at their words, like she should tell them what the psychic said. But she found she didn't know how to bring it up. What if everyone laughed at her? And would they really be wrong to laugh? The "psychic" was probably just a charlatan. And DE was silly to still be thinking of her right now.

Then she glanced at Xander. He wasn't laughing and pooh-poohing the storm like the others were. In fact, he looked . . . grim. His jaw was set, his eyes hooded and secretive. And just as she was studying him, he pushed himself away from the table and pasted a smile on his face. "Thanks so much for inviting me to lunch, guys. It's been really fun getting to know you all." Here he gave DE an extra little smile, making her face heat up like ten degrees. Dammit. "But I have something I need to get to."

"Oh," Leo and Jaya groaned in unison, then laughed.

"But you'll join us again soon, yes?" Jaya added, looking hope-fully at Xander.

"Definitely." Xander nodded to them all, then turning to DE, said, "See you later?"

She nodded coolly, but her insides were aflutter. What did he mean by that? Why did he only say that to her? *Calm down, McKinley,* she told herself the moment those questions entered her mind. It was ridiculous. They shared one class together. They'd sat together in the auditorium, and they'd had lunch with all of DE's friends. That was it. Nothing more, nothing less. She'd probably barely see him during this whole lockdown thing.

XANDER

The nice thing about Rosetta Academy was that there were usually multiple ways to access any one room. The ways weren't always highlighted or even made known to students (or even staff), but it was something the original architect had put in as a safety feature. If ever the son of a high-profile politician (or a murderer, apparently, as in the case of Tobias Huntley III) needed to get out to safety, he could be escorted out without any rando knowing exactly where he was going.

This feature was coming in handy for Xander, and he really appreciated it. As he made his way to the back entrance to the attic using a dusty stairwell that used to be part of the servants' quarters, he thought about how he'd been in here the last time when DE had come in through the main entrance and surprised the hell out of him. Before then, he had no idea any other student even realized this attic existed. Smiling at the memory of seeing her wild green eyes for the first time in that dim light, Xander came to a stop in front of the tiny half door on the top landing of the stairwell. It had been painted the color of the wall and was difficult to see unless you knew what you were looking for.

And Xander knew what he was looking for.

Taking out the small lock-pick set from his back pocket, Xander crouched down and inserted the rakes and hooks into the lock until he heard the satisfying *click* that told him he was in. Putting his tools back, Xander pushed open the minuscule door and crawled through, making sure to shut it behind him.

At this time of day, there was enough light streaming through the small diamond-shaped window that Xander didn't need to use his phone's flashlight to see what he was doing. He walked to the mess of old-fashioned steamer trunks and dust-fuzzed cardboard boxes in the west corner of the attic and sat, ready to resume his search that the power outage—and DE—had interrupted.

Xander hit pay dirt about thirty minutes into his rummaging. Whistling low, he rolled out a long piece of paper he'd found in a dusty, disintegrating cardboard tube, the kind that posters came in. It was onion skin–thin, nearly translucent with time. But he could see what it was very clearly: an ancient map of the Rosetta Academy campus—at least one hundred years old.

Not many people knew, but the Academy had changed a lot since its inception in the late 1800s. Xander thought of it as an intelligent amoeba, constantly changing shape and size, evaluating those who crawled within its belly. The thought made him shudder, and the winds whipping against the attic window didn't help.

Tracing his finger against the words "Senior Boys' Dormitory" on the map, Xander could tell that it wasn't anywhere near where the current coed senior wing was. He'd have to take a walk around campus and check that out, see where it originally used to be.

A rumbling that shook the attic floor had him distracted, and, setting the map carefully back into its tube, Xander made his way to the diamond-shaped window he'd seen DE at last night. If he squinted, he could see past the forest to the distant back entrance of the school. There was an enormous white propane delivery truck making its way very warily toward the service entrance. One of the emergency deliveries Dr. Waverly had talked about.

His mouth set in a grim line, Xander turned back to the ancient contents of the trunks in the attic. He needed to find out as much as he could before this storm descended.

CHAPTER 13

DE

Little bits of ice and snow were pelting her window in a steady drizzle, a precursor to the storm that was steadily and unwaveringly headed their way. DE paced the length of her dorm room to the floor-length window opposite and stood looking out over the beautiful vista that was currently covered in thick white clouds. You could barely see the mountains in the distance anymore.

"Shit. This is not happening." Rubbing her face, DE turned around and began to pace again. Ever since Dr. Waverly had dismissed them to prepare for the storm, DE's stomach felt like a hunk of ice from the sky had settled comfortably into it and refused to melt.

The psychic . . . the psychic had warned her of a storm. DE trailed her hand over the wooden bedposts of her king-size bed and then kept going until she was at her vanity table on the far end. Looking at herself in the mirror, she noticed her eyes looked a deeper jewel green, the way they always got when she was scared.

She was scared.

The realization made her feel a shot of anger toward that

pseudo-psychic lady who, by the way, had never even given DE her name. Now, that was just unprofessional. And what was DE letting herself get all worked up about an incompetent, no-name "psychic" anyway? She wished she hadn't thrown away the piece of paper with the snowflake so she could rip it up into a thousand tiny pieces and take them back to Madame Olivera's place.

She was *Daphne Elizabeth McKinley*, dammit. And there was absolutely no way she was letting some random lady scare her because Colorado got a few snowflakes.

There was a rumbling sound outside and the crunch of large tires, and DE stepped back up to the window. A propane delivery was being made to the north side of the school, where the service entrance was located. Another truck pulled up behind it, a food delivery service by the looks of the logo. Rosetta Academy was battening down the hatches for whatever was coming next. Swallowing, DE wiped her suddenly damp palms on her jeans.

?

She didn't take me seriously. Perhaps I was too intense, too impassioned. But I don't know what else I could've done. If she only knew what hangs in the balance, if she only knew what her inaction could do, Daphne Elizabeth McKinley would be weeping in her room.

DE

"Dudes, this is totally wild. Or as we French say, *farfelu*." Leo stood in front of the windows in the packed senior common room, his French accent lilting. Will stood next to him, his hand loosely clasped around Leo's. They turned around to regard the rest of the friend group. Leo's mouth was actually open, while Will's jaw was tense. His dark eyes looked pensive, unhappy.

He wasn't the only one feeling some kind of way about the storm. The rest of the seniors in the common room were a mix of giddy, anxious, or frenetic with nervous energy. Some of the students were guffawing, slapping each other on the back, and making Donner party jokes, which the anxious ones definitely did not appreciate, by the way they were chewing their lips to shreds. *Every*one had an opinion—Rosetta Academy had this handled; Rosetta Academy was going to get them all killed; Dr. Waverly was a genius at crisis management; Dr. Waverly was a trust fund baby who would save herself and let them all Popsicle to death.

DE turned back to her friends. "The wind's really starting to pick up." She had her legs curled under her as she sat in a green velvet armchair by one of the fireplaces. Her hands were still damp, and she rubbed them on her pants with irritation. Why was she so nervous over a storm, for fuck's sake? Storms were nothing new in Colorado. Sure, this one was bigger and stronger and was coming at an unusual time for Rosetta, but there had to be a reason for that. A *scientific* reason. Speaking of which. "Hey, Rahul," DE called.

He was sitting on the love seat with Caterina, his arm around her shoulders, her head on his chest. He was different now; he radiated a quiet confidence after the whole debacle as "RC" earlier this year. It was as if the two sides of his personality had come to a peaceful truce. It suited him, this new state of being.

As if he thought no one would notice—or didn't care that they would—he leaned over and sniffed the top of Caterina's head, then closed his eyes. When he saw DE's expression, he shrugged. "Pheromones are known to provide an oxytocin release. And we could all use some happy chemicals right now." Caterina smiled and kissed him on the cheek. "Anyway," he continued, looking back up at DE. "What's up?"

DE glanced outside the window at the wind and the shaking trees, the solid gunmetal sky that felt like an impenetrable box. "Why do you think we're getting such a late-season storm? Such a, um, big one?"

"Climate change," Rahul answered without hesitation.

DE sagged with relief. "Really? Climate change? That simple?"

"Yes. Not just the US or Colorado, but all parts of the world have been affected. It's not just global *warming*, like people think, it's also causing storms and snow and weather patterns that don't make sense for the geography of any given place. Like the heat waves in Sweden or the droughts in South Africa."

DE laughed and clapped her hands. "Climate change!"

All her friends looked at her like she was nuts. Some of the other seniors who'd been busy chattering to one another fell silent and glanced at her, their brows furrowed. Shit.

She adjusted her expression into a somber, appropriate one. "Climate change," she said solemnly this time, shaking her head.

The others all began to talk about the storm again, but DE felt a warm, gleeful relief spreading through her bones. This had abso-fucking-lutely nothing to do with that demented psychic woman. This was no prophecy. Just a coincidence. The psychic had seen some special news report, probably, and decided to use it to her advantage. DE wanted to slap herself upside the head for believing it could be anything else, even for a second. Everything was going to be just fine.

XANDER

It was three days after the announcement by Dr. Waverly, and technically he wasn't supposed to be out and about on campus. The admin had told students they could walk to their dorms or collect important items from classrooms within the next hour, but that was it. The storm was expected to hit in just a few hours, so no other outdoor activities were permitted until it had passed. Lockdown was imminent.

The other students were rejoicing because lockdown meant a chance to party, but Xander was grateful for a different reason. Lockdown meant no schoolwork or homework, which worked out well for him: he had plenty of homework of his own he needed to accomplish.

As he made his way up the small hill to the west side of campus, the solid gray sky hurled small particles of ice at Xander's face, as if warning him to turn back. It was only midmorning, but the quality of light felt like late dusk. Any part of skin that was exposed stung, and the unforgiving wind cut easily through his goose-down coat, slipping down his neck and swirling around his torso. Squinting in determination, Xander tucked his hands into his pockets, the fingers of his right curling around his phone. He'd taken a picture of the campus map he'd found, just so he could double-check himself.

At the top of the hill, he stopped and looked around. There was nothing here. It was hard to see, of course, because of the ice and the fog and the fact that he could barely keep his eyes open. But the ground barely had any snow on it yet. Xander walked the length of the top of the hill, scraping the ground with his boots. If there had been a boys' dorm here at some point, it was completely gone. There was absolutely no sign of it—no leftover foundation, no bits of brick or stone, no old signs. It was as if it had just vanished.

Frowning, he pulled his phone from his pocket and, with some difficulty, opened the picture he'd taken. Yep, this is where it was supposed to be. On Huntley Hill.

"What the hell?" Xander slipped his phone back and turned in a slow circle. How could an entire building just completely disappear? And *why*? Squinting through the ice flurries, Xander noticed what looked like a lantern bobbing up the hill toward him, an orange spot in a sea of gray and white. But then he blinked again and realized it wasn't a lantern—it was someone with red hair. Daphne Elizabeth.

CHAPTER 14

DE

Excellent. She'd forgotten her hat at the school, and she was walking across the icy green in an imminent snowstorm. She wasn't about to turn back, though, because she knew the moment she walked back into the main building, she'd get told she wasn't leaving again. The staff was doing a pretty good job keeping everyone calm, but DE could sense the thrum of panic and tension that were running through them. Most of the seniors, save for the super-anxious ones, just saw it as a cool postapocalyptic situation, though, a chance to let loose before graduation. Which made sense. Rosetta *students* wouldn't be the ones getting their asses kicked by politicians and royalty if they managed to unalive themselves. That dubious honor would be reserved for the poor staff and administration.

As the ice flew into her eyes and ears for the millionth time, DE groaned and tried to shrink into her goose-down coat. She'd stepped off the green onto a little frozen path hidden by towering pines, which were currently shuddering in the epic wind. What the hell was she doing out here, anyway? The truth was, she didn't have a clear answer to that. She just knew she needed to get out of the school, away from the admin's pinched faces and hurried footsteps, and definitely far away from students who were planning to have sex or drink or do drugs in their rooms because staff would be too distracted to stop them. She felt . . . discombobulated still, even though Rahul's climate change explanation had made her feel a lot better, at least momentarily.

Walking up Huntley Hill in the middle of a growing snowstorm probably wasn't the most *brilliant* idea she'd ever had, but moving her body felt good. Being in the quiet felt good. The cold slapping her face felt great. Really. She squinted in the wind, trying to see the top of Mt. Sama, the mountain that Grey liked to hike on. But it was lost in a thick, grim blanket of snow clouds.

"Hey."

DE let out a scream that would've made a banshee proud as she leaped backward at the male voice, nearly tumbling off the top of the hill and rolling downward. She imagined herself like a cartoon character, collecting snow around her into a giant protective snowball. But then her mind—and vision—cleared and she realized it was only Xander. She put a hand to her chest. "Xander. What the hell? Why are you trying to give me a heart attack every time I turn around?"

His look of concern morphed into an insouciant grin. Even with ice clinging to his dark eyebrows and lashes and his cheeks flushed a deep red from the bitter wind, he looked obnoxiously gorgeous. "I think you're just a little jumpy around me."

In spite of herself, DE flushed. Tucking her hands into her pockets and looking away, she changed the subject. "What are you doing up here in the middle of a storm?"

There was a pause. She looked back at him, curious, and saw that his expression had shuttered. "Just . . . getting some air."

She frowned and squinted as ice was flung in both their faces. "Does this seem like pleasant walking weather to you?"

The grin was back. "Well, I could ask you the same thing. What are *you* doing out here?"

He had her there. She shrugged and covered her ears with her hands. Damn, they were starting to hurt and she didn't want to go back yet. "Just . . . getting some air."

They looked at each other and, after a moment, laughed at the same time. "Fair enough," Xander replied, tugging off his tan beanie. Without a fuss or a word, he stuck it on DE's head and pulled it down over her ears.

She looked up at him. "But—"

"Your ears look like they're about to fall off. Keep it." He turned around and began to walk away, big boots crunching over the ice.

After a moment, she followed, her ears already thawing. "Um, thanks."

He called out over his shoulder, "Sure."

She caught up to him and they walked in silence among the frost-coated pine trees. "So, are you nervous?" she asked after a moment. "About the storm, I mean?"

He cut his golden-brown eyes sideways at her. ". . . No. The staff has it all under control, right? They always do."

DE nodded, not convinced. Despite what she'd tried to tell herself, the psychic's words *had* gotten under her skin, lodged like icy splinters there. "Right. Yeah. Totally."

Xander chewed on his bottom lip thoughtfully. They wound deeper and deeper into the little forest atop the hill, the wind thankfully dying down here as it was blocked by the abundance of trees. When they'd walked a few minutes in silence, he glanced at her, and apparently noticed her shivering lightly in her coat. "Maybe we should head—"

But he didn't get to finish his thought, because DE went pinwheeling to the ice-covered ground, landing with a huff.

"Oh shit." Xander was beside her in an instant, helping her up. "Are you okay?"

"Yeah . . ." DE could feel her cheeks heating despite the weather. *Making a great impression here. I am beauty, I am grace, I will fall down on my face.* "I'm trying to remember the last time I was around you and *didn't* fall." Xander smothered a laugh. "Seriously, though, I think I tripped on something."

They turned to look at where she'd stepped, and sure enough, there was something made of brass, poking out of the ground where decades of pine needles had previously collected and been packed down.

"Weird," DE said as they walked the few paces back together. "What is it?"

"I'm not sure." Xander squatted near the brass knob, frowning as he pushed on it. "Seems solid."

DE joined him, squatting close but not *too* close. "Huh." On an impulse, she scraped away the pine needles at the base of the knob. "Look. There's something solid under here."

Xander helped her clear more of the packed pine needles away, digging and scooping with his hands. Together, they heaved out whatever was half buried in the ground and set it by their feet.

"Interesting." DE stared at the small patinaed-metal box with ornate brass hinges and a brass topper (the "knob" they'd seen sticking out of the ground), around four foot six. She'd seen boxes like it in antique stores before; it had to be pretty old, but it was in good condition.

Xander moved to open it. Before she knew what she was doing, DE had grabbed his wrist. He looked at her askance, his golden eyes questioning, lashes heavy with ice.

"Wait." DE took a breath, her lungs filling with frigid air. "Do you . . . ? Do you think we should?"

"Open it? Why not?"

DE shrugged. "I don't know. . . ." She forced a small laugh, embarrassed. "Just feeling superstitious, I guess." It was totally moronic, now that she thought about it. Why shouldn't they open some random box they'd found in the forest? It was actually pretty cool. Maybe there'd be something vintage in there she could use in one of her outfits.

Xander didn't return her laugh. Regarding her seriously, he said, "It's up to you. If you don't want to open the box, we don't have to. We can just rebury it."

DE thought about it. There was really no reason for her to be unsettled about some box. "No, let's open it." Before she could change her mind, she reached out and flipped the lid open.

CHAPTER 15

DE

It took her a minute to figure out what she was looking at. "It's . . . it's a doll. I think." She picked up the little soft figure, made from dirt-stained cloth and burlap. There was jute string tied around it to make a head and limbs. The doll had no face or hair, but its tiny hands were folded in front of its chest, as if in supplication. To the body of the doll, someone had sewn a small brass coin with a hole in its center. The coin was stamped with the year 1873 and had a willow tree embossed on it. The willow was bending in wind, its tendril-like branches pulled toward the edge of the coin.

Just handling it made DE feel . . . weird. As if a great fog of sorrow had rolled in off the mountains, covering her in wispy fingers of sadness. Trying to shake off the sudden melancholy, DE turned the doll over. There was a sharp pricking on her index finger, and a gleaming bead of blood soaked into the back of the doll. "Ow, shit." DE squinted, but couldn't see what she'd pricked her finger on. Possibly the doll had pins on the inside, holding it together. Great. Now she'd probably end up getting tetanus. At least the sadness was fading.

"You okay?" Xander asked, concerned.

"Yeah, fine." She peered closer at the doll's smooth back. "But it looks like I might not be the only one who's pricked her finger on this thing." She gestured at a small, brownish-red spot a bit farther up on the doll.

"Ugh." Xander made a face, but DE thought it was pretty cool. This doll was kinda metal. "It's super weird-looking, too." Xander's brows were furrowed. "Why do you think someone buried it up here?"

"I have no clue. But look, this coin is from 1873. Do you think the doll could actually be that old?" The idea had DE's heart fluttering a bit. She'd always been a sucker for really old things. And the weirder the better.

Xander shrugged. "I guess. Maybe when this storm blows over, you can have an appraiser look at it or something."

DE smiled—as much as her cold, stiff lips would let her, anyway. "Yeah, maybe." She put the doll back in its box, tucked the box in her coat pocket, and stood. "But right now, I'm ready to head back to the school. I think my face is actually completely frozen."

Xander grinned and began to answer. And then everything went white.

?

She stood looking out the window at the rushing, pushing, growing wind, at the world it was beating into submission. The snow clouds were thick, oppressive, and they clotted the sky like the pale under-belly of some monstrous gray beast. There was a sudden gust, and every hair on the back of her neck stood erect. And then she knew.

It had begun.

DE

She sat bolt upright in her bed, as if she'd awoken from some horrible nightmare, but instead of memories of a dream, there was only static in her brain. DE rubbed her face. What . . . ? What had happened? Why did she feel so . . . strange?

She looked at the clock on the wall. Just past nine a.m. How long had she been asleep? She didn't even remember going to bed.

DE stared out the window, confused, at a solid wall of white. It took her a minute to realize it wasn't a wall but curtains of almost horizontal snow being pushed by an unforgiving wind. The storm. It was here.

Taking the covers off, she got out of bed—and then looked down at herself. She was still wearing her coat, her jeans, her boots. All the things she'd been wearing yesterday, when she'd gone out for a walk to Huntley Hill.

Huntley Hill.

It came back in swirls, like fog seeping into her brain. She'd seen Xander up there, and they'd found . . . She reached into her pocket and pulled out the metal box. Nestled inside was the faceless doll.

What the hell was going on? Why couldn't she remember the walk back to her dorm? Or going to bed? Or *anything* at all? And why was she in bed, fully dressed?

Sticking the box into her jeans and slipping off her coat, DE stumbled out into the hallway and down toward the common room. She needed to find Xander.

XANDER

Xander stumbled out of his room, his brain buzzing. What the actual fuck was going on? He ran into DE right outside the senior common room. Like him, DE was still dressed in what she'd been wearing yesterday, minus her coat. And she still had his beanie on. It looked adorably askew on her bed of red hair, but that was neither here nor there.

Seeing him, her face lit up with *something* for a microsecond, but then changed into the same confusion and fear he was feeling. "Xander, what the hell—"

"DE! I'm so glad you're—"

They began to speak at the same time and stopped. He motioned for DE to go first.

"What the *hell* is going on?" she hissed, her green eyes wilder than he'd seen them so far. "What happened yesterday?"

Xander pushed a hand through his hair and waited as a couple of students walked by, laughing and talking a little too loudly, a little too frenetically about the storm, as if to cover their nerves. The storm was another problem he'd have to contend with soon enough. He refocused on DE. "I don't know. I woke up in my bed dressed like this. I can't remember anything after we found the doll."

"Me neither." DE pinched the area between her eyes with a thumb and forefinger. "My head feels weird. Fuzzy."

"Mine too."

They studied each other wordlessly.

"Maybe we were attacked? Or hit by a falling tree limb or something?" DE began. "Do I have blood on me anywhere?" She turned around in a circle.

"No," Xander replied. He turned in a circle so she could study him, but he already knew what she was going to say.

"No blood on you, either." She sighed. "I don't hurt anywhere. I just feel . . ."

"Odd." Xander nodded. "Yeah. I know." He gestured toward the common room. "Wanna go in there and see if anyone saw us come in?"

DE's eyes lit up. "Yes! Maybe they can fill in the blanks for us. Come on. My friends are early risers."

CHAPTER 16

XANDER

He followed DE into the common room, frowning. This was beyond weird. Her assumption that they'd been attacked or hurt was one he'd made too, but it didn't really make sense. He wasn't in pain, there was no blood anywhere, and it was pretty unlikely both he and DE would have the exact same experience after something like that. Nothing about this added up, and Xander didn't like things that didn't add up. Not at all.

DE's entire friend group—Jaya and Grey, Will and Leo, and Caterina and Rahul—was clustered around the fireplace, talking excitedly and nervously, like everyone else in the crowded common room, about the storm that had finally descended and closed them all in.

"This is it. We're completely caged in." Will, dressed in a chunky-knit sweater, gestured toward the giant windows that were nothing but white screens. The snow was so thick, so unrelenting, that the rolling green hills of Rosetta Academy had been completely obliterated, as had the usually grand views of the Rocky Mountains in the distance. "That doesn't make any of you nervous?" He rubbed his dark jaw.

Grey grunted, and Caterina laughed breezily, though Xander noticed that she was rubbing her arms through her cardigan like she was cold. Despite the excellent insulation at Rosetta, it *was* brisk in the building. Which was another weird thing. It was like the storm had found a way to seep in.

"It's going to be okay," Caterina said. "It would be *really* bad press for Rosetta Academy if one of us got hurt. They won't let that happen. All we have to do is stay comfortable and enjoy our time off."

I'm not as confident as you about that, Xander thought, but said nothing out loud.

"Hey, guys," DE called, flopping onto a beanbag with a sigh. Xander sat beside her in an upholstered brocade armchair that looked like it was a thousand years old but was surprisingly comfortable.

"Oh, hey!" Jaya looked at the two of them, her eyes shining. "Good morning! Where have you been?"

"What do you mean?" DE asked, going still. She exchanged glances with Xander.

"I mean, we haven't seen you since yesterday afternoon," Jaya explained, threading her fingers with Grey's. She, too, was wearing a thick sweater, jeans, and boots, but nobody commented on the oddly frigid temperature. He made a mental note and filed it away. "I looked for you to see if you wanted to join us for dinner, but I couldn't find you. I texted you too, and you didn't answer. What were you up to?" Xander noticed Jaya's curious glance at him—she was obviously wondering if he and DE had been up to shenanigans together—and in different circumstances, he wouldn't have found the thought unpleasant at all. He forced his mind back to the current situation.

DE looked around at all her other friends, her pink mouth set. "Did anyone else see me after I left for that walk yesterday? Or did you talk to me, maybe through text or something?"

Everyone shook their heads.

"Why?" Leo asked, frowning. Will had taken a seat, and Leo was sitting on his lap on the love seat now, his arms around Will's neck. "What's going on? Did something happen?"

DE looked at Xander again, as if asking if it would be okay to share what had happened. He tilted his head a fraction.

Looking back at her friends, DE took a breath. "There's something weird going on, you guys." She explained about her walk up Huntley Hill, how she and Xander had run into each other, the box they'd found. Pulling the doll out of her jeans pocket (she'd put away the bulky box), she showed it to them.

"That's strangely beautiful," Jaya said. "Like something you'd find in an antique store. But it also seems . . . sad somehow. Even though it doesn't have a face." She looked around at her friends. "Right?"

The others murmured in agreement.

"Oh, wait a minute!" Leo's eyes twinkled. "I think I know what this is. That's a 'winds of change' doll. My grandmother called it *les vents du changement* in French."

"A what?" DE asked, leaning forward. Xander found himself doing the same thing. "What is that?"

"A change doll. It's a doll you make out of cloth," Leo explained, taking it from DE and turning it around in his hands. "The hands have to be folded in prayer like this—you see? And you have to sew a coin on it with a tree bending in the wind, and the year you made the doll stamped onto the coin. If you make a wish about something you want changed and then bury the doll in the earth, it's supposed to help that change come true." He smiled and handed the doll back to DE. "Someone wanted to make a change in 1873, I would say, based on the date on that coin."

"But wait . . . You said there was something strange going on?" Grey asked. "What's that got to do with the doll?"

"Because right after I found the doll, Xander and I experienced a . . ." DE looked at Xander helplessly. "What would you call it?"

He thought about it. "A time jump. A fugue state. Something that caused us to lose time and forget everything that happened after we dug the doll out of the ground."

"Right." DE nodded and looked back at her friends. "The next thing we remember, we were waking up in our beds about thirty minutes ago, dressed in exactly the same things we were wearing on our walks, down to our shoes. It's fucking weird."

DE's friends all looked agog—for about ten seconds. And then they all simultaneously burst out laughing.

"Okay, you almost had us there," Grey said, shaking his head.

Caterina gave a delicate snort. "Let me guess. You both snuck a bottle of whiskey up there and had a few sips, right? And it turned out to be just a bit stronger than you'd imagined?"

Bright spots of red appeared on DE's cheeks. But before she could argue, a girl with strawberry-blond hair interrupted the conversation. She wore a little jar-shaped pin on her sweater that said *Let's Jam!*

"Hey, guys!" She turned to Leo and Will, smiling warmly. "Look at the lovebirds."

Leo stood and gave her a big hug. "Hi, Sam! You look absolutely ravishing, as usual."

The girl—Sam—grinned. "Thanks. Listen, there's going to be a party later today. Meet in the basement at eight p.m. And pass it along."

"But we're on lockdown," Xander said, frowning. "The administration won't mind?"

"The administration won't *notice*." Samantha laughed. "They're keeping an eye on the front doors to make sure no one wanders out and dies of hypothermia, but other than that, the seniors are pretty much on their own. That's why the party's theme is 'End of the World.' What's the use of being in this perfect postapocalyptic situation if we're not going to make the best of it?" Winking, she walked off to another group, presumably to spread the news.

"Ooh, we have to go." Leo grinned. "Sam knows how to throw a wicked party."

While the others began to animatedly talk about the details, DE shifted uncomfortably on her beanbag and looked at Xander, who shook his head slightly. Xander knew what she was thinking, because he was thinking it too—her friends seemed oddly unconcerned about the weirdness the two of them were dealing with. The fugue state they'd experienced, the strange doll they'd found, and the creepy chill in the air—none of it seemed to be setting off anyone else's alarm bells. It seemed he and DE were the only ones who sensed that something really strange had happened to them, something they couldn't explain no matter how hard they tried.

?

CHAPTER 17

The secret uncovered, the gears put into motion. The story marches onward, intent on hurtling to its conclusion. Will it be a happy ending?

DE

DE showered—the hot water felt *heavenly* after the weird chill of the building—and changed into a burgundy velvet pinafore-style dress, a black turtleneck, tights, and Doc Martens, and headed down to the basement at around eight thirty for the party. A big spider ring, studded with onyx for the spider's eyes, glinted on her middle finger. She was kind of looking forward to the party— maybe it'd get her out of this odd headspace she'd been in since she woke up this morning.

The senior floor at the Academy had thinned out and cleared as the rest of the students made their way to the basement, and it lent the whole area an abandoned feeling that gave DE the creeps. The silent hallways spooled endlessly forward, the electric sconces glowing starkly against the wood-paneled walls, throwing shadows that pooled in the corners like ghosts.

She and Xander had been texting through the afternoon, but they were no closer to figuring out what had happened. Mostly DE had spent the time Googling winds-of-change dolls. There was surprisingly little information about them out there; it seemed like they were an archaic thing that had fallen out of fashion over time. She shook her head. That was enough of that. She didn't want to think about it anymore.

The basement at Rosetta Academy was buried under the main building that housed the four high school dorm floors. It was cavernous and unused and dank, and completely neglected when compared to the rest of the polished and elegant campus, but none of that bothered the seniors when they wanted to throw an unsanctioned party. The best part of the basement was that none of the admin or staff ever bothered to venture down there on a normal day, let alone during a lockdown, assuring much-valued privacy.

Tonight DE saw that someone had strung a bunch of paper lanterns around the place for a little bit—a *very* little bit—of light. Someone else had put glow-in-the-dark necklaces and bracelets in someone's (probably heirloom) blown glass vase by the door, and DE donned a pink necklace as she walked into the thumping room. Thanks to the basement's insulated and soundproof walls, the music was turned up really loud, which DE was grateful for. The beat was forcing each thought—of the fugue, the weird doll, her friends' complacence—out of her head as soon as it came in, and that suited her just fine.

She poured a mixed drink from the bottles on the card table that had been down there for ages and turned around, surveying the myriad seniors (and some specially invited juniors) dancing or sitting on the floor in groups or hooking up in corners. Their teeth and the whites of their eyes glowed in the neon lights of their necklaces and bracelets, and DE found herself suppressing a shudder.

"Hey."

She felt a touch on her arm and turned to find Xander looking at her. He had an orange glowing necklace around his throat, his sweater and jeans cloaked in shadow. His face—what she could see of it—was serious. "Oh. Hey." DE took a deep slug of her drink, not really even knowing what it was. Some kind of punch someone had thrown together. It was sweet and had a touch of alcohol, though, and that's all she needed to know about it.

He leaned against the wall beside her, his hands in his jeans pockets. "How are you doing? You know, with . . . everything."

"You mean the weirdness that has permeated every fiber of our lives and yet no one else seems to believe or see? Oh, totally fine."

Xander snorted. "Yeah. Me too."

DE gazed into her cup at the murky yellow liquid. "The thing is," she murmured, more to herself than Xander, "I keep going over her words. And they're freaking me out more and more."

"Whose words?"

DE looked up to see Xander frowning at her. "This psychic I saw the weekend before school started back up."

The music changed to something even louder, and Xander leaned in closer to her. "What did she say?"

DE shook her head, wondering if she should even share. What if Xander thought she was totally ridiculous? But then again, was it any more ridiculous than finding a doll in the woods and then losing time? She shrugged. "This psychic lady predicted this storm, first off, which I guess isn't that much of a stretch. Maybe she had a weather report from someplace. But she also said some other stuff that I can't get out of my head."

"Like what?"

DE took a sip of her drink and felt it warm her throat. "Well . . . she said, 'Souls will slumber in the perpetual twilight . . . and one will perish.' Call me paranoid, but that sounds like a warning. Right?" Without waiting for an answer, she went on. "And 'Souls will slumber . . .' Isn't that what you and I did when we lost time? 'One will perish.' Is she saying I'm going to die?"

Xander took her by the shoulders, and DE realized there were tears pricking her eyes. "Look. I don't know much about psychics, but I do know that they tend to be con artists. And all that stuff just sounds like vague occult-speak to me. You can't let it freak you out. You're *not* going to die."

DE felt a small half smile creep across her face. "We're all going to die sometime."

"Okay." Xander smiled a little too. "You're not going to die anytime soon. You can die when you're . . . ninety-eight. Of natural causes. Sound good?"

DE laughed. "Yeah. That sounds great." She shook her head. "I don't know why I'm letting it get to me."

Xander took his hands off her shoulders, and she felt cold. "Because it's been a weird couple of days. Because we found that doll and then woke up in our beds. Because we're closed in by a storm and having to bend to Mother Nature, and that always makes everyone a little uncomfortable."

DE blew out a breath. She felt a little better at the surety in Xander's voice—and by the fact that he hadn't laughed in her face for taking the psychic seriously. Something Alaric would *definitely* have done. "Yeah . . . you're probably right. What a fucking couple of days, man."

Xander raised his eyebrows in agreement. They people-watched for a while, eyes following Sam as she circled with a tray of glow-in-the-dark Jell-O shots, which most people eagerly accepted. "So, uh . . . ," he said finally, breaking the silence. "Are you dating anyone?"

DE glanced sidelong at him and then took a sip of her drink, just to have something to do. Her cheeks were burning at this sudden change in topic, but it wasn't an unwelcome feeling. "Not at the moment, no. I'm kind of on a self-imposed dating embargo." She paused. "You? I mean, do you have anyone on the outside?"

Xander stepped aside when a group of students accidentally bumped into him on the way to the drinks table, chuckling to himself. Funny, that. She'd forgotten a guy could have a different reaction to being bumped into than indignant rage.

"I like how you say 'on the outside,'" Xander said, interrupting her thoughts.

"Why?"

He shook his head, still grinning. "You make Rosetta Academy sound like a prison and we're the prisoners. Locked inside with no escape."

His grin faded, and DE felt a shiver going up her spine. It was like they'd both felt it together; the prickle of a joke that was too close to the truth. As if to punctuate their feeling, the building groaned like it was being punished by the wind outside. A few students whooped.

CHAPTER 18

DE

"Sorry." Xander swallowed, his jaw muscle tense. They were off to one side of the basement now. A few students milled near them, drinking and half dancing as they talked, but most were in the center of the basement. "Bad joke."

"No, it's—it's fine."

"But to answer your question," he continued, "no. I have no one."

"Hmm." DE nodded, not meeting his eye. "I see."

"You guys!" It was Jaya, her cheeks a deep pink in the dim light, bounding toward them. Somehow she made bounding look graceful, dressed in what looked like a cashmere dolman-sleeve sweater, skinny jeans, and glittery Prada boots. "You're here!"

Xander nodded politely while DE gave her a quick hug. "Yeah, we've just been hanging out, talking."

"Well, you can't just 'hang out'!" Jaya said, indignant. "You have to dance!" She grabbed one of Xander's hands and one of DE's. "Come on!"

"Uh, no, that's okay," DE protested, her heart already hammering at the thought of dancing with Xander. Hammering because she obviously *didn't* want to. No other reason.

Xander shrugged, muscular shoulders moving languidly. "I don't really dance."

Jaya turned to look at them, mock annoyance on her face. "What a couple of party poopers. You can't come to the secret senior snowpocalypse celebration and not dance."

"Secret senior snowpocalypse celebration," Xander mused. "Dr. Seuss would be proud."

DE snorted. "Anyway, I don't dance unless I'm very, very happy or very, very sad. You know this about me."

Jaya sighed and waved her arm, which was covered with about half a dozen of the glow-in-the-dark bracelets. "Oh, fine. But at least *try* to have fun, okay?"

DE gave her a salute. "On my honor."

When Jaya had disappeared back into the writhing crowd, Xander turned to DE. "I'm learning all kinds of things about you. Like, that you take psychic warnings seriously and you only dance when you're feeling extremes of emotion and that you're not dating anyone. It's all very interesting."

He held her gaze, and DE felt her palms getting damp. It was strangely intimate: he had to stand close to her to be heard, and the lighting was so dim, she could barely see his eyes in the reflection of his glow-in-the-dark necklace. But she could *feel* his gaze on her, like a warm hand pressed against cool skin. "Good." She took a gulp of her drink and then set it down. "I'm glad it's interesting."

"Although, I'm wondering if 'concern' would be classified as an extreme emotion."

"Huh?"

"You know. You're pretty concerned about this storm and

what happened on Huntley Hill, right? So, wouldn't that be an extreme emotion? And if it *is*, then maybe you wouldn't be opposed to a dance." He gestured at the makeshift dance floor nonchalantly, where most of the seniors were huddled together, dancing.

DE blinked. "You want to . . . dance with me? But I thought you said you don't dance."

Xander smiled lazily, and DE felt her breath catch. "I don't. Except when I do."

DE affected a similarly casual manner as him, but she wasn't sure she fully succeeded. Her heart was pounding so hard, it was almost painful. "That doesn't make any sense."

"No?" Xander moved a half step closer. His eyes were actually smoldering. Good Lord. How was she supposed to maintain her status as a celibate nun if he did stuff like that?

"N-no," DE said, attempting to sound confident, looking him straight in those smoldering, dastardly eyes. If what she'd done was an anti-love spell, then his eyes were the *anti* anti-love spell. What was she even saying? Her brain felt like scrambled eggs. "But lucky for you, I like things that don't make sense. I like a mystery."

Grinning, he held out a hand. And feeling completely helpless, she took it.

XANDER

The girl could *dance.* Xander tried not to stare, but holy shit. She was pure liquid, languorous motion, her body and the beat seeming to meld into one. The others completely faded away as he watched her, those wild, green eyes closed and keeping their secrets, a small smile tugging at her lips, most of her in shadow.

As if she could sense his thoughts, DE opened her eyes and gave him a knowing smile. "What? Did you think white girls couldn't dance?"

"Uh, no. I just . . . I guess I've just never seen anybody dance like that before. You're really good. You should definitely dance more." *With me*, he didn't add.

She smiled, looking pleased with the compliment. "I used to take ballet and gymnastics up until about two years ago."

Xander cleared his throat, in a vain attempt to clear his very foggy head. "Y-yeah, I guess . . . ah, I can see that."

DE laughed a little, because he was obviously an idiot who could barely string two sentences together in her presence. She was probably used to that kind of response. "So, what hidden talents do *you* have? I'm guessing from your reaction in the attic that you're not a government-hired assassin?"

Xander snorted as he tried to keep up with her moves. "No, not even close. I cry when I accidentally squash an ant."

"Aww." DE looked genuinely touched. "I love a softie." Then she blushed and looked away, avidly watching the other students like she had to write a thesis on bad high school dance moves.

It was weird, but there was something in the air that Xander found contagious. Like the other students' hedonistic abandon was seeping into his skin, like the storm and the dim lights and the music were making him drunk. And while he was "drunk," Xander found he really, really liked making DE blush, even inadvertently. Not good. Not good at all. "Anyway, no hidden talents, I'm sorry to say."

DE watched him for a moment, her face thoughtful. "So what

are you doing here? Why'd you transfer so late in the year?"

Xander's pulse picked up. He'd evaded that question from a few other students, by just laughing and making a stupid joke or changing the subject smoothly. But for some reason, he found he couldn't do that with DE. "Ah . . . I have my reasons."

CHAPTER 19

XANDER

Her green eyes sparkled in the dim light. "Reeeeally? I have to say, I love me a mystery."

"It's kind of a boring mystery. You wouldn't want to hear it."

DE kept swaying to the music, but her gaze was locked on his. "Try me."

They looked at each other in silence for a moment, the music and chatter from the other students fading away. "Okay," Xander said slowly, "but only if you tell me why you're on a self-imposed dating embargo."

Her face closed off immediately; she even stopped dancing with as much verve. It was like someone had turned out the lights inside her. "Yeah . . . no."

"No?"

She shook her head, glanced down at her boots. "No. It's, um . . . it's not something I like to talk about. Or *can* talk about, to be honest. Not without bursting into tears, anyway." She looked up at him, eyes narrowed. "And *nobody* sees Daphne Elizabeth McKinley cry."

The Melanie Martinez song they'd been dancing to wound

down, and Xander smiled a little as a Lizzo one began to play, to many whoops and shouts of approval from the other students. But before he could respond, the meager light from the paper lanterns winked out and the thumping music completely shut off. Outside, the storm howled, audible in the basement now that the music was off. Everybody went stock-still and eerily quiet, just for a moment.

Then the lights flickered back on and the music blared to life again, and the people all around them screamed and yelled and laughed in approval. One guy even threw his head back and howled.

"Generator must've kicked in," Xander said to DE, who looked just as startled as he'd felt a moment ago. "Just the storm, messing with the power."

"Oh." She smiled, a little wanly, he thought.

He took a breath, eager to get the conversation back on track. "Okay. I hear you about not wanting to talk about your dating embargo. I get it." But he found himself burning with curiosity and a strange protectiveness. What had happened to her? Had someone hurt her? Just the thought made him want to punch something, and he was not a violent guy.

"Hey, I kinda want to take a break." DE gestured to a quiet corner where someone had piled a bunch of beanbags and floor pillows. "Do you mind if I just go chill over there for a bit?"

"Not at all. Do you want some company?"

She smiled at him. "Yeah, sure. That sounds nice."

Xander led her off the dance floor. "I'll grab us a couple of Cokes and meet you there."

He watched her walk away, thinking, *You really don't have time for this, Xander. You're here for one thing and one thing only. Remember?*

Thing was, around DE, it was so easy to forget.

DE

DE watched him getting the Cokes, maneuvering deftly around groups of laughing, chatting students, his orange glow-in-the-dark necklace making it easy for her to track him in the dim lighting. He was so . . . unassuming. In spite of being drop-dead, model gorgeous, he seemed like the kind of guy who was content to just melt into the shadows. He'd rather be in the audience than on the stage. He was completely different from anyone she'd ever dated before, especially Alaric.

Not that Xander and I are dating, she rushed to add. *Or even going to. Obviously.* It was just a casual observation. You know. Just a mental note.

She'd have to be completely moronic to fall into anything else this quickly after being unceremoniously dumped by Alaric. She had more sense than that. It didn't matter how nice a guy Xander seemed to be. She had her heart to think about, still battered and bruised and limping along with one shoe off. Not to mention, Xander obviously had some secrets of his own. Secrets meant complications. And damn, was she tired of both secrets and complications. She'd had enough to last her a lifetime, thanks to the Alaric fiasco.

As if thinking about him had summoned him (wouldn't surprise her at all if he were some kind of demon, to be honest), Alaric suddenly appeared at the drinks table beside Xander. Too self-conscious for garish colors like pink or neon orange, he was wearing a blue glow-in-the-dark necklace that complemented his blue eyes perfectly. His blond hair was as high and perfectly gelled and coiffed as usual, in a tall mound that wouldn't move in gale-force winds. With that usual imperious look on his face, he bumped Xander out of the way and reached for the two Cokes Xander had clearly been about to pick up without so much as an "Excuse me."

When Alaric turned to leave, Xander said, "Yo. Johnny Bravo." She could barely hear him over the music, but his voice was unmistakably authoritative.

Alaric turned to him, his blond eyebrows raised. "Are you speaking to me?"

Xander slowly crossed his arms and leaned against the table. He tipped his chin at the Cokes in Alaric's hand. "Those are mine."

"There are dozens like them on the table," Alaric said dismissively. "Get another."

He began to turn away, but Xander took a step closer to him, his golden gaze unflinching. "There may be a million others like them, but those two are mine." His voice was soft and steady, but the thread of warning in it was palpable.

DE swallowed, wondering what Alaric would do. He hated to be shown up in any way, and most people, sensing this, avoided confrontation with him.

He and Xander were exactly the same height, and for one long moment, they stared at each other, neither giving an inch.

Then, finally, Alaric sighed, the most dramatic thing DE had ever heard. "Oh, fine." He thrust the two Cokes into Xander's hands. "Take them."

Without a word, Xander turned on his heel and walked toward DE. Alaric stood watching his retreating back for a moment before getting two more Cokes and melting into the crowd.

When Xander was closer, he grinned and handed DE one of the cold Cokes. "Coke, as the madam ordered." He sat on the beanbag next to DE with a *whoomph*.

They cracked their Cokes open in silence. DE felt the fizz tickling her upper lip as she took a swig, surreptitiously watching Xander over her can. She'd never seen someone so seamlessly and efficiently put Alaric in his place before. She'd never seen Alaric back down that quickly, like, ever. Who *was* this guy?

And to look at him now, he didn't look even mildly annoyed by the encounter. It was as if Alaric and his entitled arrogance had never existed. Whereas, DE knew, wherever Alaric had disappeared off to, he'd spend at least half the night sulking and grumbling to anyone who'd listen about how Rosetta Academy allowed in clueless and uncouth people who didn't know who Alaric Konig was.

As if sensing her thoughts, Xander caught her eye. "You good?"

"Fine." She smiled at him, still feeling a little off-kilter by what she'd seen. It made her feel closer to Xander somehow, as if they shared a common enemy. Which was silly, she knew. Alaric was of no consequence to Xander, and he was of enormous consequence to DE. But that was precisely *why*, in a way, she felt closer to Xander. It was like he'd shown her that, to some people in the world, Alaric was really just a spoiled rich kid, no one special. And that, to her in her current state of mind, was mind-blowing.

On impulse, DE set her Coke down by her feet and leaned forward. "You really wanna know about the whole 'self-imposed embargo on dating' thing?"

Xander immediately looked up from his soda. "Yeah. If you want to share, I mean."

CHAPTER 20

DE

DE nibbled on her lower lip, her heart thudding in her chest. The lack of light in here was definitely making her braver than she'd normally be.

The thing was, this was so hard to talk to her friends about. They all knew Alaric—Caterina had been dating him at the same time DE had (something DE didn't like to think about). And they knew DE really well. Their opinions were hardly objective. But Xander . . . Xander was a clean slate. Tabula rasa. And he seemed like he had a good head on his shoulders. She took a deep breath. "That guy you just met over at the drinks table?"

Xander's eyebrows were knitted together. "Who? Oh, Johnny Bravo?"

DE snorted. "His name's Alaric. But yeah, him. He and I . . . um, we kind of had a thing. We were seeing each other, but he had a serious girlfriend at the same time. Caterina."

Xander gestured in the general direction of the dance floor, his eyebrows slightly raised. "Caterina, the girl in your friend group?"

"Yeah." DE felt her cheeks glow with shame and guilt. As

long as she lived, she'd regret helping Alaric cheat on Caterina. She knew this with absolute certainty. Even when she was thirty years old and traveling the world in style, she'd look back on this with horrendous shame. "She and I are cool now, but . . . Alaric dumped me. It got really bad between us. He's said some things that . . ." She shook her head, a lump in her throat. The fact that the lump was there at all made her want to tear her hair out. "And he—I hate to admit it, even to myself—but he still has a hold on me. He's in my head all the time. I just . . . I feel like shit about so many things that happened between us."

"I'm sorry," Xander said quietly.

DE forced a laugh and played with the hem of her dress, not able to meet his eye. "I won't blame you if you're judging me for being the sidepiece. *I* judge me."

Xander set his Coke can down by his feet too. Leaning forward, he dipped his head until she was forced to look into his eyes. "I don't judge you. At all. Believe me, I'm in no position to judge anyone. We all do things we think are good ideas at the moment, and then we look back and . . ." He shook his head. "We feel like absolute dickheads. I get it."

DE smiled. "You sound like you're speaking from experience."

"Yeah, I am. I definitely am. But look, I've gotten to know you a little bit and you don't seem like a cheating, lying kind of person. If you lost your head and made a mistake, that's not something that gets to define you forever." He jerked his head toward the crowd. "And neither does some stiff-haired loser."

DE smiled a little. Her entire *self* felt raw, rubbed through with a pumice stone. She hated talking about Alaric; she hated admitting how weak she was when it came to him. But talking about this with Xander had, for some reason, brought some light to the darkest corners of her heart. "Thanks. Has anyone told you you're a good listener? You could probably go to grad school for therapy and charge a thousand dollars an hour for what you just did for me."

Xander snorted, picked up his soda can, and took a deep drink. "You're the first person to say *that*."

"What *do* you want to do?" DE asked with sudden interest. "When you graduate?"

Xander shrugged easily and looked out over the dancing students. The floor under their feet thumped with the beat. "I don't know. I haven't really thought about it."

"So . . . you haven't applied anywhere? For college, I mean?" She didn't mean to sound like a helicopter parent, but this was pretty significant for a Rosetta Academy student, even if he was new. Most of them had known since they were six that they were going to apply to the same Ivy League universities their parents had gone to.

Xander smirked at her, as if he knew exactly what she was thinking. "Nope. And believe me, my parents were *not* happy about that. I think I got my first Harvard sweatshirt from my dad when I turned one."

DE laughed softly. "Yeah. Same, except it's Dartmouth for me. My parents met there, so, you know. They think it's in my blood or something." She paused. Then, smiling a little, she asked, "So I guess you won't be going into the family assassination business?"

Xander chuckled. "Sorry to disappoint. My family business is living off trust funds that previous generations set up for us. And I don't know what I want to do, but I know it isn't that."

She didn't want to admit it even to herself, but DE thrilled to this bit of information, dropped like a crumb on the way to a bigger gingerbread house. Xander was so . . . opaque. And she'd just let him see a pretty big part of herself. "So what did the previous generations do that let them set up those trust funds?" she asked, hoping he wouldn't stop talking now.

He darted a sideways glance at her. "You really want to know?"

She leaned into him without quite realizing she was doing it. "Absolutely."

A smile played at his lips. "My great-grandparents and my grandparents were sort of . . . A-list Hollywood peeps."

DE's mouth popped open. Whatever she'd been expecting, it wasn't *that*. "No kidding! Oh my god! Who were they?"

He dropped a couple of names, big-name directors and actors from past decades even she'd heard of, though she was nowhere near a movie buff. "That's *insanely* cool, Xander."

DE was no stranger to Hollywood types, given that so many of them chose to stay at McKinley Hotels when they traveled. She even had a couple of A-list actresses she texted with on a regular basis. But *Xander*? *Xander* was from a dramatic (literally) family line? It was weird how much he eschewed the spotlight. In DE's experience, Hollywood stars—and their relatives—loved nothing more than to be adored. But at least now she knew the secret behind those killer cheekbones.

He studied the expression on her face. "What?"

She tried to suppress the avid curiosity burning through her eyes. Everyone always said her eyes were a dead giveaway to whatever she was feeling inside. "Um . . . nothing. I just . . . That's the first time you've ever told me anything substantial about yourself."

He continued to gaze at her for another moment, and DE found she couldn't tell at all what he was thinking. Then, dropping his head, he sighed as he cradled his soda in both hands. "Yeah. That's by design."

She frowned. "What do you mean?"

He turned to face her again. "DE, I'm here for a very specific purpose that has nothing to do with academics." And then, grimacing, he stopped abruptly and took a deep drink, as if he was afraid he'd said too much.

CHAPTER 21

XANDER

Stupid, stupid, stupid. Why had he said that? What had possessed him to hint at the *one thing* he'd promised himself no one would find out until he was done with Rosetta Academy?

An image flashed into his mind, unbidden: wild green eyes in the dark, staring into his own brown ones. Eyes that swirled with secrecy and curiosity and an unfettered *being*. DE's eyes.

She'd told him something, he knew, at great cost to herself. That thing with Johnny Bravo—Alaric, whatever—was really eating away at her. It was why her smile faded so quickly, why she laughed behind her hand, hiding, like she was afraid to fully give in to joy. It was why he could sense that every time she got even the tiniest bit close to him, she pulled away like a flower folding into its petals, afraid of being hurt again.

He had guessed she had something like a bad breakup in her history. But when she actually chose to be transparent with him, at this stupid senior party, he'd been completely taken aback. He hadn't expected it; he wasn't sure he deserved her confidence. And yet she'd placed her trust—at least in this instance—in his palms, a tiny, fragile glass bird he was determined not to break.

So it had seemed only right, in the moment, to give a bit of himself to her as well. And what was something no one else knew about him? His reason for being here, of course. The reason he'd upended his senior year and come to this strange fortress-like boarding school hidden away in the mountains.

Atticus Wakefield.

Blowing out a breath, deciding to take the leap before his logical mind could talk him out of it, he looked at DE. Gesturing at the dancing, hollering students, he asked, "Do you wanna take a walk? Get a break from the noise?"

She stood without hesitation, smoothing her palms on that velvet dress he was trying to not stare at. The neon light of her necklace lit up her high, delicate cheekbones in electric-pink spots. "Sure."

They walked together out of the basement, passing some late-arriving stragglers (who had clearly started the celebration in their own rooms). None of them paid any attention to DE or Xander, busy as they were pretending to be zombies from *The Walking Dead*, which worked well for Xander. He was wound tight, wondering what the hell he'd gotten himself into. Was he really going to tell her? He barely knew this girl. Xander glanced sidelong at her as they walked, the way she loped gracefully beside him, as if she was bouncing on soft clouds no one else could see. She had to be curious, but she didn't ask him what this was all about. She didn't pressure him. And he appreciated that.

Still, the tension of what she'd asked and what he'd said was pulled taut between them in the silence, a rubber band stretched to breaking point. In silent but mutual agreement, they wound higher and higher up the building, using the back staircase. Xander imagined them suspended in the sky, among the snow clouds and the frigid whipping wind and the squalls of snow, alone and unbothered. He found he kind of liked the image. If there was anyone he'd like to be suspended in the sky with, it was DE.

Now, that's a hell of a weird thought.

"This might be an odd suggestion, but considering we're almost there, anyway . . . Attic?" DE asked, and Xander realized with a start that they were already at the trapdoor to the attic. If he weren't aware of every thought he'd had on the way up, he'd think he'd lost time again.

"We do both seem to like to hide away up there, so, yeah." He smiled. "Sounds good to me."

DE pulled out a key on a long black thread hanging around her neck. It had been tucked into her shirt. Smiling a little sheepishly, she said, "I like to keep it with me. Sometimes the need to get away just creeps up on me out of the blue. Maybe the result of being an only child."

She opened the trapdoor and then used the piece of rope dangling from it to pull down the stairs.

The attic was almost completely dark, the small diamond-shaped window covered with a thick coating of unrelenting snow. Xander reached up and tugged the pull to turn on the lone bulb, filling the dusty space with anemic yellow light. But even in the shadows, DE's emerald eyes danced. He knew what was going through her mind because it was going through his, too—they were standing closer to each other than either of them had realized in the dark.

They stood looking at each other in silence for a beat, Xander's heart thundering. Then DE broke eye contact, wrapping her long arms around her body and shivering lightly. "It's cold." She walked to the window and tapped on it as if to dislodge the snow. It didn't work. "Feels like we're in an igloo."

Xander smiled. "I can't do anything about the snow, but I *do* have a solution for the cold."

DE turned to him, her eyes wide, her lips parted. It took him a moment to understand the double entendre of his words: a solution to the cold could be a hug . . . or a kiss. He watched in fascination as her cheeks pinked and her red-gold eyelashes fluttered. Her hand flew up to her neck, which she cupped as she finally broke eye contact. Probably because she'd just remembered her self-imposed dating embargo. As should he.

Goddamn. He needed to get out of this state of mind, pronto.

In quick strides, Xander walked over to the far side of the attic and reached behind one of the trunks he'd rummaged through not so long ago, the one that held the map that still didn't make sense to him. He turned around holding a flannel blanket.

DE's expression rearranged itself into a smile. "You stowed a blanket up here? That's genius."

Grinning, Xander unfolded the blanket as he walked back to her and draped it around her shoulders. His hands lingered on her shoulders in spite of his best expectations, her body heat radiating a warm glow, before he cleared his throat and stepped away. His pulse was flying.

DE's cheeks were tinted a faint pink again. "You, ah, want to sit?" She gestured to the window seat she'd made from old trunks at some point.

Xander nodded. "Sure."

They made their way to the window seat, again in absolute quiet. The burden of the silence was on him, he knew. He had to speak, to tell her why he'd led her all the way up here.

"So." He cleared his throat again.

"So." DE kicked her boots lightly against the trunk, her eyes searching his face, her expression carefully controlled in the shadows. She pulled the blanket tighter around herself.

"DE . . ." Xander took a breath, clutching the edge of the trunk with both hands until his knuckles turned as pale as they were capable of turning. The wind rattled the window, as if telling him to get on with it. So he did.

"I came to Rosetta Academy to solve a mystery that's plagued my family for generations." There was silence as she studied him, eyes alight with curiosity. Xander snorted. "That sounds extremely fucking dramatic, but it's true."

DE didn't laugh or even crack a smile, her eyes still blazing with the need to know. "What . . . what mystery?"

"The death of my great-great-great-uncle, Atticus Wakefield. He was a student here at Rosetta the year they opened. He died the following year, during the great storm of 1873—a storm the Academy doesn't even like to acknowledge happened. A dead student the very first year? Bad publicity. No one knows what happened to him. Atticus was found inside his dorm room, which was locked from the inside. The windows were shut. He was lying in bed, as if asleep, only they couldn't get him to wake up. The cause of death on his death certificate was listed as 'natural causes.'" Xander looked sidelong at DE. "As if it's natural for a healthy eighteen-year-old to fall asleep and never wake up. Rosetta paid off the coroner. I'm sure of it. His body was shipped back home, and then Rosetta Academy closed its doors to my family, sealing its secrets inside. I'm here to break the vault and figure out what happened."

CHAPTER 22

DE

DE studied Xander's face, waiting for him to burst out laughing or give any indication that he was bullshitting her. But there was none. He was totally serious, his golden sand-dune eyes holding hers steadily, waiting for a response, dark hair like an inkblot against his face.

"Wow." She shook her head, the word too small for what he'd told her, but it still felt big in the quiet, dusty space. "You're like a real-life Hercule Poirot." At Xander's confused look, she added, "Ah, I'm a huge Agatha Christie nerd."

He smiled at that, and DE couldn't help but notice how well that smile fit his face. "Gotcha." After a pause, he added, "Does that sound totally nuts to you? That I basically upended my senior year to come here and chase this mystery down?"

She chewed on her lip and considered this. "Not nuts, exactly . . . But I *am* curious why you felt the need to do it. This happened so long ago. Why now?"

The light bulb flickered as Xander spoke, throwing shadows across his dark, handsome face. "I guess I just realized that this is sort of the last gasp. After I graduate high school, I won't be able to 'infiltrate' Rosetta Academy as easily. My family has tried, over the generations, to figure out what happened. And all we get are condescending non-answers or silence. Rosetta has a legion of excellent lawyers, as you can imagine.

"I may not have known Atticus Wakefield, but I know the toll his death took on my family. His mother died of a broken heart six months after he passed away. Her husband was so bereft at losing his wife of twenty years that he drank himself into a slow, painful suicide. Ever since then, addiction has run rampant in my family. It's true what they say, you know. That shit runs in families like some kind of devastating genetic wildfire. If you follow the branches of my family tree, you can see the impact Atticus's death had, like poison sucked up from the soil and seeping into every branch, every stem, and every leaf." Xander paused and took a deep breath.

"And . . . about six months ago . . ." He cleared his throat, wishing this wasn't so hard. Wishing, more than anything, that it wasn't true. "Six months ago, my mom died of a cocaine over-dose. And I want some fucking answers." His eyes felt hot with tears that he'd shed over and over and over again for most of his life and especially these last six months. He couldn't bring himself to look at DE, so he kept his gaze at a middle distance on the attic floor. "My dad's completely shut down; he won't talk, he barely eats, he sits in the study all day every day with the curtains closed. The house is a fucking tomb. And maybe it's stupid of me to come all this way to figure out something that happened to an ancient relative, but I want answers about why my mom had to die the way she did. Why my family is the way it is—twisted and gnarled, like some rotted tree trunk.

"The kind of generational pain we've had to endure deserves

more than what Rosetta's given us. They legally blocked us from looking into it, issued a gag order back then so my family couldn't get any answers about what really happened to Atticus. But we deserve to know what happened, even if it tarnishes Rosetta's perfectly polished reputation. And that's why I'm here."

DE found herself leaning in as he spoke, letting each word sink into her, feeling a measure of his grief, his pain. She'd never dealt with anything of this magnitude in her entire life; she couldn't even imagine it. Her own family was fucked up and dysfunctional; her parents thought of her as a glass doll, easy to look through. But this . . . this was . . . She didn't even have a word for it. She couldn't help but see him as a valiant knight, determined to right a monstrous wrong in the only way he knew how.

"Xander," she said finally, her heart hurting for him. "Xander . . . I'm so very sorry. I know those words don't do justice after what you've been through, not at all." She turned sideways on the trunk so she was facing him. His eyes were red around the corners, his mouth pulled down in a hard line. Without giving herself too much time to think about it, DE put her hand over his. He didn't pull away. "That absolutely, monumentally sucks."

He looked down at their hands, clasped together. "Yeah, it does. She struggled with it all my life. My earliest memories are of her freaking out in withdrawal, you know? But still, I didn't want her to go. Not this way." He shook his head, a muscle in his jaw ticking.

"I think it's fucking *incredible* that you want to find answers for your family, though. That you want to break this generational . . . curse, I guess, that you guys have been dealing with."

He looked at her then, his eyes roving her face, as if wondering if she meant it. Whatever he saw there must have satisfied him, because he nodded once. "Thanks. I just, I don't know what else to do. But this . . . this feels like a good place to start." He paused and looked intently at DE. "That's why you can't tell anyone what I just told you. Okay? It's very important that none of the admin know exactly who I am or why I'm here."

DE nodded immediately. "Of course. I won't tell anyone." After a pause, she added, "Your last name . . . Murthy. That's Indian, right?"

"Yeah, South Indian. Some of my dad's side of the family is from India. But we're really all blended together—we've got Irish and Scottish and West African blood all mixed into our lineage." He half smiled. "Keeps it interesting, I guess."

In spite of the smile, DE noticed Xander's tight jaw, his fingers clamped around the edge of the trunk. She couldn't imagine what was going through his mind. "So," she said softly, "can I ask: Why did you tell me? I mean, we don't really know each other."

Xander regarded her frankly. "Why did you tell me about Alaric?"

DE's cheeks heated. She dropped her gaze, intent on the stitched hem of her dress. "Um . . . I'm actually not sure. I think it was seeing the way you talked to him at the drinks table? No one really ever talks to Alaric like that."

Xander snorted, seemingly grateful for the change in topic to something less heavy. "Yeah, I could tell by the way his jaw unhinged and fell to the floor. It took two of his little friends to pick it up, dust it off, and refit it onto his face." After a moment he added, "It was really brave of you to tell me about him, by the way. I could tell it wasn't easy."

Still not looking at him, DE let out a sigh. "It's not easy at all."

Her voice was barely audible, and it was impossible to hide the tremor in it.

Xander's voice was gentle when he spoke again. "You impress me."

DE looked up at him, her eyebrows knitted together. "Huh?"

"You impress me," he said again. "That's why I told you about Atticus and what I'm actually doing here. Seeing you share a part of yourself that's obviously super vulnerable and hard to talk about . . . It was badass. And I thought if you could do that, I could tell you about my fucked-up family."

DE smiled, feeling a little warm glow in the center of her chest.

"Besides," Xander continued, smirking, "you don't seem like the kind to go running to the establishment, anyway."

She laughed out loud at that. "Yeah, not so much."

The wind threw a tantrum outside, reminding them they weren't alone and not entirely safe. DE pulled the blanket tighter around her shoulders; it had slipped while they were talking and she hadn't even noticed.

"So . . . ," Xander said when the worst of the wind had died down. "How long do you think your self-imposed dating embargo is going to last?"

CHAPTER 23

DE

His words were casual, light as snowflakes, but DE felt the weight of them regardless. She kept focusing on the hem of her dress, the press of the trunk's hard edge on the backs of her knees. "Ah . . . I'm . . . I'm not sure. My friends keep asking me, you know. They keep wanting to set me up with cute guys." *Like you.* "Pretty sure they feel bad for me. Like I'll die alone or something."

"And you?" Xander asked quietly. "Do *you* feel bad for you?"

DE took a moment to think about this. "Sometimes. Sometimes I get scared. I've never felt this detached from . . . myself, from everything, before. I hate that I gave Alaric a piece of myself that I should've safeguarded with everything I had." She shrugged and looked at Xander. "I don't know if I'll die alone. But I do think I'll live alone. And to me, that's worse." To DE's horror, a hot tear splashed onto her cheek. She hurried to swipe it away with a fist and made an attempt at laughing. "Yikes."

Xander put a big, warm hand over hers and looked into her eyes. "It's okay. I'm not judging you. And for what it's worth, I don't think you're gonna live *or* die alone. I just . . . can't see that happening with you."

Something about the way he said it, the intent behind his words and his eyes, made DE's cheeks heat. To distract from that, DE huffed. "Yeah, sure, thanks."

"I mean it."

DE waved him away, feeling her skin prickling with sweat, her pulse racing in a way it hadn't in a very long time. She didn't like that at all. *Keep it in your pants, McKinley.* "Um. So. I was thinking, ever since you told me about your mom and Atticus . . ."

Xander quirked an eyebrow. "Yeah, that was about five minutes ago."

"Yeah." She turned to look at him, tucking one long leg underneath her. "So. Maybe I could help."

He looked taken aback; he pushed a hunk of thick hair off his forehead, but it flopped right back down again. "Really?"

"I need a project, a distraction, and this could be the perfect way to spend the last bit of senior year. What do you think?"

After a long pause, Xander shrugged. "If you really mean it . . . that would be incredible."

DE smiled. "Yeah?"

"Hell yeah. I could really use another brain on this."

"Great." She rubbed her hands together like a movie villain. "Anytime you want to take down the establishment, I'm your girl. So, what do you have so far?"

Laughing, Xander crossed to the far end of the attic. Rummaging in an old trunk there, he pulled out a roll of paper, then crossed back to DE. "It might be easier to spread this out on the floor."

DE nodded, and they both knelt on the creaking wooden planks. Xander unrolled the yellowing, onion skin–like paper, which DE saw now was a blueprint of Rosetta Academy.

"The oldest blueprint I've been able to find," Xander said, confirming her thoughts. "It's from 1872." He pointed to the date carefully printed in the corner.

"Whoa . . ." DE was afraid to even breathe on the paper. It was delicate, she could tell, thin as a whispered secret. She leaned over the design, thinking of the architect from the nineteenth century who must've so carefully pored over this, envisioning a school that was just a dream at the time.

"Yeah, it's pretty amazing. And when I'm done with it, I'm donating it to the Academy. But first . . ." His long index finger hovered in the air over the center of the paper. "You see this? This is the main building, where we are. You can see the architect designated four floors, one for each year of high school. And each dorm is indicated too."

DE nodded as she followed along.

"But the problem comes in when you look at the dorm numbers. They start at 100-A for the freshman dorms and end at 450-D for the seniors."

"Yeah?"

"Atticus was a senior. He stayed in dorm 482-D. I know that for a fact because I found a letter from Atticus's mother that referenced his address at the school."

DE finished Xander's thought. "But dorm 482-D doesn't exist. At least, not according to this blueprint."

"Right."

They both sat back and looked at each other, stumped.

"I'm kind of lost." Xander leaned back on the palms of his hands, his long legs stretched out in front of him. "And believe me, I haven't been averse to chasing down sketchy rumors. When you ran into me on Huntley Hill? I was there because I'd read online that there was a secret mystery dormitory floor either on top of Huntley Hill or buried into its side."

"I'm guessing that didn't pan out?"

Xander smiled a little. "Yeah, no. The only thing I found up there was you. And that weird doll."

DE laughed. "Sorry you got a bum deal."

"I wouldn't say that," Xander replied seriously.

DE tugged at her earlobe and looked back at the blueprint, pretending to herself that she didn't like that comment at all. No, siree. "So, listen. I have an idea."

Xander sat up.

"Have you tried the library? They have all these archives of random things. They might have more information on the hidden dorms."

"Yeah." Xander sighed. "The girl there told me I had to have special permission from the admin to see that kind of stuff. And obviously the admin isn't going to just give permission without a damn good reason." He paused. "Actually, the student assistant I talked to in the library? It was the girl you were talking to in Ms. Blackmoor's class—Anna something."

DE brightened. "Really? Then I think we may be in luck, Mr. Murthy. After all, she *is* a fan."

Xander cocked an eyebrow. "If you say so. When do you want to go?"

"Tomorrow morning. As soon as the library opens, because this is killing me and I have to solve this thing now."

Xander grinned. "Deal." He paused, scratched his nose. "Ah, you wanna get coffee first at the dining hall?"

DE found herself also scratching her nose, not meeting his eye as she answered. "Yeah, sure. Whatever."

Coffee and the library with Xander. It was definitely *not* a date, but she found she didn't mind the thought of spending time with him. She didn't mind it at all. And that was a problem.

Check yourself, McKinley. You've already given away too many pieces of yourself; how many more before you're unrecognizable?

DE sat up straighter, edged just a bit farther away from Xander on the dusty attic floor. She wouldn't give up anything of herself to this boy, no matter how intriguing or charming she found him. She'd learned her lesson very thoroughly with Alaric.

The storm howled like an angry beast outside.

CHAPTER 24

XANDER

It was close to three a.m. when Xander and DE made their way back to the dorms. He still couldn't believe he'd unloaded all that on her . . . and that she hadn't run off, screaming. It was heavy shit, he knew, and he was touched by how kind she'd been. And silly as it was, he found he was pretty excited about getting coffee with her tomorrow and then checking out the library situation.

They were halfway to her dorm room—he wanted to walk her there, just in case; the party had definitely amped up some of the students—when they passed a trio of friends half carrying, half dragging a senior boy to his dorm.

When they saw Xander watching, they smirked. "Too many Jell-O shots."

Beside him, DE rolled her eyes. "Yeah, that sounds like Paul."

But she took a good look at Paul as they passed, and once they were out of earshot of the group, leaned into Xander. "Did he look a little . . . weird to you?"

Xander frowned. "'Weird' how?"

DE shook her head, her earrings catching the light. "Not sure. Just kind of, like, waxy or something?"

Xander turned to look over his shoulder, but the group had turned the corner and was gone. "Maybe a little."

DE shrugged. "It's probably just me. I think I need to get some sleep." They were outside her dorm now, and she turned to face him. "And you do too. You have bags under your eyes."

He smiled lightly. "Okay. I'll see you bright and early?"

She pointed at him, adorably awkward in that DE way. "Coffee and the library. It's a date."

He tried not to grin all the way back to his room.

?

And so they began to fall, one by one by one. The storm threw back its head and opened its mouth, doing what it did best, taking, taking, taking. She stood there, watching. Waiting.

DE

At 7:55 a.m., DE was in the silent and empty senior dining hall, waiting for Xander. The white-aproned staff moved quietly behind the granite counters and in the kitchens beyond, cutlery clinking softly, the smell of Black Ivory coffee pervading the cool, hushed air.

The other seniors were all probably recovering from the party last night, but still. The vast, empty space gave her the creeps. It didn't help that classes had been canceled for the duration of the storm too: on a normal day, she'd be the first one to jump on a table and sing some bad karaoke to celebrate, but now

Rosetta just seemed dead to her, lifeless in a way she'd never seen it before.

Across the hall, she could see the storm pulsing and pushing against the glass of the tall windows. Shivering, she pulled out her phone and began to scroll through social media. She and Xander had agreed the previous night that they'd meet down here at eight a.m. Much as she'd tried to slow her roll while getting dressed, she'd found herself ready and twiddling her thumbs by six a.m., which was *definitely* new for her.

The thing was, a strange, electric energy was coursing through her, forcing her awake by five a.m. She didn't know if it was what Xander had told her about Atticus or the thought of spending the morning with him (again, problematic) or the storm, which had built and built until it was a monstrous thing, howling and beating itself against her windows, but DE had found herself tossing and turning, in and out of the blankets, until she'd thrown them off in disgust and decided to take a tepid shower.

Putting her phone away, DE brushed off her pants and regarded her outfit critically. She'd gone classic dark academia today, which she thought was fitting for the morning she and Xander had planned. She was wearing a blazer, turtleneck, loose trousers, and boots, all in varying shades of black, jewel green, and autumnal brown. She thought the palette particularly complemented her red hair and green eyes—and then began to worry that Xander would think she was trying to impress him.

DE sighed and mentally shook herself. *Who the hell cares what Xander thinks, McKinley? Just be yourself. Do what you want to do, wear what you want to wear.* She felt immediately better after the internal pep talk. She was here for herself, first and foremost.

Feeling a tap on her shoulder, she turned to see Xander beside her, smiling. He was dressed in straight-leg jeans and a brown sweater, which paired with her outfit perfectly, as if they'd coordinated. His dark hair was damp as it hung on his forehead, like he'd just gotten out of the shower, and he smelled like soap and a hint of laundry detergent. "Hey."

That smile. Oof.

"Good morning." She felt her cheeks heat and a weird, glowing warmth in her diaphragm, which she coughed to cover up. "Um, did you sleep okay?" His bags were gone, so the answer was probably yes.

"Yep." He chuckled. "Last night was pretty . . . interesting, huh? Hopefully that kid we passed in the hall doesn't have a killer hangover today."

DE nibbled on her lip. He was talking about Paul. Something about the way he'd looked, so still and oddly pale, kept niggling at her. "Yeah, hopefully. So, ready to get some coffee and do this thing?"

Xander nodded emphatically. "Abso-fucking-lutely. I really hope the library has what I need." They walked to the marble coffee counter, behind which were two smiling middle-aged baristas, dressed in red-and-gray-striped shirts under their aprons—Rosetta Academy colors. At Rosetta, a skeleton service staff was maintained even in emergency situations. You know, lest a royal prince sprain a pinkie getting his own cup of coffee.

"It will," DE said, more confidently than she felt. "We're going to get this thing figured out. A medium latte, please," she added to the male barista.

"Same for me, thanks." Xander turned to DE, leaning his hip against the counter. "Did you notice how much worse the storm got overnight? I have absolutely no internet. Rosetta's internal

Wi-Fi is still up, though, so we can send messages to everyone at school."

They both glanced up as the overhead lights flared briefly in intensity and then flickered back down to normal. "Yeah, and the lights doing that pulsing generator thing is going to drive me batshit." The windows at the far end of the hall shook in their panes, hunkering down against a growing wind. From what she could see, the snowdrifts must be several feet high. "Anyway, yeah, it's ridiculous. I hope it passes soon. Until then, I guess we'll all be using RA's internal messaging system."

Xander blew out a breath. "Wonder if this was what it was like for Atticus back in the 1800s."

"Somehow I think they were more used to being at the mercy of nature. I mean, our emergency supplies apparently include lattes in the middle of a fucking snowstorm."

Xander snorted. "Yeah, you're probably right."

The barista handed them their aforementioned lattes, and DE and Xander took a seat at a dining table for six, choosing to sit opposite each other near one end. Letting the steam curl around her face, DE nibbled on her lower lip. "Are you nervous at all? About finding out what happened to Atticus, I mean?"

Xander frowned and took a sip of his latte. "Why would I be?"

"Well, I mean, if there was foul play . . . it might mean a murder investigation. Right? Even though it happened so long ago? Plus, it might mean a lot of publicity for your family and the Academy, and the Academy definitely does not like to be in the media except in a very, *very* positive light. They might come after your family with their lawyers or maybe even a smear campaign."

Xander appeared to consider this, tapping his fingers on the wooden table. "I suppose that's true. I didn't really think past the solving-the-mystery part. I guess that was dumb."

"You're focused on your goal. That's not dumb. But now that you know what it might mean . . . does it change anything for you?"

Xander took a deep breath and held DE's eye. "No. Not one thing. My family still deserves to know what happened to Atticus. Beyond that . . . we'll take it as it comes. It's not like my family doesn't have resources to fight back."

DE nodded and took a deep drink of her latte, relishing the warmth coating her throat and pooling in her body. Even though the storm was being kept at bay by Rosetta Academy's superior construction, she still felt as if cold tendrils were making their way in, cooling her blood. "I was hoping you'd say that."

Xander grinned. "Didn't take you for such an anarchist when we first met."

DE laughed. "Stick around and you'll learn a lot more about me than you ever wanted to know."

CHAPTER 25

DE

They finished their coffees quickly, DE burning her tongue and cursing under her breath. But they were both eager to get to the library.

"The archives are one floor lower than the main area of the library," DE explained with a slight lisp from her burned tongue. They approached the double wooden doors with the gold sign above them that said ARCHIVES. "I've actually never been here."

"They really lean into the Hogwarts vibe, don't they?" Xander murmured as they stepped into the cool interior, complete with dark cherrywood floors, high ceilings that boasted massive golden crystal chandeliers, and an imposing polished oak desk behind which sat a student, her head bent over a book. The sign on the desk said STUDENT ASSISTANT, and behind the desk was another set of double doors, tightly shut.

"Hi!" DE called out in her most cheery voice, and the student looked up.

It was Anna, from Ms. Blackmoor's class, just as Xander had said. As soon as she saw DE, her brown eyes lit up. "Oh my gosh, DE, hiiii!" She closed her book—something about fashion design, DE saw—with an adorable owl-shaped bookmark. "How *are* you? Isn't this storm wild? OMG, I *love* your outfit! I'm a dark academia *nut.*"

DE chuckled at the barrage of questions and compliments, immediately deciding that Anna was her favorite freshman. Not that she knew any other freshman, but still. "Hey, Anna." She propped her elbows on the high desk and gestured with her chin at the owl bookmark. "I adore that aesthetic. The drawing, the colors, the folk-artsy vibe . . . It all just *works.*"

Anna's mouth fell open. "Oh my god, you really think so? Thank you!! I made that myself when I was bored. I could make you one if you want!"

DE was going to end up with a little sister if she wasn't careful. "Oh, you don't have to do that."

"I do, and I will," Anna countered firmly. "What animal or bird should I do? And give me a color palette too."

Seeing that the indomitably cheerful Anna would not be dissuaded, DE gave it some serious thought. "Is a spider too weird?" she asked after a while, thinking of her favorite spider ring. "And maybe an autumnal, witch-core color palette?"

Anna immediately and very seriously jotted something down on her phone. "That's going to be *fabulous.* I can't wait to work on this."

DE grinned. "Hey, thanks. Can I pay you?"

"No!" Anna looked genuinely aghast as she reached around to grab her cardigan off the back of her chair. She shivered slightly as she shrugged into it, DE noticed. "It's a *gift,*" Anna continued. "Absolutely no charge."

"What about if I just promise to tell people about this new, fresh, upcoming talent? Especially some Parisian fashion-industry friends I have who are going to be staying at McKinley Park Avenue this summer and with whom I will definitely be dining?"

Anna looked like she might faint. "That . . . would be . . . *amazing*."

DE smiled. "Awesome."

Xander had been waiting patiently beside her throughout this exchange, and now she glanced sideways at him as if to telepathically send a message: *I'm working my way up to it, don't worry.* To his credit, though, he didn't seem concerned at all. In fact, he looked like he was enjoying the conversation. There was a small smile on his face, and his golden-brown eyes were crinkled at the corners just the tiniest bit.

"So, Anna . . ." DE set her hands flat on the cool wood of the desk and leaned in, as if letting the other girl in on a secret. "I've sort of run into a problem, and I'm really not sure what to do about it. But I think you may be able to help me."

Anna's eyes were wide. "Absolutely. What do you need?"

She was such a sweet kid. "The thing is, I'm looking for blueprints that are kind of really old."

"Especially to do with the old senior dorms," Xander added, pulling out his phone to show Anna a picture of the blueprint he'd found up in the attic. If Anna was curious about why Xander had a picture of the blueprint, she didn't say anything.

DE explained quickly about the dorms and how they were numbered on the blueprint. "But see, I'm pretty sure there must've been another wing of senior dorms somewhere on campus. I have this relative who went to Rosetta in the 1800s, and I'm pretty sure he stayed in dorm 482-D. But that number doesn't exist on this blueprint."

Anna frowned. "Are you sure you have the dorm number right?"

"Yep," DE replied. "We have an old . . . um, report card from him that lists his dorm number." She wasn't even sure they *had* report cards back then, but she plunged ahead. "And I just think it'd be really cool if I could see the place where Great-Uncle Daphne . . . son stayed while he was here."

Xander coughed a little beside her, but Anna looked intrigued. "Daphneson? So you're named after him?"

DE nodded solemnly. "Yes. You see why it's important to me."

"Absolutely," Anna said again. "Let me poke around on the computers, and I should have an answer for you soon about where you can start searching."

DE made a face. "But don't I need, like, special permission or something to access these archives? I mean, won't we get in trouble for doing this?"

Anna glanced over her shoulder as if checking that they were still alone. "To be honest, the teachers and staff are completely consumed by this storm. No one's been down here except me for two days, and I think it's going to stay that way until everything's back to normal. I could send you a message on the Rosetta Internal Messaging System when I find something, if that works?"

DE clapped her hands. "That would be so great! Thank you!" She reached forward over the desk and gave Anna an impromptu hug. It wasn't even a show; she really, really liked this cute-as-a-button freshman.

Anna grinned, her cheeks going a delightful pink. "No problem."

"Talk soon!" DE waggled her fingers at Anna, and then she and Xander exited through the double doors, the same way they'd come in.

Xander turned to DE, his jaw hanging open, as they walked away. "Okay, that was straight-up magic. I don't think she even remembered turning me away a couple of weeks ago. And then you float in there and all the locks magically unlock?"

DE laughed. "I told you, Anna and I have a special bond. The question is, will you be able to sleep before she sends us that message?"

Xander blew out a breath and rubbed the back of his neck. "That is an excellent question."

DE opened her mouth to respond, but her phone chimed with the distinct *ding-dong!* that meant she'd gotten a message via RIMS. "Whoa, that was fast," she said as she slipped her phone out of her trousers pocket and checked the screen. But it wasn't a message from Anna. It was from Jaya.

Where are you?? it said. **Something's wrong with Leo. I think it's serious.**

DE frowned down at her screen. "Oh shit. Gotta go."

"Wait, what's going on? Can I help?"

"It's my friend Leo." DE waved her phone around as if that would explain anything. "Jaya says he's sick or something? I—I don't know. It sounds bad."

"I'll come with."

Without another word, they dashed off together to the senior dorms.

CHAPTER 26

DE

DE felt sick as they rounded the corner to Leo's dorm room. There was a gaggle of students at the entryway, and even more spilling out into the hallway. They were all talking at the same time, the air thick with sentences she caught only snippets of:

"—wake up—"

"—poisoned?—"

"—infirmary—"

She pushed her way through the crowd, vaguely aware that Xander was right behind her, a solid, if silent, presence.

When she got close enough to see Leo's bed, with Will, Jaya, Grey, Caterina, and Rahul clustered around him in a tight circle, the first thing DE felt was a wave of relief. He was lying peacefully in it, tucked under the covers, both hands folded over his chest. His eyelids fluttered lightly as if he were in a tranquil dream.

But then she realized the absurdity of the situation. With all the chaos in his room, why would Leo be asleep?

A hand grabbed her by the elbow, and she spun to face Jaya. Jaya's face was drawn, her mouth in a tight line. "Oh, thank god you're here," she said in her clipped English accent. "I was worried something awful had happened to you, too."

"What's going on?" DE asked as Will knelt by Leo's bedside and smoothed back his hair, looking frantic. The rest of her friends were in a similar state, all of them talking animatedly together. Rahul, especially, looked incredibly anxious; he and Leo were like brothers. Grey, too, looked uncharacteristically shaken, his mouth drawn into a hard line. No one except Jaya had noticed her arrival. "What's wrong with Leo?"

But even as she asked the question, faint alarm bells were going off in DE's head. Because there was something awfully, eerily familiar about the way Leo looked: skin waxy pale, his form deathly still, much too still to simply be asleep. In a flash, it came back to her—Paul. She'd seen him being carried by his friends after the party, and he'd looked just like this. *Wrong*.

"We don't know." Jaya shook her head. "Will came by ten minutes ago and Leo was like this. None of us have been able to wake him up. We just called the infirmary; the medics are on their way."

"Was he acting sick at all last night?" Xander asked, and DE suddenly remembered he was there.

Will looked up at them, shook his head. "N-no, not really. I mean, I guess toward the end of the night, he was acting a little . . . zoned out. He had this faraway look in his eye, and he wasn't as animated as he usually is. But that was all of us!" He looked around at the friend group for confirmation and got several nods. "We were all tired; we didn't leave the party until two in the morning."

"Yes, Leo was acting lethargic, but well within the normal bounds of his behavior. This should not be happening," Rahul put in, and DE could tell he was trying hard to maintain his usual state of factual logic. His voice trembled, though, giving him away. "There was no indication of pathology, at least to my layman's eye. *None*."

Grey clapped him on the shoulder. "None of us noticed any-thing," he confirmed, his voice low and troubled.

"Where are the medics?" Caterina said severely, glaring toward the door. "This is a completely unacceptable response time—"

But she hadn't finished her sentence when two people, a Black man and a Middle Eastern woman, both dressed in red-and-gray scrubs, came rushing in, holding medical bags and wheeling a stretcher. The students in their way dispersed like smoke.

With clinical efficiency, the man had a blood pressure cuff on Leo while the woman tried to rouse him and checked his breath-ing. "Leo Nguyen," she called loudly. Whoever had made the call to the medics had obviously told them who the patient was. "Can you hear me, Leo?" She rubbed his sternum with her knuckles, but there was absolutely no response. "His airway's clear," she said quietly to her partner, who nodded.

"Pulse ox is 97, BP 123/80."

"Has he taken any drugs or alcohol? It's vital that you be hon-est with us if you want us to help your friend," the woman said to their friend group, her gaze piercing.

"He—he had some alcohol last night," Will admitted, looking worried. He rubbed his forehead. "But it was just one serving, maybe two, of wine. And he drank loads of water with it. He didn't seem to be sick at all, and I was with him for hours afterward."

"Yes, we were all together," Grey said, his voice ringing with authority. "Leo wasn't even drunk."

The medics exchanged a glance, clearly not believing Will's or Grey's story. They were probably used to being BS'd by teenagers.

"Well, we'll need to take him downstairs to figure out what's going on," the male medic said. In a matter of moments, he and his partner had Leo's sleeping form loaded and strapped into the stretcher, and they were wheeling him into the hallway.

"Can I come with you? Please." Will looked like he was about to cry.

"And me as well," Rahul said, his eyes shiny. "He's . . . he's my best friend."

The male medic nodded after a moment of hesitation, his expression softening.

The others squeezed Will's shoulders and patted him on the back.

"We'll come visit as soon as we can," Grey said, concern etching lines around his eyes. "Keep us posted, yeah?"

Will nodded, and then he and Rahul were running down the hallway with the medics and Leo.

DE watched them go, her head full of jumbled thoughts, all jostling for attention. What the hell had just happened? Why had Leo looked just like Paul? "I—" she began, but then there was a commotion from farther down the hallway.

"Help!" someone yelled. "We need help in here! Paul won't wake up!"

And then someone else shouted, "And Penelope and Samira, too!"

DE and Xander exchanged a glance. Her hunch had been right. She turned to Jaya. "I'll text you soon, okay?"

Jaya nodded, her hand twined tightly with Grey's, before turning back to comfort him.

Then Xander and DE dashed out into the hallway to check on the other students who wouldn't wake up. What the *hell* was happening?

CHAPTER 27

DE

DE paced the length of her room, rubbing her tired face with one hand. It was the only place she could talk to Xander in total privacy. "This is wild. And by that I mean *completely* batshit. They *all* had that weird mannequin look I noticed on Paul last night after the party. And they were all way, *way* too still to just be sleeping, Xander. It was like—I don't know, like they'd gone into hibernation or something." She shivered at the memory.

Xander, sitting on the armchair by the window, bent forward with his forearms resting on his thighs, shook his head. His hair flopped in his face. "Four students. What the fuck is happening here?"

"Right? Four students. *Four*. That we know of." DE stopped and took a swig of water from the custom Bling H2O water bottle on her desk, with the Rosetta Academy insignia encrusted on it in gold. The school supplied all the students' fridges with them, and the storm hadn't disrupted the supply—yet. She stopped, put her hands on her hips, and looked at Xander. Her underarms prickled with sweat. "I have something to tell you that's probably going to make me sound just as batshit as this situation."

Xander lifted his head, studied her expression. "Okay."

"You know how I told you about that psychic I visited who predicted the storm?"

"You said she probably just had weather reports before the school did."

"Right." DE began to pace again, muttering to herself. She briefly stumbled into some half-finished calculus homework she'd tossed onto the floor—in all this madness, she'd forgotten calculus even existed, to be honest—and kicked it to the side in irritation. "Dammit. Why didn't I keep it? I should've kept it."

Xander frowned and straightened in the armchair. "Kept what?"

"The thing!" DE flung her hands out and kept pacing, faster and faster. "The square piece of paper she gave me. I threw it away like—like a complete idiot. And it had some writing on it, writing that I can't quite remember. . . ."

Xander narrowed his sand dune–colored eyes. "Okay, you're gonna need to rewind and catch me up."

"Okay, yeah, right." DE took a deep breath and then blew it out, slowing her pacing a bit, trying to calm the fuck down. She took off her blazer with jerky movements, tossed it onto the bed, and said, "It's just . . . I can't stop thinking about what the psychic said." DE screwed up her face, trying to remember the exact words. "'Souls will slumber in the perpetual twilight . . . and one will perish.'" She looked at Xander, raising her eyebrows. "Does that sound like the shit that's happening around here?"

Xander rubbed his chin. "I don't know. . . . Like I said, that could be taken any number of ways."

"Taken any number of ways?" DE couldn't believe he didn't see it her way. "I think it's a little too on the nose! In fact, it could plant a flag on the fucking nose. She literally said people are going to be falling asleep once the storm comes." DE began counting off on her fingers. "Leo. Paul. Penelope. Samira. Xander, what if that's not the end? What if more people are going to—fall asleep, or go into hibernation, or whatever?"

Xander considered her four fingers and then shook his head, running his hands through his hair. "I don't know, DE. Why would the psychic even tell you that?" He blew out a breath. "If you really think this has merit, do you think we should go to the admin?"

DE put her hands on her hips, cocked her head. "And tell them what? That I went to a shady psychic on Main Street and she called down a magic storm and now we're scared? I mean, they'd just laugh at us. And honestly, I wouldn't blame them." She walked closer to Xander. "Look, I *know* this sounds really out there. I'm just saying, there are a lot of coincidences at play here. And even the medics didn't seem to know what was going on. I just think it's worth looking into."

Xander rubbed his square jaw slowly, thinking. "Okay. Say you're right. Say the psychic predicted . . ." He waved his hands around. They were big, but elegant somehow. Like he should play piano. *Focus, DE, Jesus.* ". . . all of this. What next? What should we do?"

DE looked down at her boots as she began pacing again. "I don't know. I mean, I would *like* to go back there, to her store. But . . ." She gestured at the windows, caked with snow and ice. The world beyond was a white sheet. "Obviously that's a no go."

Xander stared at the unforgiving snow, deep in thought. "Wait a minute." He looked back at DE. "She said, 'Souls will slumber . . . and one will perish.'"

"Yeah." DE nibbled on her thumbnail. "Like we need any more fucking stress." She was cursing way more than she usually did in a conversation. But circumstances were dire, dammit.

"Atticus died during a snowstorm almost a hundred and fifty years ago. And just like now, there are no details about the storm or his death. Everything I've been able to find has been carefully bland or straight-up empty. Like they had no idea what to make of what was going on."

DE waited, but he didn't say anything else. "And . . . you think there's a connection?"

Xander shook his head. "I'm not sure. But like you said, we need to do something."

Twin *ding-dong!* sounds filled the room as both their phones chimed. RIMS. They checked their phones, and then DE looked up at Xander. "Dr. Waverly's calling another meeting."

Slipping his phone back into his jeans pocket, Xander stood. "Well, let's go hear what she has to say."

CHAPTER 28

XANDER

Since going to Huntley Hall would require walking out into the storm, the assembly was in the senior dining hall. But the dining hall was too small to fit all the students from all four grades comfortably. As a result, there were people standing four deep against the walls and windows. Anna, the girl from the library and his History of Rosetta Academy class, was huddled with a few friends in the back, who were all gesticulating wildly. Anna herself, though, had her arms crossed around her middle and was staring distractedly out the window at the storm.

By some unspoken law of high school, the seniors had all managed to sit in seats at tables, so Xander and DE walked toward them. Most of the seniors were chattering to each other, nervously bouncing their legs or tapping their fingers on the table. But some kept to themselves, gazing off into the middle distance, as if lost in thought. One senior boy was chugging a gallon bottle of orange juice, extolling the virtues of vitamin C and how it would keep him safe from whatever germ was going around.

The energy in the dining hall was an unsettling mix of chaotic and muted, nervous and distracted.

"This is fucking weird, isn't it?" DE murmured in his ear, and Xander nodded.

"Definitely weird."

DE's friends—minus Leo and Will—waved Xander and DE over as soon as they saw them.

"Saved the two of you seats," Jaya said as they approached. Her face was drawn, serious, as were the faces of the rest of the friend group. There was a pall over them, thick as a blanket.

"Thanks." DE sat and Xander took a seat beside her. She turned to Rahul. "How's Leo?"

Rahul ran a hand through his hair. "No change. Will's still in the infirmary with him. He said he'd send a RIMS text if anything changed." His voice was tightly controlled, as if he were afraid to let his true emotions show. Caterina had her arms around him, and she was rubbing his back absently. Comforting him, Xander thought. "The doctors are completely stumped."

"And there's been nothing about the other three students either," Grey added, his hand intertwined with Jaya's on the table.

"This is—wow," Xander muttered, and he and DE exchanged a glance. He assumed she wasn't telling her friends about the psychic's prophecy because of how they'd laughed the fugue state story off. That was fine with him. The fewer people that knew about it, the better, for now. Maybe he and DE could uncover some kind of answer, something to do with Atticus or the previous storm. Answers were good; answers were actionable and combated panic.

"Thank you for coming at such short notice, everyone." Waverly's somber voice boomed over the mic clipped to her lapel. People's voices got quieter and then silenced completely. Dr. Waverly stood at the head of the dining hall, in front of the marble counter where, just a few hours ago, he and DE had gotten coffees. Scattered on either side of her were the rest of the Rosetta Academy staff and high school teachers. "I know it's a tight squeeze here, but we appreciate your patience and accommodation."

Her voice and countenance were crisp and unflappable, as always. Points to Waverly for appearing confident and in charge, even at a time like this. But, Xander saw, her face was a shade paler than usual, and the lines around her mouth were especially pronounced. She looked around at the high school student body with her pale blue eyes.

"I've called this meeting to address the concerning situation you've no doubt heard about by now, which has affected . . . *some* of our seniors." DE and Xander glanced at each other. Four seniors had been affected, but Waverly seemed to want to keep that information nebulous. Cagey as fuck. "As you know," the headmistress continued, "we retain two world-class physicians in the infirmary. They assure me that they do not foresee any long-term complications . . . at this time." She cleared her throat, adjusted a button on her suit. "Still, it has come to my attention that there was an unsanctioned party last night, during which alcohol was available." Her eyes caught and held a few of the senior students', but no one flinched. Dr. Waverly looked away and continued speaking. "Needless to say, this is a breach of several of Rosetta Academy's rules, as outlined in the student handbook and to which you have all agreed to abide. As such, the staff and I are applying a strict moratorium on any unsanctioned gatherings of more than six people. Parties of any kind are strictly prohibited, as, of course, are alcohol or illegal substances. Any students caught in violation will be disciplined at the highest level, including the possibility of expulsion."

There was a stirring through the crowd, like autumn leaves skittering along a sidewalk in a cool breeze. Xander could tell the rest of the students weren't used to hearing Waverly threaten them with expulsion. Some of the students wore open expressions of outrage. Xander chewed on the inside of his lip to keep from smiling. Entitlement was such fun to watch when it got challenged.

He felt an elbow in his side and turned toward DE, who was looking to the front of the room but leaning her head in toward him. "Hey," she whispered. "Look."

Xander followed her gaze and saw she was looking at Ms. Blackmoor, their History of Rosetta Academy teacher, who was standing slightly removed from the rest of the staff. She was wearing another long black skirt and a long-sleeved gray turtleneck tucked into her skirt. Her hair was in an old-fashioned bun, and her thin hands were clasped at the front of her skirt. Xander couldn't tell what she was looking at, or if she was even listening to Dr. Waverly. Unlike the other staff, she wasn't fidgeting or shifting. She looked like she might be posing for a Victorian photograph.

"Yeah?" he whispered back to DE, not following what she was trying to say.

"Ms. Blackmoor! Remember that story she told us about the Huntleys? She obviously doesn't feel any kind of need to be loyal to the Academy. She might have information on the 1873 storm that isn't biased."

Xander sat up straighter. Now, why hadn't he thought of that? "That's brilliant," he murmured to DE. "Let's go talk to her after this is over?"

DE gave him a thumbs-up and turned back toward Dr. Waverly, who was finishing up her speech.

Xander found he could barely pay attention anymore. His foot wouldn't stop tapping on the wooden floor. And then, as if his impatience and his gaze had called out to her, Ms. Blackmoor's eyes moved to him, and the tiniest hint of a smile grazed her thin lips.

CHAPTER 29

DE

Ms. Blackmoor was an oddball. Even after Dr. Waverly had made her speech and all the teachers and staff had dispersed, she stood rooted to her spot at the front of the dining hall, her hands still folded over her long skirt, making eye contact with DE and Xander, smiling softly. It was as if she *knew* they were coming to talk to her, as if she'd overheard them. Which was weird and totally impossible.

DE caught her eye over the heads of the other students who were walking out of the dining hall in a big swarm and found she couldn't look away. Not even when Jaya caught her elbow and said, "Hey, come to my room at lunch. We're gonna order some food from the dining hall and just hang out. Bring Xander, too."

DE nodded but kept moving toward Ms. Blackmoor. She was aware that Xander was beside her, but neither of them said anything to each other. When she glanced at him, she saw him gazing straight ahead at Ms. Blackmoor too. The woman was more than a little hypnotizing. Strange.

"Hello," Ms. Blackmoor said serenely when they had reached her. People parted and went around them, jostling DE and Xander lightly but avoiding Ms. Blackmoor. "How are you both far-ing?"

It was a weird question to ask. How were they 'faring'? Kind of old-timey but also as if this storm was some kind of game-show challenge they were going through. But maybe DE was overthinking things; it wouldn't be the first time. "Um, good. Thanks. We were wondering if you could help us with some-thing. Some . . . information we were looking for."

Xander nodded. "It's from a long time ago, around the time of the school's founding."

Ms. Blackmoor held his gaze and then, after what seemed like a long minute, nodded. "Indeed. Why don't we go to my class-room to talk further?"

Her classroom was quiet—almost *too* quiet after the buzz and chaos of the dining hall. The tall windows barely let in any light, thanks to the snow and ice covering them. But still, Ms. Black-moor didn't turn on the overhead lights. Instead, she walked to her chair and sat, turning to DE and Xander in the grayish gloom.

"Now. How may I help you?"

Xander and DE looked around awkwardly and then perched on a couple of desks, facing Ms. Blackmoor. Xander cleared his throat, the sound echoing in the deserted classroom. "Well, like we were saying before, we're looking for some information and we thought—we hoped, anyway—that you might be able to help us. There was a storm, a big snowstorm like this one, a century and a half ago. Rosetta Academy doesn't really talk about it, but I know it happened because my great-great-great-uncle was a student here at the time."

"I see." Ms. Blackmoor looked toward DE, her dove-gray eyes

piercing. "And you are also interested in this storm?"

"I am." DE fiddled with her many stacked rings as she spoke. "I think maybe we can figure out what's happening at the school if we look at the previous storm. Maybe it'll give us a clue or . . ." She trailed off, shrugging. "I'm not sure. But I know I can't just sit around and wait for it to blow over while my friend is in the infirmary in a coma."

Ms. Blackmoor didn't say anything for a minute. Then, softly: "The past *can* hold answers to the present. But one has to be willing to look. To see." Ms. Blackmoor's eyes seemed to cut over to DE's pants pocket. DE realized with a start that the change doll was nestled there, and she'd been holding on to it. She let go of the doll in her pocket, startled. Did Ms. Blackmoor *know* something? But then the woman's gaze continued on. *Dammit, McKinley, your paranoia is the last thing this situation needs.*

DE coughed, mainly because Ms. Blackmoor was freaking her out a little and her spit had forgotten which pipe it was supposed to go down. "Um, yeah. Totally."

Xander just nodded solemnly.

Smiling, Ms. Blackmoor gestured behind her toward a closed door that DE was only now noticing. It was nondescript, and blended into the wall, except for its brass doorknob. "You're welcome to help yourselves to my archives. I hope you find what you're looking for. As long as you work on this together, I think you will."

"Oh, uh, great, thanks. But, I mean . . . could you help us look? Three heads would be better than two." She flashed Ms. Blackmoor her best puppy-dog eyes.

Ms. Blackmoor only smiled in that irritatingly serene, slightly mysterious way she had. "Ah, but I'd just be in the way, my dears."

Whatever that meant. And actually, maybe it was better she *didn't* help them look. DE couldn't imagine enduring that smile and those odd eyes much longer. "So, we just . . . go through there?" DE pointed at the door.

Ms. Blackmoor didn't answer, just kept her hands folded on her lap, a hint of a smile still at her lips. Weirdo.

"Okay." DE shrugged at Xander, and they both hopped off their desks and made their way to the door.

Xander turned the knob—DE fully expected it to be locked—but the door swung open without a sound. Inside, the room was dark and smelled of dust. DE felt along the wall until she found the light switch, then flipped it on.

"Whoa." She blinked. Old wooden shelves stretched out in straight lines, stacked haphazardly with dusty files, cardboard boxes, and yellowed papers. It seemed like all of Rosetta's history might be stuffed in here. "Thanks for letting us use your—" DE began, looking back out toward Ms. Blackmoor. But the woman had slipped away in silence, like dusk into night. "Um, okay then."

DE and Xander stepped farther into the storage room, and the door shut behind them with a heavy *thunk*.

CHAPTER 30

XANDER

Xander whistled and rubbed the back of his neck. Everywhere he looked in the small room, there were shelves crammed with boxes and files and papers, all of them yellowing and nearly falling apart. It didn't look like Ms. Blackmoor believed in a traditional filing system.

"Jeeesus. I'm not sure where to even start. I mean, there must be *centuries*' worth of stuff here." He felt like he'd hit pay dirt, only the pay dirt was an enormous, tangled ball of yarn that he had to disentangle bit by bit in a very short amount of time. "I guess we better get started. The records from around the time of Atticus's storm aren't going to just fall into our laps."

DE took a deep breath behind him, where she was poking at some shelves. "Yeah. This is for your family and all the students at Rosetta. We can do this. Easy-peasy."

Xander chuckled darkly. "I don't know about the easy part. I wish Ms. Blackmoor had wanted to lend a hand. She probably knows where all this stuff is." He paused, frowning. "Hey, why do you think she's storing all this back here instead of turning it in to the Rosetta admin?"

DE made the verbal equivalent of a shrug in the back of her throat. "I guess because she's the Rosetta history teacher." She paused and said, more quietly, "And let's face it. She's a bit of a kook."

Xander looked back at her and they laughed together. Shaking his head, Xander took a breath. "Okay. Let's get to work, McKinley."

"On it, Murthy."

They each turned back to their separate shelves and studied the contents.

"1950–1959," Xander read on the label affixed to a box that looked like it had suffered some water damage. "First female students; Donation for aquatic center; Huntley Hall renov."

A few feet away, DE called out the contents of the papers she was looking at. "This sheaf says, 'Food and bev. receipts; 1922 fundraiser; Hockey team founding.'" Xander heard her sigh. "Fuck. You weren't kidding. This is going to take for-fucking-ever." She threw an arm out toward the chaotic shelves before them. "I mean, *look* at this fucking place."

Xander grinned. "Anyone ever tell you that you curse a lot when you're stressed?"

"It's been noted a time or two," DE said primly, and Xander's grin grew even wider. He hadn't expected to be smiling at a time like this, but he found it hard to be too grim when he was around DE.

DE reached into her pants pocket and pulled out the change doll, which Xander had all but forgotten about until that moment. Looking down at it, DE mused, "You know, this thing's always in my pocket, but I never quite remember putting it in there." She shook her head. "This storm is getting in my head. Hey, maybe

I should whisper a prayer into its ear or something. Think that'll give us some good luck?"

Xander laughed, but she looked at him seriously, those wild green eyes intent and clear now. His laughter fading, he shrugged. "Yeah, sure. Why the hell not?"

DE pulled the side of the doll's head to her lips. "Please help us find the answers, magical change doll," she whispered, her voice holding a ring of sincerity Xander hadn't been expecting. It was really kinda cute.

They both waited in the silence, although Xander wasn't sure what they were waiting for.

When DE's phone let out a *ding-dong!* that reverberated in the storage room, they both jumped, then laughed nervously. Shaking her head, she slipped the change doll back into her pants pocket and pulled her phone out. Studying the screen, she hissed. "Oh shit. I totally forgot about the lunch with Jaya." Looking up at Xander, she added, "You're invited too. It's just the group having lunch and chatting in Jaya's room. Wanna go?"

Xander couldn't help but notice the faint pink tone that had seeped across her face. It made him think of strawberry candy and summer skies, happy things. "Sure."

"Great." Not meeting his eye, DE tapped in a response and returned her phone to her pocket. Her cheeks were still pink. "Um, good." She smoothed her hair down and looked around at the as-yet-unexplored shelves. "I guess this will keep another hour or two until we can get back."

Xander followed her gaze, feeling his spirits deflating. How the hell were they ever going to get through all this information in time to make a difference to anyone? "Yeah," he said mutedly, not wanting to infect her with his defeatist thoughts. "I guess so."

They turned to go, and Xander held the door open for DE. But just as he was about to step over the threshold into Ms. Blackmoor's classroom himself, he heard something. It was a sibilant whispering followed by a muted thud almost too quiet for his ears to pick up. He looked over his shoulder, not expecting to see anything.

On the floor, centered between two weathered wooden shelves, was a yellowing canvas bundle held together with string.

"Hey, wait a minute," Xander called to DE, who came back into the storage room.

"What's up?"

Xander walked toward the canvas bundle. He realized that, for some reason, he was walking carefully, tiptoeing almost, as if the thing might suddenly rear back and strike like a snake. "Was this on the floor the whole time?"

He knew what her response would be, but it still chilled him.

"No. Definitely not." DE's voice held the note of confusion he was feeling himself.

On reaching the canvas bundle, Xander saw that it had been stamped with the numbers 1872, though the black ink had faded with time. He looked back at DE before kneeling to pick it up. It was heavy, full of papers whose frayed and torn edges stuck out at the top and bottom. Xander gathered the bundle into his arms like it was a precious baby and walked to DE.

"Aren't you going to open it?" she asked.

He shook his head as she turned off the lights and closed the door behind them. "Let's go to Jaya's room and do the lunch first. We can take our time looking over all this later. It feels like there's a lot of stuff in here."

Nodding, DE followed him back into the darkened classroom and toward the door.

?

A helping hand, reached out. But will she take it? A word of advice, planted in her ear. But does she hear? Time knocks on her door.

DE

Although she was itching to see what was in the canvas folder, DE understood Xander's hesitation to open it up just then. She knew herself—she'd want to spend as much time as possible poring over every single scrap of paper in there, analyzing and reanalyzing everything they found. The thing had been sitting in the *middle of the floor*, in a spot that DE and Xander had walked over and past at least a dozen times during their foray into the storage room. It was like it had a mind of its own or was being powered by . . . something else.

She gave the folder a sideways glance as she and Xander walked upstairs toward the senior dorms, passing only a few other students along the way. It seemed most people were either in the dining hall or huddled in their rooms after everything that had happened.

Xander was cradling the canvas file gingerly, strong hands gentle, as if he was afraid the whole thing would poof into a pile of dust. And to be honest, she felt the same way. Ever since the storm had started, DE had the distinct and unsettling sense that her entire environment was precarious and odd, a fun house of mirrors that might rearrange itself into something unrecognizable with a flick of some cosmic wrist. She reached into her pocket and touched the change doll again. She didn't know if doing that was what had precipitated the appearance of the canvas folder, but she wasn't about to give up any positive superstitious habits now. The nice thing was, the doll didn't make her sad anymore. But like she'd told Xander, it had a funny habit of turning up on her person. It was just always . . . there.

Help us solve this thing, she pleaded silently, hoping the doll was listening. *Please don't let anyone else get hurt.*

CHAPTER 31

DE

When they rounded the corner to Jaya's room, the first thing they saw was Caterina dragging Rahul in by the wrist. Frowning at each other, they followed the couple in.

"You *have* to take a break from the medical journals, Rahul," Caterina was saying, a tiny wrinkle of concern between her carefully threaded eyebrows. "I could barely see you at your desk, between the stacks of *JAMA* and *Lancet*. And, actually, I've barely seen you at all these last few days. Have you even eaten today?"

Rahul pushed a hand through his hair. "I don't need to eat. I'm just sitting at my desk, reading. That doesn't expend too many calories."

"Your brain still requires calories to function, bud," Grey put in, patting the floor beside him. He and Jaya had made themselves comfortable there on the carpet, a pile of sandwiches and a bunch of sodas between them.

Rahul flopped down, heaving an inconvenienced sigh. Caterina sat beside him, still looking worried. DE and Xander followed suit, Xander setting the canvas folder carefully on the floor. Their knees brushed a little, and DE found herself taking comfort in the solidity of him, the body heat emanating from him and wrapping around her.

Jaya, dressed in a thick turtleneck sweater that was pulled up over her chin, gestured to the food. "We've got about a zillion sandwiches here, so take your pick. Fair warning, though, a lot of them have smashed avocado in weird combinations. Like avocado–peanut butter–bacon." She made a disgusted face. "Apparently, they were a bit overzealous in their assumption of how much avocado we'd consume during the storm, and now they're trying to get rid of it before it goes bad." She attempted to smile, but DE saw how wan and pinched her face was. The others were all shades of the same, but Rahul looked the worst. He fidgeted with his phone and his hair and then his phone again, as if he didn't know what to do with himself. Caterina now had her arms around him.

"Mm," DE said. "I'm not really that hungry."

Jaya sighed. "That makes all of us." It was true; no one was eating, though Caterina had placed a sandwich in front of Rahul.

DE reached over and squeezed Rahul's knee. "Hey, dude. How are you holding up?"

"There's no reason to think Leo won't make a full recovery," Rahul said in response, looking up into her eyes. He pushed his glasses up on his nose. "He's a healthy eighteen-year-old with no underlying pathologies."

DE nodded. "I agree. He's going to kick this thing in the ass. They all are."

Grey drummed his fingers on his knee, a nervous habit he'd never exhibited before, in all the time DE had known him. When he spoke, his deep voice was pressing, urgent. "I heard today that three more students have fallen into comas." DE noted absently that Grey's blue sweater matched his eyes perfectly. At another time, she might've teased him about this. "Another senior and two juniors this time."

"What?" DE asked, staring at him. Her mouth went dry. "Who?"

Grey named them, all people DE knew, though not well, and then added, "Word is that their vitals are incredibly low. Even Leo's are now, though his vitals were fine when the medics came to his room."

DE blinked, not wanting to ask the question, but knowing she had to anyway. "What . . . what does 'incredibly low' mean?"

Grey cleared his throat and hazarded a glance at Rahul, obviously worried what he was about to say would affect his friend even worse. "Ah . . . they said their vitals are barely above . . . above death. Just enough to keep them alive, but not much more."

DE saw Xander balk at this new information. Her throat felt tight, as if she couldn't get enough air. Discreetly, she unbuttoned the top button of her shirt. She and Xander needed to quickly dive into that folder they'd found. Whatever this was, it seemed to her like the pace was picking up.

Rahul nodded at Grey's words, his face going even paler than it had been, though he'd heard this already. "Yes." He glanced at Caterina. "I really should get back to the medical journals."

Caterina shook her head, that wrinkle still present. "You need to rest, too. You won't be of any help to Leo if you pass out from exhaustion, right?"

Rahul nodded reluctantly. "Fine. Five more minutes, then."

"Reading medical journals is better than anything the rest of us are doing." Grey pounded his fist on his leg, his jaw set. "I just feel so fucking helpless. Will says the infirmary medics and doctors aren't telling him anything. Just that no news is good news.

Which is total bullshit. They're just as baffled as we are."

"Leo's parents are physicians," Jaya sighed, pulling her sleeves down over her hands. "But of course, that's useless when there's no way to get in touch with the outside world. It's like we're in an opaque bubble, suspended in a world of white. No one can see in, and we can't see out. How horrible a coincidence that this had to happen during the worst snowstorm this state's seen in . . . forever."

It was funny, DE thought. Jaya's suite was really big, one of the biggest the Academy had to offer students because she was royalty, and yet they were all huddled together in a little clump. As if they were seeking safety in numbers.

Her eyes alit briefly on Xander, those thoughtful, kind golden eyes, his full mouth pursed. DE wondered if he was thinking the same thing she was . . . that the more she thought about it, the less this seemed like a horrible coincidence. She just couldn't shake the feeling that the storm was here for a purpose, for a reason, though what that reason might be, she had no idea.

"Are you guys okay?" Jaya asked, looking from DE to Xander and back again.

DE ran a thumbnail over the plush carpet. "Fine. Just worried like everyone is right now. And trying to figure out all this stuff." She didn't want to tell her friends what they'd uncovered—which really wasn't anything so far—because she didn't want to give them false hope. She was intimately acquainted with false hope, and it sucked. "We're not having much luck, though."

Grey's blue eyes pierced hers. "You've been keeping to your-self a lot these last few days," he remarked. It could've been taken as an offhand remark, NBD, but DE knew Grey. In his even tone she knew there was a question, probably one they were all asking: What was going on between her and Xander?

She wanted to laugh and cry and run screaming out into the blinding snow. This was the worst time for her to be thinking of anything remotely romantic. The psychic's prophecy, Leo and the others falling into unshakable comas, the change doll, the weird canvas folder, the storm—they were all pointing to something, but she couldn't see what that something was, and it was frustrating as fuck.

But the truth was . . . there *had* been times lately when she'd wondered what it'd be like to . . . to give in. To let Xander in. Obviously an insanely bad idea. Because not only were they dealing with the freakiness of the storm and the sleeping sickness, but there was also the whole "protecting herself from devastating heartbreak" bit that she couldn't—shouldn't, wouldn't—forget. The anti-love spell that she'd done had been for a *reason*, dammit. And that reason was that she couldn't trust herself to make good decisions.

And the worst part was, she couldn't tell her friends any of it. Not unless she wanted to worry them sick about the storm and the sleeping thing and even herself, even more than they already were. DE glanced at Xander. He was looking surreptitiously at the folder next to him, as if he was trying to use X-ray vision to see inside. In spite of the turmoil she felt around him sometimes (a lot of times?), she was glad she had him, at least. They may not have known each other very long, but she felt closer to Xander than she felt to most people at the school. As the only two people who knew about both the psychic's prophecy and Atticus, they shared something together now, something that felt . . . big. Monumental.

Ding-dong!

The sound of the school's internal messaging system made DE's stomach twist in a knot. *What now?*

It was Jaya's phone that had pinged, so she pulled it off the nightstand and glanced at the screen, her face immediately blanching. "It's—it's Isha, my little sister. She says—she says even more students are falling into comas. Her boyfriend Elliot's one of them. Freshmen, sophomores, and juniors. Sixteen so far. The infirmary's nearly overrun. I must go." She rushed to the door, Grey close on her heels.

DE stood. "Want us to come with you?"

Jaya shook her head, her hand on the doorknob. "No. You lot stay here. I'm going to talk with Isha and see what's going on. She's a mess; I'm sure she'll just want to talk to me." There was no question that Grey would go with her, though; he and Isha were like brother and sister.

DE nodded. "We'll try to figure this thing out, Jaya."

Jaya's lips trembled. "Do it quickly. I have a feeling we're running out of time."

DE watched as her friends rushed out into the hallway and disappeared, knowing in her gut that Jaya was right.

CHAPTER 32

XANDER

They made their excuses to Caterina and Rahul—who immediately returned to his room so Rahul could pore over his medical journals—and walked quickly to Xander's room. He had the canvas folder tucked under his arm, and it felt hot, like it was a glowing ember. DE was quiet as she walked beside him, nibbling on her lower lip.

He opened the door to his dorm room, and they slipped inside. He flipped the light switch on, and DE looked around his room appraisingly, as if curious what kind of decor he'd have in here. But Xander had made sure there were no clues to his personality here; his room was completely bare, on purpose. Nothing on the walls, nothing in the bookshelves. His desk was bare too, except for a Rosetta brochure he'd been looking through. He'd attached a plain, bare-bones white clock to the wall, purely functional.

DE pursed her lips at the end of her inspection. "Welp. Message received."

Xander frowned. "What message?"

She gestured around his bare room. "That you came here

with just one objective in mind, and it wasn't fitting in or having a good time."

He let a smile slip at that. "You're not wrong. Shall we?" He lifted the folder at her, and she nodded.

Both he and DE walked to the small settee by the gas fireplace, which he also flipped the switch for. They sat beside each other, and Xander took a deep breath as he put both hands on the rough surface of the canvas folder. Part of him was afraid to open it; afraid that it would be full of disappointment, afraid that he and DE *had* just overlooked it on the floor, that it was just a folder that had fallen out of its shelf, nothing special.

But another part, a much stronger part, was *sure* the folder contained at least a fraction of the puzzle he wanted to solve. He was sure whatever was in here would lead him closer to Atticus, to an answer to the question his family had been asking for generations.

"Ready?" DE's voice was soft, and she nodded toward the folder as Xander sat frozen.

He blinked, shook himself out of it. "Yeah. Absolutely." He flipped the folder open on his lap.

The yellowed, brittle papers inside the folder smelled like age and decades of silence.

DE huffed a nervous laugh as they gazed upon the top page—a receipt for bed linens, from the looks of it. Lots and lots of bed linens.

"Can you believe I actually expected a swirl of gold dust to rise up from in there?" she asked, clutching Xander's shoulder for a moment. The presence of her hand, the warmth of it, the weight, felt good. Her perfume—something warm and smoky, like vanilla and incense smoke—drifted over him, and that felt good too. Unbelievably good. He wasn't in this alone, like he'd thought he'd have to be.

He laughed lightly. "And if there *had* been a swirl of gold dust, I would've totally just gone along with it. Nothing is out of the question at this point." He put the bed linen receipt to the side, facedown. "Do you want to divide the rest of these in half so we can go through it a little faster?"

"Sure."

He handed DE the top half of the stack of old papers, handling them as gently as he could, and began to peruse the bottom half on his own. They worked quietly for a few moments, their breathing falling into unconscious tandem, the scratch and crackle of carefully turned sheets of paper the only thing that punctuated the silence.

Then Xander sat up straighter. "Look at this." He held the piece of paper closer to his face, reading the fine print. "An extra-large order of food for their cellars and extra kerosene and lanterns." And at the bottom of the receipt, someone had scrawled, simply, *Storm*. Xander pointed out the word to DE, whose eyes flashed with the excitement he felt. "Waverly may have sidestepped my question about the previous storm, but this is concrete evidence that it affected the school. Or at least they were worried enough about it that they ordered extra rations."

"Keep going," DE said, her voice rushed. "Maybe we'll find other good stuff."

Xander set the receipt for the food and lanterns away from the receipt for the bed linens, so they could begin to mount evidence of the storm and what may have happened to Atticus. Like DE, he couldn't shake the feeling that the closer they got to solving *that* mystery, the quicker they'd solve the one unraveling in the school currently.

They worked in silence for a few more minutes, and then Xander found another bulk delivery. "This one's for firewood," he told DE. "Definitely prepping for the storm."

A few minutes after that, DE held up what looked like yellowed cardstock. "Check this out," she murmured, tilting the cardstock so the font on the front glimmered gold. "It's an invitation for a spring dance at Rosetta Academy."

Xander peered at the invitation. There was a gold foil crest of the Academy from the old days—two crossed swords with a crown over them—and below it, a gold foil picture of a boy and a girl in Victorian-era clothes slow dancing. In black type, the invitation said:

You are hereby invited to a most royal celebration and dance at the Academy on March 24, 1872. Gowns and gloves, please!

"Weird," Xander said, frowning. He turned the invitation over, but the back was blank. "Who was this invitation for? The Academy was a boys' prep school in the 1800s."

"It was," DE said, nodding, "but there was a girls' prep school in Aspen. It closed when Rosetta began to accept girls, but it was pretty popular with the upper-class set back in the nineteenth century. It's where girls were sent to study comportment and etiquette so they could be married off to the most eligible bachelors."

"'Comportment'?" Xander asked. "What the hell's that?"

"Oh, you know. How to be dashing and irresistible, mostly." She fluttered her eyelashes at Xander and tucked her hands under her chin, and he snorted. More seriously, she added, "I guess they had socials and dances so the students at the two schools could mingle. Huh."

"The dance was on March 24th," Xander said, checking the date on the invitation. "When were those receipts dated for the kerosene and food?"

DE checked the paper. "March 22nd. I wonder if they even had the dance, since they knew the storm was incoming."

"The firewood was dated for March 22nd too. And maybe they didn't know how bad it was going to be," Xander mused. "They didn't have Dopplers back then."

A *ding-dong!* interrupted their conversation. Feeling a familiar dread, DE pulled out her phone and checked the screen. "It's just Anna," she said with a sigh of relief, glancing up at Xander. "She found something in the library she wants to show us."

CHAPTER 33

DE

In the library, Anna the bubbly freshman looked . . . well, frankly, she looked stoned. Her eyes were half-lidded, dark purple half-moons under them. She was just sitting there, staring off into space, when DE and Xander walked up.

"Oh," she said, blinking repeatedly, sounding surprised. "Hey." It was like she'd forgotten she'd sent DE that text at all.

DE exchanged a look with Xander, who was frowning, his thick brows pulled together. "Um, hey, Anna," DE said, turning back to her. "Are you okay? You look a little . . ." She didn't know a polite way to say "high."

"Tired," Xander put in discreetly, noticing DE's struggle.

DE nodded vigorously. "Yeah, uh-huh. Tired."

Anna smiled absently. "Oh, I'm fine. Just . . . late night. You know, doing research. For you guys."

"Well, we really appreciate that," Xander replied, leaning his elbows forward on the desk. "And I'll bring you a coffee right after this, I promise."

Anna's smile got a bit brighter. "Thank you."

There was an expectant pause, but Anna didn't rush to fill it. So

DE cleared her throat. "Your text said you found something . . . ?"

"Oh, right. Right." Anna tugged at the sleeves of the brown sweater she was wearing. The tag was clearly visible at her collarbone; she had put the thing on backward and inside out. "Come with me. I'll show you." She lifted the desk's lid to the left, making a gap that DE and Xander could walk through.

Anna led them to a thick, closed door a few yards from the counter, using a keypad to open it. "The archives," she said. "Dusty things that no one ever asks for."

"Until now," Xander muttered, and DE felt goose bumps roll along her skin.

They entered a storage room that was much bigger than the one in Ms. Blackmoor's room and much better organized. There was row upon row of heavy-duty metal shelving, outfitted with dozens of gray metal file drawers. Each drawer had been carefully seen to with a label maker, and everything smelled antiseptic, like it had been recently dusted and sprayed with cleaning chemicals.

Behind the shelves were four largish oak tables, each with four wooden chairs pulled neatly in. One of the tables had a large roll of paper straightened on it.

"Here it is," Anna said slowly, walking over to it.

DE and Xander joined her and leaned over the paper, studying it. "Looks like an old blueprint," DE observed, squinting to see the small writing at the top. The paper was yellowed, and the writing was barely visible, even in the bright overhead lights of the room.

A pause, and then Anna responded. "That's exactly what it is." Another pause, and then she reached over and pulled a pair of blue nitrile gloves out of a box DE hadn't noticed on the table. "Here, let's all wear these to keep our finger oils off the paper. I don't know if it's strictly necessary, but it's standard procedure in here."

Xander and DE obediently donned their own gloves, and then the three of them returned to the blueprint.

"So, what you see here," Anna said, pointing to the top left corner, "is the date the blueprint was made. 1870. Two years before the Academy officially opened. What I think is interesting is this annotation, on the top right."

DE read it out loud. "Senior boys' dormitory." She looked at Anna. "So that would be . . . the fourth floor of this building where the seniors currently have their rooms?"

Anna smiled broadly, though it still managed to look hazy. "That's what you'd think, right? Only, check this out." She pointed to the orientation of the floor. The current senior floor was shaped like a wide, curving U. This one, however, was a sharper U, with angled edges and corners.

"That's weird," Xander said. "Were the senior dorms housed in a different building back then?"

"Not a different building, exactly," Anna replied. "But look at this." Adjoining the blocky U was a box that said "backfill." "I think the senior dorms used to be housed here, in the main building." Anna looked at the two of them, her gaze a bit unfocused. "But it wasn't on the fourth floor, like it is now. It was in the *basement* of this building."

DE frowned. "The basement? But we've been down there lots of times. The senior party was there just a few days ago. And there was no evidence of boys' dorms. It's just one big, open, unfinished space."

Anna shrugged. "Yeah, I have no idea *where* in the basement or how it could be possible. I just know—this is what this blueprint shows. That's how the original architect meant to build it."

"And there's no chance this plan was discarded for a newer one?" Xander asked, looking down at the blueprint.

"I have no way of knowing that for sure, but I've been told by the librarians that everything in the archives room was kept because of its actual historical context and value for the Academy. So this should be accurate—the missing boys' dorm rooms are in the basement."

"The basement," DE mused. She tried to think back to the party, but it had all been so dark and full of people and she hadn't really paid much attention to whether there might be more to the large, dank space.

"Do you mind if I take a picture of this?" Xander asked.

Anna shrugged again, a little vaguely. "Sure. Be my guest."

CHAPTER 34

DE

While Xander pulled out his phone, DE turned to Anna. "Thanks for doing this for us," she said, infusing as much warmth into her voice as she could. "I'm so grateful. You have no idea."

"It's no trouble." Anna's distracted smile slipped. "Do you mind if I sit down? I just feel a little . . . weird."

"Yeah, of course." Concerned, DE pulled a wooden chair out from the table, and the freshman girl sank into it. "You've been working too hard on this for us."

Anna shook her head, but her gaze remained straight ahead, not on DE. "No. Not at all. All the people, falling asleep . . . Maybe it's having an effect on me, too. I feel exhausted. Like I could sleep standing up."

DE watched her in alarm, realizing just how young she was and how scared she must be of everything going on at the school. She scooted closer to Anna. "It's a really scary thing. I'm freaked out too. Have you . . . have you had any friends fall asleep?"

"Some." Anna looked away, but DE saw her lip quivering. "My friend Jonas is really close with one of the admins—they're like distant relatives—and he told me she said there are a lot more students falling into this weird sleep. But the Academy's trying to keep it quiet for as long as they can. They don't want to start a panic." She sighed, slow and deep, the eerie sound of flutes playing against a rib cage. "I don't know what to think."

"It's so hard." DE tried on a soothing voice, hoping it worked. She wasn't a naturally maternal person. "One of my good friends is in the infirmary too."

Anna turned away in her chair, and DE supposed she wanted to conceal the fact that she was crying. But then, abruptly, the freshman stood and walked to the information desk where she usually worked, where they'd found her that day they'd come downstairs and spoken with her.

DE walked over, confused. Anna didn't seem to be doing anything. She was just standing there, staring straight ahead at the double doors. Her hands were on the counter, palms facing up, fingers loosely curled. Xander hadn't noticed anything; he was still poring over the old blueprint.

A ripple of gooseflesh washed over DE's skin. "Anna? Are you all right?" DE turned to Xander, panic beginning to thrum in her veins. "Xander, I think there may be a problem."

To DE's growing horror, Anna didn't respond to her words at all. Even a clearly false "No, don't worry, I'm just having a weird day" would've been preferable to this complete silence. Anna didn't turn to look at DE or Xander, even though it was obvious they were talking about her.

Xander went to stand directly in front of Anna, frowning. His voice was gentle, but firm with authority. "Hey. Anna. Are you okay?"

Anna smiled beatifically—and faintly—at the two of them. It was like she was in a pleasant dream, and all she saw were fuzzy shapes and inoffensive pastel colors. "Of course I am. Most people don't like change, but I thrive on it."

Xander looked about as flummoxed as DE, and for that, she was thankful. "Um . . . okay. Great, I guess."

DE stepped closer, her hip pressing against the wooden information desk. "Anna, you'll put the blueprint back, right?"

Anna turned that unnerving, unfailing, pleasant-as-pie smile on DE. "Of course I will." She kept her word and walked to the tables in the back. Gently she rolled the blueprint up and stuck it into a storage tube. Then she put the storage tube under the wooden table and resumed her smiling position at the front desk. Her eyes were slightly unfocused, her palms, again, turned up and resting on the desk. The most eerie part was that her smile hadn't slipped the slightest.

DE made a sudden executive decision. "Look, we need to take you to the infirmary. Something's not right here."

"The infirmary?" There was only the slightest negative inflection in Anna's tone. "For what? Besides, I have to stay here, at my job. I don't get off till five." As she spoke, she kept her body in the same position—standing tall, palms on desk, etc. It was more than a little creepy.

DE looked at Xander. Yep, from the expression on his face, he was definitely tracking the strangeness that was going on. Almost unconsciously, DE and Xander moved closer together, as if presenting a united front to this bizarre situation—and maybe even drawing a bit of comfort from each other. "Humor me, then," DE said. "Please?"

No sooner had she finished her sentence than DE's, Xander's, and Anna's phones chimed with a *ding-dong*. The message that had just come in from Dr. Waverly made DE's stomach drop.

There was no room in the infirmary. People suffering from the sleeping sickness could and should be taken there, but anyone else with more minor concerns needed to stay away. The medical personnel were already overtaxed.

Xander held his phone up to DE. "Well, shit." He tilted his head toward Anna, who was staring straight ahead, between DE and Xander, at nothing. "She's not exactly suffering from the sleeping sickness. I mean, she's not *asleep*."

"Yeah." DE rubbed her hands over her face. "Anna, are you *sure* you don't want to go to the infirmary? Just to get checked out?"

"Of course not. I'm perfectly fine. Just a bit tired." Anna's smile didn't grow, nor did it fade. It was like looking at a plastic doll.

"Right." After the slightest pause, Xander slipped his phone into his pocket. Turning to DE, he added, sotto voce, "I mean, there's really nothing we can do if she doesn't want to go?"

"Yeah. Fuck." DE turned to Anna. "Thanks for your help, Anna. We're leaving now, but if you need *any*thing, anything at all, you text me. Okay?"

Anna just kept on smiling.

CHAPTER 35

DE

"What the hell was that, Xander?" DE said as soon as the double doors closed behind them. They walked quickly down the hallway, arms swinging in tandem.

"I think it might be what we're hoping it's not. The beginnings of the sleeping sickness. Though *when* she actually falls asleep is anyone's guess. This thing seems to affect people at different rates." Xander sounded tense, his syllables clipped and hard. "Something is seriously fucking unright with this place." He adjusted the collar of his sweater, weighing his next words. "I keep wondering when one of us is going to be next."

"I know." DE's voice was barely above a whisper. Much as she hated the thought of falling prey to this weird-ass disease—or whatever it was—she found she hated the idea of Xander falling prey to it almost as much. Somewhere along the way, she'd begun to consider him a true friend. A real fondness, a warm affection for him, bloomed in her chest at the thought.

Slightly stunned by this state of affairs, DE cleared her throat as they wound through the carpeted hallway, her boots and his shoes whispering on the thick burgundy carpet. Obviously, this called for a change of subject. Pronto. "Hey, I want to stop by the infirmary."

Xander stopped short, forcing her to stop too. "What? Why?"

DE twisted her fingers together as she talked. "You totally don't have to come. I want to check on Leo. And also . . . I just want to see what it looks like down there." The thing was, she felt seeing how it really was might help answer some things for her; it might bring some clarity about this bizarre *Twilight Zone* episode they seemed to be stuck in.

Xander rubbed the back of his neck with a big hand and studied her, his expression still not fully convinced. But as he looked into her eyes, she saw his hesitation slowly melt away. Finally, he took a breath. "Okay. I'll go with you."

DE couldn't help the relieved grin that spread across her face. "Really? Because I'd understand if you didn't. This whole thing is fucking creepy."

Xander raised his eyebrows and huffed. "Yeah, no shit. But I want to come." He ran a hand through his hair, holding her gaze. "I want to be there for you."

DE nodded, that warmth seeping into her chest again, a feeling that was becoming very, very familiar when it came to Xander. She could just tell her cheeks were pink with it. "Okay, um, thanks. Follow me."

XANDER

The message sent out by Dr. Waverly about the conditions of the infirmary was a warning bell. It was pretty obvious what she was saying—things were bad and getting worse by the hour.

But still. *Seeing* it was a whole different matter.

Xander had never witnessed anything like it in his life. He liked to think of himself as a pretty together guy—and 99 percent of the time he was—but this definitely, *definitely* fell into the other 1 percent. Even the full-grown adults didn't seem to know how to deal with it.

The large, oddly beautiful, no-expenses-spared infirmary at Rosetta had been made to look like a gleaming bubble of white. Every surface was polished, sparkling, and spotless. The walls, floor, and ceiling were all a seamless, calming, pure white. There were windows at each end of the long rectangular space, tall and narrow and framed by ornate white molding. Currently, with the storm raging outside and the snow that had encased the window-panes, there was no view. Just more whiteness. Xander had the disorienting feeling he'd materialized in some different realm, a kind of nightmare fairy-tale land.

Machines of every kind and caliber, most of which he had no name for, were set along the walls and the beds in which dozens of occupants lay motionless. They beeped and chimed while small screens glowed gently, which medical personnel, dressed in red and gray scrubs, checked every so often.

It was chaos in here, but it was a weird kind of chaos, where half the population involved was completely and deathly still and silent. And yet, the sheer number of catatonic students—at least two dozen, easy—spilling out in gurneys into the hallway, stacked shoulder to shoulder on little hospital beds in the vast expanse of the infirmary itself, all of them with their arms by their sides, their faces waxy and immovable . . . it was a lot. It was more than a lot. And judging by the way the medics were snapping at each other and the few curious or worried students who had wandered downstairs, even those in the medical profession found it unsettling.

Most of the students who'd drifted down to see what was going on in the infirmary were talking quietly to each other; some were even holding hands and praying, their heads bowed. But, Xander noticed, there were a select few who looked lost in a trance, standing in odd places—facing walls or corners—or just gazing into the room without a single expression on their faces.

"Holy shit." DE was pressed up against the wall in the hallway, a few feet away from a comatose female student Xander didn't recognize. She looked really young, though—probably a freshman or a sophomore. "Ho-ly shit, Xander." DE's green eyes were riveted to their fellow Rosetta students, in their own sort of horrifying limbo as the storm raged on outside, throwing the natural world into a similar purgatory.

A young male medic with short blond hair—not either of the ones Xander had seen respond to Leo—ran by, clutching a printout, probably a medical report of one of the patients. Xander made room, watching as the medic walked up to a Black female doctor and presented the report to her. She ran her finger down the paper, her brow furrowed. "Dammit," Xander heard her say. "It didn't work. Nothing is working. What the hell is going on?" She shoved the printout back at the medic and turned to administer to the patient closest to her. "We only have a couple of gurneys open that we pulled out from storage, and even those are going out in the hallway. Soon we'll have to . . ." She brushed her hand through the air, her mouth a straight, tight line. "I don't know. Improvise."

He could feel their futility, their frustration, their confusion. And if the doctors were that stumped, what hope did all of these sleeping students—did *any* of them at Rosetta—have?

Xander ran a hand through his hair. "This is freaking wild."

"It's . . ." DE shook her head. Then, pushing herself up off the wall, she stepped carefully to the doorway of the infirmary proper and looked in. "There he is," she called softly over her shoulder.

Xander joined her to see Leo lying three deep in the white bubble of the infirmary space, his face just as masklike, his skin just as waxy, as it had been upstairs. His breathing was extremely slow, his chest barely rising and falling. The heart-rate monitor attached to him beeped lethargically. There was no hint of the energy, the bubbling vivacity, that made Leo himself. Will slouched next to him, looking absolutely exhausted in a rumpled sweater and jeans, texting someone.

Before Xander could respond, DE walked in and touched Will on the shoulder. When he looked up, she gave him a hug, which he returned, his eyes shut tightly behind his glasses.

Feeling like he was infringing on a private moment, Xander turned away. His gaze fell on the many students in the hallway, sleeping through what was probably the biggest mystery of their lives. What the hell was happening here that modern medicine couldn't even touch?

At least he knew now where Atticus had spent his final moments, down in some basement dorm room. Xander couldn't help shake the feeling that if he could just find out what happened to Atticus during the last storm, he could help all these people. He could ease DE's pain. He glanced at her, her eyes shiny as wet emeralds as she looked down at her friend. He remembered what the psychic had told her . . . that souls will slumber and one will perish. Xander hadn't voiced this to her, hadn't wanted to worry her more than she already was, but . . . who was the "one"? Who was going to die? And what if it was DE? The sickness didn't seem to discriminate about who it attacked.

The moment he had the thought, he felt a pain in his chest so severe, he was sure his heart had turned to glass and burst inside his rib cage. There was no way, no *way* he would let anything happen to Daphne Elizabeth McKinley.

He had to figure this thing out.

DE

DE lay on her side on the floor in her room, breathing in the smell of carpet freshener. It had been a while since anyone had cleaned the carpet, but then, she had barely been in her room, so everything was still virtually untouched. It was the day after she'd witnessed what was going on in the infirmary, and she felt sick.

Anna. Anna was down in the infirmary now. DE had gone down to see Leo again this morning, and . . . there was Anna, lying on her back, her black hair fanned out on the white pillow. She looked like an Asian Snow White. The innocence and the horror, the combined mindfuck of the whole thing, had made DE weep. So she'd come up here to take a break, to figure out what the fuck was going on and what the fuck she was going to do about it.

The wind howled and beat against her windows, which were still covered in thick, white snow like a giant hand pressed against the glass, punishing and unforgiving. The first thing DE had thought to do was to somehow go into town and find Madame Olivera. Maybe she could demand answers, ask the woman what she knew and how. But there was no way to make the walk or drive into town. They were all prisoners of Rosetta Academy and the storm, whether they wanted to openly acknowledge it or not. The thought made DE's throat close up; it made her want to throw her desk through the window and scream. But, of course, she didn't. She had to keep her head about her. She had to figure this out for her friends, for everyone she cared about and had known for almost all her life.

A question had begun to sprout in her mind over the last few days, gnarly and poisonous and incessant: When Madame Olivera had told her that one soul would perish, who had she meant? DE couldn't help but think of Atticus Wakefield. How he was related to Xander, how Xander was now here, trapped at Rosetta in this storm, just like Atticus had been. And Atticus had *died*. What if . . . what if Xander was the one Madame Olivera had been talking about? But *she'd* been the one to go to Madame Olivera. She was the one to whom the message was delivered. Maybe it was her. Maybe there was a chance—big or small—that she wouldn't make it out of this.

DE squeezed her eyes shut, her heart hammering in her throat. No, dammit. She wasn't going to let that happen. She and Xander were both going to get out of this unscathed, along with everyone else at Rosetta. She would figure this thing out, period.

Her phone chimed, mercifully interrupting her thoughts, and she slid it out of the pocket of her jeans. It was a calendar reminder; she was eating breakfast with Jaya and Grey in the senior common room. Jaya was supposed to get them all breakfast biscuits from the dining hall to share.

She got herself off the floor with some effort. It was weird, this strange ennui that was starting to settle in at the same time that sheer panic was taking hold, two competing, twining feelings that had a talonlike grasp on her brain. She didn't want to think about what would happen if she failed to stop whatever was happening at Rosetta Academy. But not wanting to think came with a price—the mental sludge that was gradually taking hold, the deep and thick elixir of denial that she was slowly being dipped in by a mind that didn't want to deal with the consequences of reality.

"Stop that weak shit, Daphne Elizabeth McKinley. Remember who the fuck you are." She'd always taken care of herself, looking out for herself because no one else was going to do it. Not her mom, not her dad, not any of the adults in her life. This was no different.

DE stood with purpose and looked at herself in the mirror. Her green eyes were gleaming, hard and focused. She wouldn't go down without one hell of a fight.

CHAPTER 36

DE

DE clutched the change doll in her fist as she made her way down to the common room. It was a strange little thing, ugly and old-fashioned. But for some reason, it had started to bring her comfort. It was always just *there*, like a ride-or-die friend. And right now, DE really appreciated the support.

Plus, if its whole thing—its raison d'être—was change, it had to help her *change* this situation around, right? Maybe if she talked to it or held it enough, built up a connection with it, matched her vibe to its ancient one. Or something. If she had the internet, this would be a lot easier. There were probably entire YouTube playlists about how to activate your winds-of-change doll.

As she passed dorm room after closed dorm room, DE began to notice something: no one was in the hallway; none of the students were leaning out of their dorm rooms calling out to each other; nobody had propped their doors open to allow friends to come and go freely, as was the custom at Rosetta.

Turning into the common room, DE noticed how eerily still it was in here, too. The snow-whitened windows lent a general pallor, a glum dimness, to the room, but it wasn't just that. It seemed like everybody was lying low, waiting to see who the "sleeping sickness" (as it was coming to be called) would hit next. It was as if they could avoid detection by whatever malevolent entity was stalking the halls of Rosetta Academy if they just played it cool, kept it quiet.

In fact, the common room was empty, she saw at a second glance, or nearly empty. She could see the tops of Jaya's and Grey's heads, but besides them, there was only another senior named David Lancaster reading listlessly in the far corner. He didn't acknowledge DE's entrance.

Jaya and Grey were sitting in armchairs by the giant floor-to-ceiling window, facing away from DE and the door, looking out at a solid wall of snow. Their hands were intertwined lightly between the armchairs.

"Not a great view right now," she called as she walked toward them.

A tingle of warmth and relief wrapped around her heart at seeing someone she knew, someone she was going through all this with, even if they really hadn't had a chance to hang out since all the chaos had begun. She needed to spend some time with Jaya, she decided, just her and Jaya. They could talk this whole thing out, and DE knew she'd feel better. She always did after hearing Jaya's measured, wise words in that posh accent.

Neither of them turned at her voice, and she felt a pang of empathy. They were probably lost in thought, worried sick out of their minds for Leo and all the other students.

"Hey, guys. It's your favorite human." DE walked around their armchairs so she was in front of them, forcing a smile onto her face.

The cold light from the window showcased their waxy,

mannequin-like skin. For a horrifying moment, DE thought she was staring at two life-size dolls shaped to look like her friends, placed in these chairs by some weirdo. There was absolutely no expression on either of their faces. Their eyes were open but blank, unstaring, unseeing; their mouths slack and lips slightly parted.

DE's mouth went instantly dry. She stared at them for way too long, waiting for them to do something, to laugh, to tell her they were playing a terrible joke. She squeezed the change doll, squeezed and squeezed and squeezed, not knowing what to do, her underarms and upper lip and palms all prickling with sweat. Her mind didn't want to accept this—was, in fact, railing against the evidence before her. She knew what was happening, but no, it was too much; it couldn't be happening, not to Jaya, whom she considered a sister, and not to Grey, who was one of the best people she knew.

"Jaya. Grey." Their names were just whispers, whimpers really, escaping her lips. Their shapes shifted and blurred as her eyes filled with tears. But once the tears fell, she saw that her best friends still sat immovable and impassive in their chairs, unaffected by anything she could say.

CHAPTER 37

XANDER

The door to his dorm room burst open, hitting the wall on the other side. Xander dropped his phone with a "What the *fuck*?"

He'd been sitting on his bed, zooming in on the picture of the blueprint Anna had given him in the library. It felt weird, wrong somehow, to be doing this when Anna was downstairs in the infirmary. DE had texted him about that. But what else was he supposed to do? Sit around twiddling his thumbs? Let her hard work go to waste? What better gift to Anna than to figure this whole thing out and get her out of whatever trance had taken over the school?

DE stood at the doorway, her eyes wild and wet with tears, her nose red, her hands balled into fists at the sides of her thighs. "This is bullshit!" she cried, her voice much too loud for the space.

Xander hopped off his bed and approached her, his entire being igniting with concern. "What's wrong?" A stupid question, because what was *right* lately?

She stepped into his room and pushed the door closed, using her fists to wipe at her eyes. "Jaya and Grey." Her voice broke as she said their names. And she didn't have to say any more. Xander understood.

His heart broke for her. He knew how much her friends meant, especially Jaya. "Shit. *Shit.* I'm so sorry."

She shook her head, back and forth, as if she were attempting to deny reality. And then she covered her face with her pale, many-ringed hands and began to sob.

For just a moment, Xander stood there, his brow furrowed, his heart aching for her. And then, pushing aside any doubts, he walked forward with purpose and gathered her into his arms. She was still for a minute, but then she melted into him, wrapping her arms around his waist, burying her face in his neck and letting out sobs that racked her entire frame.

Xander felt a lump in his throat as he bore witness to her pain. He found himself tightening his own arms around her, cinching her close to him, trying to erase her hurt with his touch, as if that were possible.

"I'm sorry," he whispered again, rubbing her back. He was surrounded by her perfume, smoky and dark, whispered secrets and lingering regrets. "I'm so sorry."

"I don't know why this is happening," she said, her breath fanning against his neck. "Why is this happening, Xander?"

"I don't know. But we'll figure this out." He spoke with much more optimism than he felt.

DE, her arms still around his waist, pulled back a little until she was looking into his eyes. "How? How are we *ever* going to figure this out? We don't even really know what 'this' is. The doctors don't even know! We're fucking stuck in an episode of *Supernatural*." Her eyes, those beautiful green eyes, filled with tears.

She spoke with such despair that Xander found himself saying, "Let's go find the basement—where Atticus's room used to be. I'll bet we can find something useful. What we read about Atticus's death sounds a lot like what's going on now. Maybe there's a connection, a solution there." He wasn't sure of that at all, obviously. They were talking about a 150-year-old dorm room, not a curated museum. But he only knew he had to offer DE *something* at that moment, and this was all he had. "Okay?" Without thinking about it, he gently brushed back a strand of soft hair off her forehead with the tips of his fingers.

DE blinked at him, her red-gold eyelashes laced with tears, like dewdrops on blades of autumn grass. "Okay." She kept staring into his eyes, and Xander felt something inside him shift. In a quiet voice she added, "Why are you so nice to me, Xander?"

He shook his head and said simply, "Because it's what you deserve."

DE's gaze drifted from his eyes to his mouth. Xander froze, his heart beating so hard, he was sure she could feel it through his shirt. But the next moment, her lips were pressed against his, soft and pliant, her mouth falling open.

She tasted like tears and longing. Xander found his tongue exploring hers, her mouth warm and familiar as if they'd been kissing forever. His arms tightened around her waist, his kiss conveying everything he wanted to but couldn't: *I like you. I'll keep you safe. You deserve better than you got from Alaric.*

But in the next moment she pulled back, gasping quietly. Stepping away from him, she covered her mouth with one hand, her eyes averted. Xander's arms felt cold, empty. He wanted her with a ferocity that took him aback.

"I'm sorry," DE whispered, now hugging herself around her

waist as if she was cold too. As if she missed his arms too. "I shouldn't have . . ."

"Don't be sorry." He stepped forward and then stopped, not wanting to scare her away. He gazed at the delicate planes of her face and was startled by how familiar they were to him, how much they already felt like home. "I . . . I wanted that too, DE. I've been wanting to kiss you since the first time I saw you in that attic."

She looked at him, shaking her head before he was even done speaking. "We can't. I can't."

Her eyes had drifted to his mouth again, but he bet she wasn't aware she was doing that. The expression on her face was the dictionary definition of the word "torn": she looked like she was being pulled, almost violently, in two opposing directions. Wanting to fly into his arms and run and hide. He wished he could show her he was safe, that this was safe, that he'd rather maim himself than ever hurt her.

Xander mustered up every ounce of courage he could find within himself to ask the question and ask it in a gentle way: "Why not?"

"It was a mistake." Her words were like a spear to his heart. "I already told you what it was like with Alaric."

"I don't see what that has to do with me—with us."

DE's eyes flashed. "There *can* be no 'us,' Xander. You don't know what I've been through, what it's taken for me to—to keep myself safe. To make myself feel halfway whole again; to make myself feel halfway *human* again." Her voice broke, and his heart broke with it. "I've been taken apart into little pieces so many times. I don't think I could p-put myself together if I got taken apart again. I can't take that chance." A pause, and then she whispered, "I'm sorry." The brief blaze of anger he'd seen was gone, like her tears had doused it. She looked absolutely shattered now, tired to the bone.

He wanted to gather her in his arms, to soothe her, to help her see what he saw when he looked at her: not a broken woman, but one who'd been strong enough to piece herself back together. He opened his mouth to say this but then closed it again. He could see in her eyes that no matter what he said, he wasn't going to convince her. "You don't have anything to be sorry about, DE. I understand." His voice was low and even. But he found he couldn't meet her eye any longer. His chest felt hollow, like his heart had flown away, unable to take the pain anymore. Walking past her, he opened the dorm door and took a breath. "Should we get going to the basement, then?"

After just a moment's hesitation, during which a thousand emotions seemed to swirl in those green eyes, DE nodded. "Yeah," she whispered, unwrapping her arms and swiping at the tears on her face. "Let's go."

Outside, the growing storm shrieked and battered the windows, demanding to be let in.

CHAPTER 38

DE

Xander pulled out his phone and tapped at the screen. "According to the old blueprint Anna showed us, there used to be a stairway in the archives section of the library that led to the basement dorms. Anna probably missed the stairway because she wasn't feeling well." He looked up from his phone, and DE wondered if he'd ever look at her with that gentleness and fondness in his eyes again. "So let's head to the library."

Her sidelong glances at Xander as they walked down to the library revealed one thing: she'd cut him to the quick. His face was a mask of politeness, but she saw the muscle ticking in his jaw, the way his eyes, those beautiful, golden sand-dune eyes, glistened with pain.

The thought that she'd done that to him made her feel nauseated, like she wanted to run to the nearest bathroom and vomit. But what choice did she have? What she'd told him was true—she was tired of being broken apart. She was tired of the pain, of the heartache, the nights lying awake wondering why she wasn't good enough. She couldn't walk down that path again. She just couldn't.

Xander didn't understand why—why she had pulled him close

just to push him away, why they couldn't be together when they obviously got along so well, why DE kept a wall up when she obviously wanted to let him in.

He wasn't wrong about any of those assumptions. She *did* like him. She could admit that now, watching him out of the corner of her eye. He walked tall and proud, like he and the world were on good terms. He had an easy nobility about him, a pure *goodness* that shone out from every pore of his perfect skin. Alaric never had that. Alaric had a permanent sneer at his lips, just a faint thing you saw when the light caught it. Alaric assumed the world wouldn't appreciate him in all his glory, and therefore he had to be an asshole to make sure people *got it*, that they got who he was and all the money he had that made him worth something.

Xander had an ease about him, a languid confidence that said, *I am who I am. If you like me, great. If you don't, that's cool too.*

And DE found that a thousand times more attractive than she ever thought she could. She had never liked a guy before who actually thought she deserved good things. And she knew this, his simple and genuine declaration, was throwing her. Ever since she was little, all she'd known was being dumped places like she was an inconvenience, a burden, like a mangy cat no one wanted to bring home. Her parents had basically used Rosetta Academy as a holding cell for her as soon as she turned five years old. When they couldn't be bothered to spend vacations with her, they left her there or arranged for her to stay with friends or far-flung relatives in various countries. She had no siblings. She'd never known a steady, unconditional kind of love. She wasn't sure such a thing even existed.

They turned the corner that would eventually lead them to the library's entrance.

Part of her felt guilty for even thinking these things while

Jaya and Grey had now joined Leo and Anna and all the others down in the infirmary. Who was next—Rahul? Caterina? She herself? DE needed to focus on this new crisis at hand, not the ongoing crisis that was her love life.

"After you," Xander said politely but stiffly, holding open one of the double doors to the library. DE ducked inside without meeting his eye.

"Thanks," she mumbled, trying to keep her mind on what they were there to do. Inside, the library was empty, Anna's friendly face conspicuously absent from the reference desk. DE opened the flap in the desk that would let them pass through and left it open for Xander to come in after her. "The door to the archives has been left open."

"That's good for us," Xander said from behind her, still being unfailingly polite. "I guess Anna wasn't really in the mindset to lock up when she was last here."

DE shivered a little at that. Poor Anna.

"So according to the blueprint, there should be a hidden stairway at the back of the archives room." He crossed the main room of the archives at a diagonal, and she followed him, past all the neat shelves and boxes they'd seen before.

Xander crossed to the clean, neutral beige wall at the back of the room and began to knock on it, possibly looking for something hollow.

DE stepped away from him, looking around at the towering shelves lined with boxes and poster tubes.

She turned a corner at the end of a row of shelves, the smell of old paper flooding her nostrils like ancient perfume. She was almost to the end of the second row of shelves now, with absolutely no idea where this secret passage might be.

At the end of the section, by the wall, was a large marble

statue of Coeus, the Greek Titan of knowledge and inquisitive minds. She'd never seen the statue before, but then again, DE spent as little time in the library—and by extension, the archives section—as possible. She was more into modern technology than dusty old papers.

"A little on the nose with the whole academic theme here, Rosetta, but okay," DE muttered. Absently, waiting for Xander to be done, she ran her hand over the carved folds of Coeus's white robes. And then paused. A faint memory tugged at her, insistent.

One of the first things Madame Olivera had said when DE walked into her store came back to her: *an inquisitive mind, a seeker of knowledge.* Coeus, as established, was the Greek Titan of knowledge and inquisitive minds. That couldn't just be a coincidence, could it?

Her pulse pounding, DE began to peer more closely at the statue. Coeus was poised on a white marble stand of sorts, his feet planted firmly on the stone. And around his ankle, just barely visible, was a white button.

"That's an anachronism if I ever saw one." Kneeling, DE peered closely. Yep, definitely a button. It was white, nearly impossible to see, unless you were really looking. And even then, you'd probably just dismiss it as a repair done to an ancient statue. DE reached a finger out to push the button, then stopped.

"Xander," she called, in a voice that sounded quavering even to her. "I think I may have found something."

He was beside her in a flash, his eyes avid with expectation. "What? What is it?"

DE pushed the button. And beside Coeus, on the wall, a small, nearly invisible door swung open soundlessly.

CHAPTER 39

XANDER

Xander felt his whole chest expand with exhilaration as the door swung open. "I knew it! The blueprint had this stairway that had no obvious doors leading to it—it's gotta be this."

There was a small, dusty wooden staircase that wound down into the darkness. It seemed ill-advised to actually go down it, but what choice did they have? After just a moment's hesitation, Xander led the way. It smelled like rot and disuse, musty and claustrophobic. And he could swear the stairs were creaking with just his weight on them. When DE came in after him, the small door swung shut, leaving them in pitch-black darkness. He heard DE gasp softly behind him. Xander turned on his phone's flashlight and they kept going.

At the bottom, he stood blinking for a good ten seconds, not really able to believe they'd done it. They were actually *here*.

The basement dorms sprouted off a dark, dusty hallway that smelled of mildew and desolation, which made sense, considering no one had been down here since forever.

DE turned on her phone's flashlight too. "Hopefully we leave here tetanus-free," she half joked, carefully kicking at a rusty nail that stuck out from one of the floorboards.

Xander managed a laugh; he knew she was trying to make things okay between them again, and that's what he wanted too. He wanted to pretend the last forty-five minutes had never happened, just like she did.

The problem was, his heart hadn't gotten the memo. He was trying *really* hard to not look at her, because if he looked at her, he knew his gaze would linger. Yes, she'd turned him down. Yes, it stung and it sucked, majorly. But his heart wasn't really connected to his brain—it never had been. And his heart wanted DE. No matter what.

He half smiled to himself. It was funny that when he first arrived at Rosetta, he'd thought she'd be a distraction. He'd warned himself not to get tangled up with her because he couldn't afford that. But now . . . now he was the one chasing after her. He was the one realizing just how much he needed her in his life.

But that didn't matter. She'd said no. That was that.

Xander realized he had goose bumps. It was cold in the basement, colder than he thought it should be. He'd guess it was maybe forty degrees, which was odd. He remembered reading somewhere that far enough underground, a basement would be around fifty-five degrees regardless of surface conditions. Filing that away, Xander turned his attention to the many damp-swollen doors lining either side of the hallway. Using the flashlight on his phone, he could just about make out the dorm numbers. It looked like the even numbers were on the right side. Once he figured that out, he found Atticus's dorm room—482-D—without much trouble. The door to 482-D was firmly shut, unlike some of the other rooms. From underneath the door, swirls of frigid air curled out and wrapped themselves around Xander's ankles.

Xander stood staring at the door for a few moments, as if he could will himself to see inside it. He heard DE rustling around behind him and took a deep breath before he spoke. "I found it."

She was by his side in an instant. "482-D," she read aloud. "Whoa."

"Yeah. Whoa." Xander was having trouble catching his breath. He clenched his lightly trembling hands into fists.

In his peripheral vision, he saw DE turn to him. "Hey. You okay?"

He glanced at her and then away. "Yeah. Fine."

There was a long pause, and when he looked back at her, she had an eyebrow up, the planes of her face stark in the blue-white light from her phone's flashlight. "Really? You don't think I'm that gullible, do ya?"

"Okay, I'm a little . . . shook." He blinked hard, trying to clear his head. "I mean, it's *right here.*" He gestured toward the door just two feet before him. "This is where Atticus spent his last days. This is where it all went down. I've been chasing this for years, and now that I'm finally here, I don't know how to feel about it." He snorted. "I sound like a total fucking mess."

"No, you don't." DE's voice was firm. "I've never had a family member die under mysterious circumstances that were then covered up, so I won't pretend to know exactly how you're feeling. But Xander, this might be the precipice of the solution right here: to solving your family's mystery, to solving the mystery of this storm, to helping everyone at Rosetta who's caught the sleeping sickness. Jaya and Grey and Leo and Anna and countless others. We could be literally standing before the key to this whole thing. Of course you're feeling some kind of way. I am too." He felt her fingers entwine around his and squeeze, briefly, before she pulled away.

His heart rammed against his chest. Xander nodded. "All right. Let's do this." Reaching for the doorknob, he turned it, expecting it to not budge at all. But it did.

It was stiff and hard to manipulate, but it did turn. And then . . . nothing. "The door's stuck." Xander tried pushing the doorknob again, but the door remained tightly shut.

"Do you think it's locked?"

Xander shone his phone's flashlight on the doorknob, trying to see what was going on. It would be so much easier if it wasn't so freaking dark down here. "No, it doesn't feel locked. I think the door's just swollen in its frame." He shone the flashlight upward along the doorjamb and saw a thick forest of spiderwebs. "I'm going to have to force it." Turning the doorknob again, Xander put his shoulder to the door and heaved with all his might. With a great, groaning creak, the door swung open, tearing the spiderwebs as it went. A gust of icy air blasted them in the face.

They both stood staring into the darkened dorm room, a relic of a time long past. Xander saw his breath cloud out in front of him, a mist of white. There was still furniture in the room: a bed along the wall to the right, a small wooden desk straight ahead, and a small wooden armoire next to it. There was a small window, too, but the glass was so grimy, it was completely opaque. The freezing, trapped air felt thin here, stale and musty, and Xander imagined a crypt must smell exactly like this. There was something else, too, something he couldn't quite put his finger on. It was like the room was cloaked in a miasma of despair and anger and helplessness. Just standing here, he felt an intense wave of sadness roll over him.

Beside him, DE let out a small sigh. "It's so . . . awful in here," she whispered, her breath visible too. "Not just the cold, but the *feeling*. It's the same thing I felt when we first found the change doll. This endless, dark sadness." She wrapped her arms around herself, the beam of her flashlight bouncing along the walls.

"Yeah, I feel it too. Fuck." Xander took the first step in, holding his phone out in front of him like a talisman. The smell of decay wrinkled his nose, but he pressed on, his feet guiding him almost thoughtlessly to the center of the room.

"What do you think we're looking for?" DE asked behind him, her voice hushed.

He understood the need for hushed voices; he felt it too, a certain ethereal quality to the room, like it existed in another dimension not usually accessible to people. "I'm not sure. . . . Maybe we can just start looking around and see what we come up with?"

"Sounds good to me."

Xander crossed the room to the armoire and yanked on the handles. Like the door to the room, it took a little pressure before the double doors finally gave way, releasing a cloud of dust and the camphor scent of mothballs.

CHAPTER 40

XANDER

Xander sighed. "Empty." The armoire stood stark and bare, lit up in the flashlight's beam.

"Should we look in his desk?" DE asked hesitantly, pointing her phone toward the small wooden desk that sat quietly like a well-behaved dog in the corner.

"Feels weird to be poking around his stuff, doesn't it?" Xander asked, and DE nodded vigorously.

"Yeah. I mean, I know he's been dead for a long time, but . . ."

"But you still want to respect his privacy. Yeah, me too. But this is the only way we can find some answers to help everybody. And I'd like to think Atticus would be on board with this."

DE met his eye. "You're right. He would want his people to know what happened to him."

His people. She'd said it casually, but it struck a chord deep inside Xander. He'd never known Atticus Wakefield, but his death had left a tangible hole in the family. How would Xander's own parents feel if he died with no explanation or cause? It was difficult to conceive such a thing happening, but it *had* happened to Atticus. Besides that, Rosetta Academy had actively hidden

Atticus's death from the press and everyone outside the family, as if it were some dirty secret. That wasn't right. Xander had the opportunity to right that wrong, in some way, not just for Atticus and his family, but for everyone at Rosetta now. If something were to happen, if someone were to die in this storm, he didn't want Rosetta closing ranks again. He didn't want this to be the end of the story.

With new determination in his step, he crossed the room to the wooden desk. It had a small hutch with two drawers on either side. The top of the desk opened on a hinge so you could store stuff inside.

Holding his phone in his left hand and searching with his right, he began with the two drawers. The one on the right held only a small stub of a pencil. The one on the left held a book.

His heart thundering, a light sheen of sweat on his brow in spite of the frigid air in the old room, Xander attempted to understand what he was looking at. It was as if finally being granted access to Atticus's stuff was short-circuiting his brain. It took him a full three seconds to realize what his great-great-great-uncle had left in the drawer.

"A journal," Xander gasped when the rectangular shape of the tiny book finally made sense to his brain. "They must've missed it when they cleaned out his room."

DE blew out a soft breath and looked at him expectantly.

His hands trembling a bit, Xander lifted the small leather-bound notebook from the drawer. It was held closed by a string, also made of leather, that had been looped around it several times.

Xander smoothed his hand over the pebbled cover. He swallowed, the sound echoing in his head and then spiraling outward into the dusty old room. "Okay. Okay. Here goes."

His fingers shook as he unwound the string and then slowly cracked open the journal cover. A small shimmering tornado of dust motes rose and twirled in the air, and then Xander's eyes were reading Atticus's name in his own hand, written in scratchy fountain pen on the first yellowed page.

> *Atticus Wakefield*
> *1872, Rosetta Academy*

CHAPTER 41

XANDER

Xander blew out a breath that seemed to be stuck in his chest. Running his fingers lightly over the neatly printed handwriting, he shook his head. "Wow. That's his writing. When he was right around my age."

DE nodded beside him but didn't say anything.

Xander swallowed and turned the first thin, yellowed page. After a moment's pause, he got out his phone and turned on the flashlight to be able to read better.

> *January 1, 1872*
>
> *To pen one's thoughts on paper in this fashion seems to me to be a strange pastime, and yet, here I find myself. What do I hope to achieve? Perhaps nothing more than a sense of peace and stillness, which I find more difficult to grasp with every passing year. I am thankful for the presence of steadying forces in my life, good friends and mentors.*
>
> *I must go—Tobias and I are meeting before dinner.*

"Tobias," Xander murmured. He looked at DE and pointed at the journal with his chin. "Check this out."

She walked forward and read the journal entry, her lips moving silently as she went. Then her eyes widened. "Tobias?" DE looked at Xander, her green eyes dancing with questions. "As in, Tobias Huntley III? The alleged serial killer?"

Xander shrugged. "Maybe. Wouldn't that be a weird coincidence?" He flipped the page and frowned. "What's this?"

There was a square piece of loose paper stuffed into the journal. On one side was printed an image of an ornate silver snowflake and, at its center, a small silver key.

Xander heard DE's sharp intake of breath beside him and turned to face her, the square paper in his hand. "You okay?"

DE reached forward and grabbed the paper from him in a very DE move. Xander couldn't help but smile a little, in spite of still feeling the sting of disappointment from what had happened earlier. "Holy shit. That's, um, that's exactly the same piece of paper that psychic I told you about gave me. I mean, like, down to the key in the center of the snowflake and everything."

She turned it over in her hands, running one finger along the edges. On the back, in silver script, it read: *The blood of lost souls wakes the storm. You have the key to vanquish it. Open your heart. I will guide you.* "Jesus. It's the *exact* same thing. The weight of the paper, the feel of it, the message on the back, everything. And I threw that piece of paper away. I know I did." She handed the paper back to him. "So how is this possible?"

He looked down at the silver script, glinting in the beam of his flashlight. "I . . . Maybe you're remembering it wrong?"

But she was shaking her head vehemently before he was even done talking. "No. I studied that piece of paper very closely. I know what I saw. Damn, I wish I'd kept it so we could compare the two."

Xander stuck the paper carefully back into Atticus's journal and then closed the book. "I'm going to take this with me, give it a careful read-through. Maybe he'll mention where the paper came from."

DE nodded, nibbling on her lower lip. "Yeah, good idea." She took a breath. "Is it just me or does it seem like things get weirder every time we go looking for answers?"

DE

DE sat beside Jaya, holding her friend's limp, cool hand. "I wish you'd wake up," she said, her eyes filling with tears. "I'm so lost, J. I can't . . ." A hot tear dripped onto her cheek and splashed onto Jaya's hand. "I don't know how to fix this."

Jaya continued to breathe deeply, peacefully, as if she were having the best sleep of her life. She was out in a gurney in the hallway leading to the infirmary, and they'd put Grey in another gurney next to her. DE looked from Jaya's face to Grey's, noting the equally serene expressions on both their faces. A shiver rippled through her.

"You know there isn't enough space here anymore?" she murmured to Jaya, smoothing back her hair. "People who get the sleeping sickness now are being kept in their rooms, and the medics are just checking up on them a few times a day. Some of the staff are pitching in to do the checkups too, because the doctors and medics are completely overwhelmed." She shook her head, feeling more tears spilling. "This is such a fucking mess."

DE realized she felt intensely guilty, walking around with agency and thought while her friends languished here. Standing, she squeezed Jaya's hand one last time and returned it to her side. Then she patted Grey on the shoulder and went to check on Leo.

Will was sitting beside him, looking as despairing as DE felt. "Hi." He managed a wan smile.

"Have you eaten today?" DE asked, noting the dark circles under his eyes.

As if he could feel her assessing gaze, Will took off his glasses and rubbed them. "Not yet. I'll get something soon."

DE reached into the pocket of her sweater tunic and pulled out a protein bar. "Here. I'm not going to eat it, so you might as well."

He took it. "Thanks."

DE pulled up a chair and sat beside Will, both of them gazing at Leo as if he might wake up any minute.

"I shouldn't have just dropped him off at his dorm room," Will said finally, his voice low. His hands were clasped between his knees, and he was leaning forward, his eyes on Leo. "I should've gone in, made sure he was okay. Maybe he wouldn't be here, in this bloody infirmary, if I had."

"No." DE put her hand on his back. "You can't think like that, Will. This has nothing to do with what you did or didn't do. Look around." She gestured around them at the bay filled with quiet, still bodies. "No one knows what's happening; no one knows the cause. But you not checking up on Leo isn't it."

Will took off his glasses and pinched the bridge of his nose. "I just don't know what to think. I feel so fucking helpless, and I hate that feeling. *Hate* it."

DE put her hand on his. "I know what you mean. My best friend—no, more like my sister—is lying out there in the hallway." She gestured toward where Jaya lay. "And I can't help but feel like there's more I should be doing." What she really wanted to be doing was reading the journal, mining it for clues to solving this thing. But Atticus was Xander's relative, and so she was giving him some space to look at it before she took a turn. She took a deep breath. "You can't do any more than you're already doing, Will. Soon enough, this storm will pass, and we will get help for everyone here." But even as she said the words, DE felt them ring untrue.

Surreptitiously, she pulled her phone out and checked the screen. Nothing from Xander yet. She had a feeling, though, that whatever next step had to be taken would be spelled out in Atticus's diary. She just hoped they didn't figure it out too late.

CHAPTER 42

XANDER

Xander set the journal down and rubbed his eyes. He was sitting in an armchair by the window in his dorm room, the fire in the fireplace dancing merrily. In spite of that, he was cold—freezing cold. It was like the chill from Atticus's room had seeped into his bones, turning his marrow to frost. He'd put on an extra sweater, and now he pulled the sleeves down over his fingertips, blowing on them. He'd been reading Atticus's journal for the last couple of hours without pause, and his eyes felt gritty and dry. Xander watched the snow flurries beating against his window, the unrelenting wind screaming in frustration at being denied the right to claim everyone inside the building.

It was weird, but Xander realized he couldn't quite put his finger on how much time had passed since he and DE had found Atticus's journal in the basement. Had it been just this morning? Yesterday? Two weeks ago? It all felt equally possible. He checked the date on his phone. No, it had definitely been this morning. He was . . . pretty sure.

So far, Atticus seemed to be just an average Rosetta Academy student, concerned about friends and grades and "courting." There was nothing to suggest anything more sinister lurking around the corner, and Xander was frustrated. Should he keep reading this journal, hoping it would shed light on the storm and Atticus's death, while all around him, people were getting sick and falling into comas?

He looked down at the journal, clenching his jaw. But what was the alternative? He couldn't just run around without a plan, hoping things sorted themselves out somehow, especially knowing that the answer—or a hint of it—might lie in the pages of this book. Taking a resolved breath, he picked up the journal and began to read again.

> *March 2*
>
> *I had the opportunity to call upon Emma Rose today. It is her eighteenth birthday. One day I will prove to her family that I am worthy of her. One day I will be a self-made man, owing his fortune and his name to no one but himself. But for today, I simply gave her a special doll I had made for the occasion and told her to keep it with her always, in lieu of my presence by her side. I shall dream of the blush that colored her cheeks so prettily for the rest of my days.*

Xander smiled lightly; Atticus had it bad. Then he paused. The "special doll." Could it be the change doll he and DE had found on the hill?

Frowning, Xander turned the page and kept reading.

> *March 5*
>
> *It was a beautiful day today, sunny and cold, and so I asked Emma Rose if she would accompany me on a stroll around the gardens. Though we didn't talk*

much of us, I did notice she carried the doll I gave
her, and the sight of it brought me much joy.

On the way back to my dormitory, I saw again
that strange washerwoman who has taken to staring
at me with the most unnerving look in her eye. I
waved my hand in greeting, not knowing what
else to do, but she did not wave in return. When I
got close enough to hear, though, I realized she was
muttering something under her breath. I caught
but a gist of what she was saying, this madwoman,
but it sounded like, "Souls will slumber. One will
perish." She repeated those words under her breath
until I had passed by. How very odd.

Xander sat up straighter and reread the last few lines. *Souls will slumber. One will perish.* Wasn't that what DE said the psychic lady had told her? In fact, he was pretty sure those were the *exact* words DE had recounted. What the hell? His palms suddenly sweaty, Xander kept going.

March 9

Tobias said today that I should ask Emma
Rose if she'd accompany me to the spring dance on
the 24th. Although my friendship with Tobias is
quite new, I do trust him in matters of the heart.
According to Tobias, he has courted many young
women already and seems to have quite a special
touch with them. Perhaps I would do well to follow
his advice.

But I am once again stymied by my own
doubts. What have I to offer a lady like Emma

Rose? I am not as handsome as Tobias, nor do
I come from the sort of fortune he does. Would
someone like her truly want to be with someone
like me? Can I truly offer her all she deserves?

Xander felt a cold finger press against his spine as he reread the entry. Tobias definitely had a "special touch" with the ladies, but maybe not in the exact way Atticus had imagined. The other stuff, though, the self-doubt and the worry that he couldn't offer Emma Rose everything she deserved . . . That was something Xander could identify with. Something he could identify with *too* well, in fact. And if Atticus were here today, Xander wondered what he'd make of this entry. Would he say to his past self, *You idiot, you have such limited time, you should make the best of it while you can*? Xander had a feeling he would.

Setting the journal aside, he picked up his phone, opened RIMS, and clicked the "compose" icon. He typed DE's name and then tapped out a message quickly.

Can we meet up tonight? 7 PMish? -X

His phone dinged a second later.

Sure. I can bring a couple of sandwiches from the dining hall to your room? Guessing this is about A's journal . . .

Xander responded quickly.

Yeah, all that sounds great.

He didn't think he'd have an appetite, but he couldn't explain that to her over text.

Xander appreciated the fact that she was trying to get back to their easy friendship. He wasn't quite there yet—he still had one last thing to say to her—but that was okay. Tucking his phone into his pocket, he sat back in his chair and watched the snow fall. If only he wasn't so cold.

CHAPTER 43

DE

The bag of avocado-and-turkey sandwiches hung from DE's wrist as she made her way to Xander's room. She was five minutes early, but she was hoping he wouldn't mind; she was just too excited to hear what Atticus had to say in his journal.

She'd been *trying* to be sensitive and patient. Finding your mysteriously dead ancestor's diary wasn't something that happened every day, and she knew Xander would need time to process. So when he'd messaged her so quickly after, she'd been ecstatic. Hopefully he had some good ideas on what to do about the sleeping sickness.

When he answered his door, she burst in without waiting for an invitation. They were past all that now; things were way too serious. DE tried hard to block out the last time she'd been in here, when she'd been . . . ah, distracted. Despite her best efforts, the memory of the kiss and the conversation they'd had right after broke into her thoughts. She pushed them away, feeling her cheeks heat. *Not going there. Nope, nope, nope.*

"Hey," she said, holding out the bag of sandwiches.

Xander stood in front of his window, dark hair falling onto

his forehead. His eyes were shadowed, hooded, and DE couldn't make out the expression in them.

She stepped forward hesitantly. "Hey, Xander . . . are you okay?" Had there been some unspeakably bad news in the diary?

He rubbed his face and strode to the fireplace. She could see his eyes now—they burned with determination and . . . something else. Something she couldn't quite identify.

"Yeah, no, I'm fine." He gestured to the sandwiches. "Can I take those from you?"

"I got it," DE replied as she unwound the bag's handles from her wrist and set it down on Xander's nightstand. "Was there . . . was there something bad in the diary?"

Xander glanced at the book, which was on a side table by an armchair facing the window. "I'm still reading it. But, um, listen to this—Atticus met a strange 'washerwoman' who said the words 'Souls will slumber. One will perish.'"

"What?" Goose bumps rushed up DE's arms, her body reacting before her mind had fully understood Xander's words. "But that's exactly what Madame Olivera said to me. And we found the same piece of paper that she'd given me in Atticus's journal. How is that possible?"

Xander shook his head. "I don't know. I also found out that he gave Emma Rose, the girl he loved, a 'special doll.' I'm pretty sure it's the change doll we found. I've been trying to piece it all together and it's not clicking for me yet. I'm going to keep reading, though."

DE looked over at the journal, took a step toward it. "If you're too tired to keep going, I could take over?" She knew she sounded eager, and that's because she was. She really, really needed to know what the hell was going on.

Xander held up a hand. "I'm going to get back to it soon, I

promise." He cleared his throat. "But, um, I have something I need to say first."

DE's eyebrows were knitted together. "Oh. What?"

Xander rubbed his palms on his thighs and took a breath. He was starting to make her really nervous. What was this? "DE, this storm, the sleeping sickness, what Madame Olivera told you about one person dying . . . It's all made me think. Made me realize." He licked his lips before continuing. Seeing his nerves made DE's pulse race. "No one knows where life's going to take them. Atticus thought he had all the time in the world to be with his love, and he died at eighteen. I guess . . . reading his journal has put things into perspective for me."

Xander's golden eyes were intense now, focused. "I don't know what's going to happen, DE. I don't know if this weird sickness is going to claim us all or if the storm's just going to keep raging or—who knows what the future holds. The one thing I've learned from Atticus's death is that you can't ever predict when your time's going to run out. And if mine ran out today, I know there's only one thing I'd regret: not telling you how I feel."

DE felt her knees go soft. She walked on wobbly legs to the armchair by the window, turned it so she was facing Xander, and collapsed onto it. "Xander . . . I . . ." She shook her head, at a loss. Her mind was reeling with a thousand thoughts, a thousand emotions, all flaring and blazing and burning with an intensity that left her breathless. The maddening push-pull that she'd managed to suppress was back—she wanted Xander more than she'd wanted anyone in her entire life; she was terrified of what he could do to her heart.

"I know we've dipped a toe in this river already. And I know you said you weren't interested. But in my heart, deep down inside, I know there's a spark, a glow, every time we're together. It's a real live thing, lighting up everything around me. Tell me you don't see it."

DE looked down at her hands, so tightly clasped in her lap that they were bloodless and white. "I see it," she replied, her voice barely above a whisper. She looked up at Xander, and he was shimmering. That's when she realized her eyes were full of tears. "I know we have something between us. It's kind of impossible not to notice."

Xander's face was so vulnerable, so full of hope, that she wanted to bawl. "Then . . . then could that be enough . . . ?"

"Enough to overcome my misgivings?" She half smiled. "No. Can't you see, Xander? I'm broken. There's no putting me back together. And I'm tired of relying on other people to hold my pieces together."

He pushed a hand through his hair, his expression torn. Then, as if deciding something, he came forward and knelt beside her. "This is because of Alaric and what he did to you, right? DE, I'll never, ever hurt you that way. I'd rather eat a bag of wasps."

DE laughed, then sniffed. "You're a real poet, you know that?"

Xander placed a careful, warm hand over hers. "I never thought I'd feel this way about anyone, especially not now, not with Atticus and the storm and—" He stopped and took a breath. "From the first moment I saw you in that attic, when you threatened me with expulsion, I was . . ." He shook his head, smiled as if to himself. "I was completely, utterly smitten. I was lost. And I was yours."

DE searched his eyes for a long moment. At that moment, she could see it all—giving herself over to this feeling, to those golden eyes, to Xander. But . . . hadn't she been here before, and not all that long ago?

CHAPTER 44

XANDER

Xander had been joking about that bag-of-wasps thing, but now he really did feel like he'd eaten one. There was a sudden buzzing in his ears, a pain in his sternum.

He could see the exact moment when DE decided to say no. Her eyes, those beautiful, wild green eyes, shuttered. Her entire being closed off from him, as if she'd put up some internal wall to keep herself safe.

She bit her lip and looked at him, her eyes glittering with tears again. "I'm sorry," she whispered. "I can't. I can't ever open myself up that way again."

Xander slowly moved his hand from atop hers. He nodded and stood, his jaw clenched against the hurt.

DE grabbed his hand. "It's not you, Xander. I promise. I . . . I like you. Very much. But . . ."

He looked at her, his face solemn. "You don't have to explain," he said gently. He was hurt, but this was still DE. And she deserved gentleness. She deserved for him to meet her where she was. "It's okay." He took a breath. "Telling you was something I had to do to feel right within myself. And you . . . you have to say no to feel right within yourself. To protect yourself."

"It's not that I think you're anything like Alaric," DE rushed to say. "I mean, of course you're not. But I . . . I'm not a full person anymore, Xander. And you deserve better. You deserve someone who can give you all of herself."

"Don't do that," Xander said, feeling a flash of anger that he worked to quell. "Don't put yourself down, or make it out like you're not good enough. You are. *More* than good enough. You're one of the best people I know, DE."

DE looked down at her hands. "Just know that turning you down is one of the hardest things I've done."

Xander felt the breath whoosh out of him. They were right there, on the cusp of something incredible. As soon as he'd had a glimpse of what lay on the other side, the door had closed on him, on them. Forever.

He opened his mouth to respond, but no words came out. Xander had never been speechless before, but at this moment, he found he had absolutely nothing to say.

An explosion of knocks interrupted the moment. "Daphne Elizabeth? Are you in there?"

DE turned to Xander, eyes wide on her pale face. "That's Caterina." They both leaped up for the door, though Xander got there first.

When he flung it open, Caterina was standing in the doorway, her face ashen. "I thought I might find you here. Come quickly," she said, her voice strained. "Something really strange is happening."

DE

"Where are we going?" DE followed Caterina down the hallway at a breakneck speed, thankful for her long legs. "What's going *on*?"

Caterina shook her head, her long brown waves undulating, and looked over her shoulder at DE and Xander. "I can't explain it. You have to see for yourself."

DE's stomach dropped. Without thinking, she reached into her tunic pocket for the change doll and rubbed its head. Hazarding a look in Xander's direction, she saw he looked exactly like she felt: harried, distracted, stressed, unhappy. She could barely believe they'd been in the basement together only that morning, thrilled at finding Atticus's journal.

They followed Caterina down the stairs to the first floor. Then she turned a corner, and they found themselves outside the teacher's lounge. Just as they got there, Rahul exited through one of the double doors. His rumpled shirt had been misbuttoned, she saw, with one tail hanging lower than the other. The new Rahul never dressed this way anymore. DE felt a knot of ice form in her stomach.

Immediately Rahul took Caterina's hand. "Hey, DE," he said, his voice uncharacteristically subdued.

"What's going on?" DE said again. "Who's in there?"

Rahul and Caterina shared a look, and then each pushed one of the double doors open in answer.

DE stepped in, with Xander close behind on her heels, and then stopped short.

"Holy shit."

The teacher's lounge had a large sitting area as soon as you entered, furnished with plump, comfortable couches and armchairs, a large brick fireplace, and lots of potted plants. Beyond this sitting area, past an arched entryway, lay a conference room with a long, rectangular table and a dozen chairs around it.

Right now, eleven out of those twelve chairs were occupied.

In each of those chairs was a Rosetta Academy teacher, sitting completely silent and absolutely still, hands resting in identical positions on the table—palms up, fingers loosely curled. There was no expression on their faces besides a slightly dreamy, unfocused sort of stare. If DE were to close her eyes, it would feel like she were in an empty room.

"Mannequins," she found herself saying as she stared at them. Her lips felt wooden. "They look like mannequins."

"I came in to look for Dr. Waverly," Caterina said. "A dozen more students have succumbed to the sleeping sickness overnight. But when I came in . . . I found them like this."

"It's speeding up," Xander said from beside DE. "The rate at which people are getting sick, I mean."

"Yes." Caterina met both of their gazes. She wasn't one for overly emotional displays, but DE saw the corner of one of her eyes twitch. In Caterina-speak, this may as well have been a scream. "I've written letters to my father and my half sister, and I'm saving them in the desk drawer in my room. I wanted you to know, just in case."

Rahul's face fell, as if just the thought of a world without his precious Caterina was too much to bear.

"Great. You can give the letters to them yourself." DE made sure her voice was matter-of-fact.

Caterina shook her head. "Don't do that. We're not in a war zone and you're not my comrade-in-arms. This is a really fucking strange situation, and it doesn't look like anyone's immune. But if one of us does get out, I want my family to know what happened to me, what my last days were like."

Xander cleared his throat. "If I get out and you don't, Caterina, I'll make sure the letters get to where they need to go."

"Thank you." Caterina smiled faintly at him. "Now, if you'll excuse me, Rahul and I are going to spend some time alone together." What she didn't say, but what all of them heard anyway, added on to the end of that sentence: *while we still can.*

The moment they were gone, DE turned to Xander, eyes flashing, face hot with emotion. "Why did you say that? Why did you promise to send those letters?"

Xander looked utterly flummoxed. "Because . . . it was the right thing to do?"

"No. The right thing to do is to tell her—to tell anyone who'll listen—that we're all going to make it through this safely. All the people in comas are going to wake up, and—and we're going to get the help we need, and this stupid, shitty storm is going to blow over. . . ."

"DE . . . hey. Hey, it's okay."

It was only when Xander put his arms around her that DE realized she was sobbing. She let him comfort her for a moment before she remembered their last encounter and realized this wasn't fair to him. Letting him comfort her, letting him close. She pushed back against his chest and stepped away when he loosened his arms.

"I have to go," she said, swiping at her cheeks with her fists.

Xander frowned. "Go where?"

"I have to try everything I can to fix this. I—I'll see you later." And before he could stop her, DE turned on her heel and stalked out of the lounge.

CHAPTER 45

XANDER

Xander paced his room, looking at his phone, just in case. Just in case she sent him a message. Just in case she tried to reach out. Just in case . . . something.

But, of course, his blank phone screen stared back, mocking him. He had no idea where DE had rushed off to. Damn it, he should've offered to go with her. Or to help her. But after she'd rejected him (for the *second* time, his asshole brain reminded him), he didn't want to become a hanger-on, someone who couldn't take a hint. She was a strong woman. She could do whatever it was herself, couldn't she?

Sighing, he looked around his room—and stopped. Atticus's journal still sat on his side table, waiting. In all the chaos of the last few hours, he'd forgotten what he'd been doing when he'd asked DE up to his room.

Checking his phone screen one more time—still blank—he walked over to the armchair and sat, pulling the journal over into his lap. He might as well finish what he'd started.

March 10
    I walked the gardens with Emma Rose again,

but this time, Tobias came along for, as he put it, "fortifications." He seemed genuinely interested in Emma Rose, asking questions about her family and her time at Llewelyn School for Girls. He even hinted rather robustly that Emma Rose should consider coming to Rosetta Academy for our spring ball on the 24th, a suggestion that caused her to blush and look up at me from beneath her eyelashes. I cannot stop thinking of her.

March 16

I had dinner at the tavern in town tonight and as I sat there, savoring my stew, Tobias entered. He joined me, and after our meal, asked if I'd accompany him to a neighboring jeweler. He had a pocket watch to pick up there that had been in need of repairs.

At the jeweler's, Tobias guided me to the ring display. He asked if any caught my eye, and when I asked why, he laughed and replied that he thought Emma Rose would be expecting one from me soon. So shocked was I by this suggestion that all I could do was gape at him like a fish taking its dying breaths. He laughed uproariously at that, Tobias, and I must admit, I didn't much like the gleam in his eye. It seemed like he was having a laugh at my expense and I didn't quite understand the joke.

March 20

In spite of the biting and vicious cold, it is a glorious day. Emma Rose sent me a *letter by messenger, asking if I could meet at the gardens—our usual spot. I was there ten minutes early and watched as she walked up the path toward me, her cheeks rosy and pink, her smile shy and beautiful, as always.*

Once we'd walked for a while, she hesitantly stated that she'd love to go to the spring ball. Apparently, Tobias had asked her friend Isabella, who'd said yes. This was news to me, as Tobias hadn't mentioned asking Isabella. But I expect he did it to encourage Emma Rose to accept my request whenever I made it. Of course, once Emma Rose told me she wanted to go, I wasted no time at all in asking her. She said yes and then we clasped hands and smiled at each other like a pair of loons until it was time for her to go.

In four days, I will be dancing with Emma Rose in my arms. I must thank Tobias for his clever engineering. I have decided, I will tell Emma Rose how I feel the night of the ball. I can't stand this tossing and turning any longer. I must know if she will be mine forever. I won't be able to rest until I do.

Mr. Thompson, the porter, was complaining today that his bad knee ached. Apparently, that only happens when we're in for a big snowstorm. I do hope he's wrong this time. I don't want the ball to get delayed on account of weather.

March 24

It has all gone so horribly wrong. I can only

hope that I am stuck in a nightmare, from which I will mercifully awaken soon. Otherwise . . . otherwise, how am I to go on? How am I to ever forgive myself?

The girls from Llewelyn were brought over tonight for the spring ball. Emma Rose was ravishing in a black-and-bloodred silk gown, the rich crimson bringing out that warm hue in her cheeks. Her lovely long hair was pulled back and hung in waves to her waist. Her dark eyes sparkled when she saw me, and my heart hitched in my chest. This is her, I remember thinking. My future wife, the mother to my children. This is how it all starts. I must remember so we can tell them one day.

We danced the evening away—oh, how we danced. When the music was playing, everything else faded away. The stern escorts from Llewelyn, the watchful teachers, the other students. No one existed except me and Emma Rose.

"Look," she said quietly, shyly. Reaching into the pocket of her gown, she pulled out the doll just a little, so I could peek at it.

"You brought it with you," I said to her, smiling.

"Yes." Her cheeks aflame in the sweetest pink, she smiled coyly back. "It reminds me of you. I never leave it behind."

Now is the time, I remember thinking. I must tell her how I feel. I must make sure she knows my intentions.

Oh, why did I not seize upon my instinct and my courage? Why did I let that moment go to waste? I have no answers to those questions. I knew only that I was suddenly overcome by fear, by doubt. What if Emma Rose said no? What if she did not feel the same way? What if she was only being nice to me, as was her kind nature?

During a break, as I was fetching us both some water, I saw Tobias.

"Have you told her?" he asked me, his eyes intent and avid with curiosity.

"Not yet." I looked back at Emma Rose; she was speaking with Isabella, who had come with Tobias.

"Well, what are you waiting for? A girl like Emma Rose isn't going to wait around for you to work up the nerve, you know. She must have a dozen other suitors."

I know it was meant to be helpful, but his words really had the opposite effect on me. Whatever dregs of courage I was working on disappeared. Suddenly I was filled with the cold, awful realization that I wouldn't be confessing my feelings to Emma Rose—at least, not that night. The moment had passed me by.

I shook my head. "I can't," I said to Tobias. "It's just not the right time."

He gave me a shrewd look, his blue eyes glittering. "Are you certain?"

I nodded, miserable. "I'm certain. It's not going to be tonight."

"Very well," he said, thoughtfully, as he took a sip of his ale.

It just wasn't the same when I returned to Emma Rose. We danced and talked, but from the look in her eye, she could tell something was amiss. Of course, being the elegant lady she is, she couldn't ask me outright what it was. And neither could I say. What would I say, even if I could? That I was a coward and was now backing out of the agreement I'd made with myself? That I couldn't share the feelings of my heart, though the girl in my arms was all I could think of lately?

When it was obvious that the magic between us had dampened, Emma Rose told me that she would be going home with the next round of girls who were being transported back to Llewelyn. She said she'd made plans to meet up with Isabella and that the two of them would be sharing a carriage back. Of course, I escorted her to the door. And then Tobias came with word that Mr. Pembroke, our headmaster, had been searching for me, so I left her after I said my goodbyes.

Why didn't I wait until she was safely ensconced in the carriage? Why couldn't I have stayed just a few moments longer?

I cannot remember much from the rest of that night. Only that, sometime later, a scream filled the hallways. I ran to the door from whence

*the sound came, only to see Isabella, clutching
her throat as she looked at something beyond my
vision, something in the snow off the path.*

*I rushed forward to lend my assistance
but stopped short when I saw what Isabella
was looking at. It was a crumpled form, in a
snowbank, in a darkened corner of the vast lawn.
The crimson silk was like a bloodstain against
the pure snow. When I looked closer, I saw that
her cheeks were no longer pink with health; her
skin was now the exact hue of the snow. Her
dark eyes, once so full of life and vivacity, were
open, unstaring, unblinking. A thin trickle of
blood leaked out one corner of her perfect mouth.
And around her neck was a cruel ring of night-
black bruises. The doll I'd given her lay facedown
beside her, a small bead of blood staining its back.
Without thinking, I picked it up and slipped it
into my pocket.*

*My Emma Rose. My darling, darling Emma
Rose. Who did this to you?*

*I will never forgive myself for deserting you
in your time of need. I am so deeply, deeply sorry.*

CHAPTER 46

March 27

The storm has enveloped us. As I look out at the world, washed out and without color, I imagine this is how I will feel for the rest of my days. No color can replace the pink of her cheeks. No sunlight can compare to the way her eyes sparkled. Why did she have to die? Of all people, why her? She was so pure, so very good.

I feel a raw, pulsing anger within me, cold and deep as the driven snow. A world without Emma Rose should have no color. It is right that all is cold and stark and white. We should all be buried, suffocated, forever.

March 28

Something quite odd is happening. People are slipping into long slumbers, from which they cannot be awakened. Mr. Pembroke, our headmaster, succumbed today. We cannot reach the outside world; we are utterly closed in. I cannot help but think this is just. If Emma Rose had to die the way she did, then we should all suffer for our evil.

March 30

> *The snow spins and whirls, dashing itself*
> *to the earth in pirouettes and hazy streams.*
> *I watch from my room, through the window.*
> *The storm is violently beautiful. It is my cold,*
> *hungry anger, made manifest. I clutch Emma*
> *Rose's doll close to my chest. I breathe sweet*
> *words of revenge in its ear. I tell Emma Rose*
> *that the world is suffering for what it did to her.*
> *Perhaps I will join her before long. I welcome*
> *the end, if it is coming for me, for I am so very*
> *tired. So very, very tired. Perhaps I can close my*
> *eyes, just for a bit.*
>
> *Good night, Emma Rose. I will be with you in*
> *my dreams, my love.*

Xander turned the page, but there wasn't any more. The rest of the blank sheets stared up at him, an unwritten story, a lifetime, paused.

He felt a lump in his throat he hadn't been expecting. "Holy shit." Putting the journal aside, Xander rubbed his numb face. Emma Rose . . . She'd been killed by Tobias Huntley, hadn't she? He could feel Atticus's pain and horror and anger and love through the pages, and he felt like he himself had seen Emma Rose lying there in the snow, her neck puffy and bruised from the hands of whoever had killed her. But that really wasn't so much a mystery anymore, was it?

Poor Atticus. Poor Emma Rose. And Tobias Huntley was never even brought to justice. He got to live out his full life, privileged and protected, while Atticus and Emma Rose had theirs snatched away from them. Xander felt a deep thrum of anger within him. So this was what had happened to Atticus. This was why generations of Xander's family had suffered, and continued to suffer. This was the genesis of why his mom had died. He'd take this book back to his family. He'd show them what had really happened. Sure, the genesis of the sleeping sickness was still a mystery, but at least he knew now how Atticus had passed his last hours. That was more than any of his family had ever known. He hoped he could deliver some sense of peace.

Outside, the wind whooped. Xander looked up, jerked back into this reality. What if his family instead was left mourning his own death at the end of all this? He'd come here to find answers, to bring them some peace, but now it was looking like . . .

He thought of Atticus's last written words. *I am so very tired. . . . Good night, Emma Rose.*

Goose bumps ran up Xander's arms and legs. He couldn't let that happen. He had to solve this thing. He had to get them out of this. Atticus's journal hadn't shed light on how he might do that, but now that he knew Atticus had faced a storm just like this, with the sleeping sickness claiming people . . .

But what could he do? How could he protect everyone? DE's face flashed before his eyes, and he imagined her cold and still, lying in her bed, unable to waken . . .

No. He wouldn't let that happen. He was going to stop this thing. He'd figure it out. Somehow. Xander stood from his chair, his muscles bunching with energy, with purpose. But in the next moment, he felt exhausted. Maybe it was reading about all that Atticus had been through, what poor Emma Rose had had to endure. He sat back down slowly and stifled a yawn.

DE

The wing holding the teachers' quarters was located on the south side of the main building, attached to the building by a glass walkway. On a nice day, when it was light out, you could enjoy the sights of the Rosetta Academy campus's rolling hills and precisely manicured jewel-green lawns as you walked the length of it. Now, however, it was dark and cold and gloomy, the many inches of snow pressed against the sides and the ceiling of the walkway turning it into a long, white coffin.

DE huddled into her sweater as she strode along, feeling the icy cold reach into her body and wrap itself around her bones. It was like the storm itself was creeping into her, claiming her. She shuddered at the thought.

The walkway shook with the force of the wind, rocking slightly in its foundation. Was it just her or did the storm seem more . . . malignant now? Like it was gaining strength and momentum?

Shaking her head, DE refocused her mind on the task at hand. She couldn't afford to become distracted, and she definitely couldn't afford to let her fear take over. Things had to be dealt with.

She walked into the warmth of the teachers' wing with a shudder and a sigh, her body relaxing and thawing as it came in out of the cold. On the wall to her left was a series of small gold nameplates, indicating which teachers currently lived in the wing and which rooms they occupied. She ran her finger down the list and stopped at B. Blackmoor, Room 4A. That was up in the turret.

With renewed vigor, DE turned and marched to the far end,

where there were stairs that would take her up to the turret room of the wing. The turret room was the least favorable of all the teachers' residences, DE knew, and was generally reserved for new or temporary teachers. DE climbed the stairs, feeling her anger heating up all over again.

At the top, Ms. Blackmoor's door was closed. DE banged on it with a closed fist, holding nothing back. "Ms. Blackmoor! Open up!"

A moment later, she heard quiet footsteps, and then the door swung open. Ms. Blackmoor stood in the doorway, her expression neither surprised nor annoyed. She looked serene, as if a student beating on her door, demanding for her to open it, was an everyday occurrence.

"Hello, DE." She smiled a little, folding her hands neatly over her long skirt. Her hair was still in that old-fashioned bun, and she looked as if she'd been enjoying a pleasant evening in her room in spite of the chaos all around her. "How can I be of assistance?"

CHAPTER 47

DE

DE sputtered. "How can you 'be of assistance'? Are you kidding? Do you have any idea what's going on out there?" She thrust her arm in the general direction of the main building.

"I do," Ms. Blackmoor replied, her face solemn. Then she opened the door wider. "Why don't you come in?"

DE brushed past her, walking into the small (by Rosetta standards) room. Unlike the extravagance of the student dorms, which were filled with designer furniture and ornate wood-work, this one was plain and neat, a pile of books on a desk the only real clutter she could see. There was a cup of tea beside an armchair by the window, steam curling up and above it like a soft white hand. The room smelled like jasmine and sage.

Turning to Ms. Blackmoor, DE said, "All the other teachers have been affected by the sleeping sickness. And I noticed you weren't among them." The empty twelfth chair at the conference table. It had been meant for Ms. Blackmoor. So why wasn't she there? Why was she here, sipping tea and reading a book without a care in the world?

Ms. Blackmoor gazed steadily at her with those colorless eyes. "Do you have a question?"

DE huffed a laugh. The woman was incredible. "Um, yeah. The question is: What the hell is going on? Why have you been spared when none of the others have? Why did you have the folder we needed in that weird little back room of yours, and why did it land in the middle of the floor, as if it had been placed there for us to find? Why did the psychic say the same thing that's in Atticus's journal?" She hadn't meant to blurt the last question out loud, but there it was all the same. It was a question that had been floating around in her mind all evening, ever since Xander had told her what he'd read.

"Why don't you have a seat?" Ms. Blackmoor gestured at the armchair. "I could brew you some tea. Would you like that?"

"No, I wouldn't." But DE took a seat anyway. She was really tired. She couldn't remember the last good night's sleep she'd had. "I just want to know what the fuck is going on."

The teacher studied her appraisingly. "You know, you don't look well."

"Wow, you're observant. Maybe I don't look well because people I care about are falling into weird-ass comas and I have no idea what to do about it. And right now, you're the only adult awake apart from a few eighteen-year-old seniors." DE was being undeniably rude, but she couldn't help it. All the emotions she'd been feeling, all the things she'd been bottling up, were rushing to the surface.

Ms. Blackmoor remained unflappable, however. "And what would you like me to do about it, DE? I assume that's why you're here? To ask for something?"

DE leaned forward, clasping her hands together between her knees. "I want to know what your role is in all this."

The teacher sighed and took a seat in a wooden chair that had been pushed into her desk, turning it first to face DE. "And why do you think I play *any* role in all of this?"

"I'm not stupid. You weren't present with all the other teachers when we found them in comas. And then I got to thinking . . . I haven't really seen you do *any*thing since this all started. You've been on the sidelines, watching, observing, but not much else. You know more than you're letting on. Am I right?" She held her breath. The truth was, she'd come here on a wing and a prayer. There was nothing concrete she could hold up to say that Ms. Blackmoor was definitively involved in any of this.

Ms. Blackmoor gazed at DE, steadily and without any inflection of expression. It was like the woman felt none of it—none of the fear, the anxiety, the uncertainty, that had enveloped everyone else.

"Fine." DE stood. "Then I guess we've got nothing to talk about." She strode to the door.

When her hand was on the doorknob, Ms. Blackmoor spoke softly. "Where are you going, DE?"

"I'm going into town," DE said. "I'm going to find that stupid psychic I talked to, who warned me of a storm."

Ms. Blackmoor didn't blink. "How are you going to brave the winds and the snow?"

DE threw up her hands. "I have a coat! I'll figure it out! And if I die of hypothermia, at least that'll be better than sitting around waiting for something to happen to me and all the rest of the people I care about."

Ms. Blackmoor smiled at that. "You're brave, aren't you?"

DE rolled her eyes. "Spare me the pep talk, okay?" She turned to go again.

"Stop."

Turning to face her teacher, DE narrowed her eyes. "Why?"

"Because I have something I'd like to show you."

Her voice was somber, and it carried a weight to it that had DE walking back to the armchair to take a seat. Her palms had begun to sweat, though she didn't know why. There was a strange energy in the room now, a crackling kind of intensity that made the hairs on the back of DE's neck stir.

Once DE was seated, Ms. Blackmoor held her arms out to either side. "I am one with many names," she said, her voice suddenly not her own at all. It was like two or three or a dozen women were speaking at once, all of their voices coming from Ms. Blackmoor's throat. "I am one with many faces." Suddenly DE wasn't looking at Ms. Blackmoor at all. She was looking at an old, bent-over woman, her silver hair covered with a scarf. In a flash, before DE could react, she changed to a tall, statuesque woman, with odd purple eyes and black hair. Another blink and she was the psychic Madame Olivera, a veil over her face, her eyes glittering behind it.

DE gasped. "What—how . . . ?" She wanted to run. Her blood was ice in her veins, her skin rippling with goose bumps as the thrill of fear took hold. But no matter how she tried, she couldn't force herself out of the chair. Each limb weighed a thousand pounds.

DE shook her head, back and forth, back and forth, hoping some ray of light would pierce through the fog in her brain. "Who *are* you?"

CHAPTER 48

DE

Ms. Blackmoor studied DE for a moment. "If I asked you who *you* are, what would you say? Maybe something about your personality traits, or the fact that you're a student, or perhaps your family's lineage. But if I asked you where you came from, what the genesis of *you* is, which I suspect is what you're asking me, could you answer? I don't think so. 'You' are a concept that's fully formed in your mind, and yet you have no clue about your early years, do you? You don't remember your birth or how you came to be."

DE nodded.

"I'm the same way," Ms. Blackmoor continued. "I don't remember a time when I wasn't. I don't remember how I came to be. I consider myself a guardian of the Academy. But other than that, I have no answers for you."

DE swallowed, her throat making a dry, clicking noise. She didn't know whether to be terrified or intrigued. "Did you cause the storm? And the sleeping sickness?" It was a legitimate question. She had no idea what Ms. Blackmoor was capable of. *If she caused the storm, if she caused all this misery to my friends, I'm going to kill her,* she decided. She didn't care if Ms. Blackmoor was an all-powerful witch or demon or whatever the hell she was. She'd die trying to take her down.

But Ms. Blackmoor only shook her head. "No, Daphne Elizabeth. I'm not responsible. But something you hold near to you is."

DE frowned, confused. "What do you m—" she began, and then it came to her in a flash. She pulled the change doll out of her pocket. "Are you talking about this?"

Ms. Blackmoor nodded solemnly, her gaze on the doll, wary, focused.

Still confused, DE looked down at the doll. Its faceless head, its nubby arms and legs, the coin sewed into it. It looked utterly harmless to her. But then realization began to dawn, slowly, like sunlight seeping into the sky. "Wait a minute. The square piece of paper Madame Ol—you—gave me. It said something about how the blood of lost souls will begin the storm. And I pricked my finger on the doll the day I got her."

Ms. Blackmoor just looked at her, waiting.

"And Xander!" DE continued, the realizations coming hard and fast now. "He said Atticus had given Emma Rose a special doll before she died. It was this doll, wasn't it? Xander thought it might be." She paused and took a breath, her pulse racing, her thoughts all jumbled. "But I don't understand. How is this doll responsible for everything that's happened? The storm, the sleeping sickness . . . ?"

Ms. Blackmoor sat in her chair again, sighing, a sound that reminded DE of wind blowing through old trees. "Atticus Wakefield. After Emma Rose died, his life was barren, he himself a frozen husk of a young man. His love for her was immense; his anger at her death even more so. It consumed him. He couldn't move on, couldn't find a single reason to go on living. He died of a broken heart. But not before he whispered into the doll's ears about his hatred of the world that had taken his precious Emma Rose from him. Not before he breathed a soul into the doll. Emma Rose's blood was already bound to the doll. And when you found it, Daphne Elizabeth, you pricked your finger, adding your blood to hers. You awakened the curse that Atticus had begun all those years ago. The curse of lost souls, of unrequited love."

DE's heart pounded. She had so many questions, but she felt her time running out. All of their time running out. All those people in the infirmary, all the people yet to make it in there. "So, okay. When I came to visit you in the psychic store, you said I held the key to vanquishing this storm."

"You do."

"What key? What does that mean? Is it a literal key? Or is that, like, a metaphor?"

Ms. Blackmoor studied her with an infuriatingly blank expression.

DE threw her hands up. "Come on! You have to give me *some*-thing! Atticus died—are people here going to die too?"

Ms. Blackmoor got up from her chair, picked it up, and moved it close to DE. When she sat again, their knees were almost touching. Leaning forward, Ms. Blackmoor took both of DE's hands in her own cool, dry ones. "Not *people*, DE. Just one person. If you don't vanquish the storm, one person will die. The rest will awaken when this is all over, remembering almost nothing of it at all."

"One will perish," DE muttered, remembering part of the prophecy, the part that had made her extremely uneasy. "Who?"

Her lips felt wooden, immovable. "Who's going to die?" The possibilities unspooled in her head like a horror movie she couldn't turn off. Which of her friends would she lose? Whose death would be her fault? Jaya's? Grey's? Xander's?

When Ms. Blackmoor didn't respond, DE looked up into her eyes. They were watchful, but full of sadness and . . . pity. With a shock, DE realized why.

XANDER

Tick. Tock. Tick. Tock.

Xander sat up straighter in his chair, his eyes dry and gritty, stiff muscles creaking in his body. Blinking, he gazed blearily at the clock on the wall. Holy hell. He'd been sitting here, staring at nothing, for close to an hour. It was late evening now. Maybe he needed caffeine. Dining hall. He'd go get some coffee from the dining hall. He needed to do *something*.

He wasn't just going to sit around hoping that something would happen, that someone would help. The so-called adults had all succumbed to this weird sleeping sickness. How long before the rest of the people at Rosetta Academy did too?

A flash of DE's beautiful face, slack and drained of vivacity, flew through his mind. He couldn't allow that to happen.

Xander forced his stiff legs upright, forced himself to focus. He would go to Atticus's dorm room, pick it apart, rip up the floorboards if he had to. *Some*thing down there had to give him a clue about how to stop this storm, how to set things right again. He knew from Atticus's journal that the sleeping sickness had gone through Rosetta Academy back in Atticus's time too. So there *had* to be something in those old dorm rooms that would light the way to a solution, right?

It was the only thing he had. His Hail Mary pass. Maybe it was ridiculous, but this whole situation was ridiculous. Xander walked to his door. But the moment his hand was on the doorknob, he was overcome by a fatigue so intense, it actually made him woozy. The world swam.

"Whoa." He tottered backward, his limbs feeling like they were filled with wet cement. He could barely move. "What the hell?" He was mumbling now, he realized, his words running together, hardly audible.

Trying to fight through it, he attempted to reach for the doorknob again. He had to help DE. He had to.

But it was pointless. As if of their own accord, his limbs kept moving him backward. Like his body knew he couldn't keep going or he'd collapse.

Xander walked to his bed, sitting down quickly as his knees buckled. "I . . . can't . . . I need to . . ." But he couldn't finish his thought. It took too much energy. Maybe he'd just lie down. Just for a bit, just until he felt a little stronger.

Just a little nap.

CHAPTER 49

DE

She stumbled back down the walkway to the main building. DE barely remembered leaving Ms. Blackmoor's—or *whoever* she was—room. She huddled into her sweater, cold spots blooming behind her chest, her stomach, in her thighs. She felt the storm might possibly consume her, a hungry beast with its jaws wide open, a black maw she'd slide down and never crawl back out of.

All the stuff that Ms. Blackmoor had told her—it was insane. It was completely, 100 percent Grimms' fairy-tale shit. And yet she'd been right about so much. She'd known about the doll. She had *changed her appearance* right in front of DE. And so, DE had no choice but to believe it. An ancient curse, put in place by Atticus Wakefield and his pain, had taken hold of Rosetta Academy. And now someone was going to die.

The fatigue creeping into her limbs made her feel like she weighed as much as a planet. An entire galaxy. And yet she kept marching forward through sheer force of will, knowing she had to get back to the dorms. She had to.

I've never fallen in love.

The thought zipped through her mind before she could stop it. But was that really true?

As she walked unseeing down the length of that gloomy, icy walkway, DE thought about the last few weeks. To be honest, she'd been happier than she'd been ever since . . . no. She'd been about to think *ever since she and Alaric broke up*. But that wasn't really true, she realized. These last few weeks had been her best weeks since ever. The storm had dampened her happiness some-what, of course, but underneath it all, underneath the stress and the fear, she'd still felt treasured. Respected. Seen. Heard. Loved. For the very first time in her life, she'd felt important. She'd felt like she mattered. She'd begun to realize that maybe, just maybe, she had inherent worth as a person. That she was worth time and attention. And that was, in large part, thanks to Xander Murthy.

As she pushed her way into the warmth of the main building, DE thought about how he'd put himself out there—twice—to tell her how he felt. And how, each time, she'd turned away from him.

She could feel the fatigue beginning to weigh her eyelids down; she felt her breathing slow. She knew what was happen-ing. The curse had her in its arms; it was cradling her, crooning an eldritch lullaby. It wouldn't be long now. Right then, climbing the stairs to the senior wing, DE knew what she had to do.

As she wound her way past the senior common room and the senior floor kitchenette, DE realized something hazily. She hadn't seen a single person since she'd walked into the main building. Sure, student and teacher numbers were depleted right now, but she'd usually at least see a few students, gathered together, talking worriedly about everything that was going on. Currently, though, it was quiet as a tomb.

Frowning, her mind fuzzy, she walked to the first dorm room and knocked on the door. No response. She tried the door, found it unlocked, and peeked her head in. Trenton Ashwood, the senior who lived there, was lying on his bed, his hands neatly by his sides. His face was placid and still.

"Trenton?" DE called, noting the querulous sound to her voice. She blinked hard, trying to focus past the fatigue, past the confusion, past the fuzziness. But Trenton didn't move.

Fear clotting the back of her throat, DE stumbled to the next dorm room. Knocked. No response. Inside, another senior lay on his bed, asleep, a copy of the Bible in one limp hand. The next room held a senior girl, her windows covered over with thick quilts and bedspreads, like she'd been afraid the storm would burst in and get her. It had gotten her anyway.

DE stumbled, almost falling multiple times, the length of the hallway, knocking on doors, opening them, checking on the people inside. Asleep. Every one of them. Even Rahul. Even Caterina.

On legs that felt like melting rubber, DE walked the length of the hallway to Xander's room. She could hear her own heartbeat, thudding slowly, painfully against her rib cage. Her blood, trying to rush, rush, rush through veins clogged with slush. Her breath, quavering, gasping, choking. Her vision tunneled until all she could see was what was right in front of her: Xander's room, his dresser, his bed.

And on the bed . . . Xander.

DE stood above him, looking down at his sleeping body. He looked completely still, motionless. His strong hands, those piano-player-esque hands she'd so admired, were limp on his chest, thick eyelashes resting on his sallow, waxen cheeks. There was a hint of stubble on his jaw, just a subtle darkening of the skin there. His chest rose and fell with each breath, but barely. He was still Xander, but barely.

Her legs suddenly giving way, DE dropped down next to him. The change doll rolled out of her pocket, though it had been snug in there, and lay against a wrinkle on the bed, seemingly watchful. DE's hand hovered above Xander's for a second before she covered his freezing fingers with her own chilly ones. Burning remorse filled her up, its flames licking at her slowing heart, eating her alive. Why hadn't she been more honest with him, with herself, sooner? Why hadn't she seen what she saw now—that loving someone was an act of strength? How had she let this happen to them?

"Oh, Xander." Her voice was just a whisper in the quiet room. She couldn't even hear his breathing. "I'm so sorry. I'm so, so sorry."

Outside the window on the far side of the room, the storm had gone quiet.

"I should've told you this before—when you kissed me, or when you were brave enough to tell me how you felt." She swallowed, struggling against the encroaching blackness that was at the corners of her vision now. "But I didn't, not because I didn't feel the same way, but because I was afraid. And somehow I hadn't stopped to consider a greater truth: that never giving your heart away at all is a way scarier prospect than having your heart broken. Having your heart broken means you took a chance; it means you tried something. That you decided to be an optimist in a world that would much rather you be a cynic."

Stopping to take a deep, almost painful breath, she went on, gazing at his beautiful, still face like she could memorize every curve, every plane, every divot and freckle. "I couldn't see it then, but you came into my life when I needed someone to show me a different way. When I needed someone to shine a little light on me and whom I could shine my own light back on. We were destined to meet, Xander—I believe this with my whole heart. You changed me. By looking at me differently, by seeing me for who I truly am, you helped me see myself that way too. And I realize something now I'd never realized before: I don't need *anyone* to validate me. I don't need my parents or a boyfriend or my friends to show me I'm worth something, because I can see it for myself. I don't need anyone to piece me back together because I'm *not* broken. And because I'm not broken, because I'm not in pieces, I can give you my whole heart. I *want* to give you my whole heart." Her voice gave way as she spoke. "But now it's too late."

"You deserved better," DE continued, even as it got harder to hold her head up, to keep her lips moving. "You deserved better from me, and I'm sorry. You deserved the truth." She smoothed his hair back with a shaking hand. "The truth is, Xander, that I love you. I know that probably sounds completely unbelievable; we've only known each other a few weeks. But I think our hearts knew maybe what I didn't, or couldn't, see. That we are—we were—a perfect match." She sniffed, her eyes growing hot. "I'm sorry I didn't see that in time. I'm sorry this is where we are now."

Her tears spilled onto her cheeks then, hot and furious. "I don't know how much longer I have, Xander, so I better say this quickly: I love you, I love you, I love you. And wherever I'm going, whatever's next for me, I'll carry you with me. Always."

Before she lost her nerve, DE leaned over and kissed Xander tenderly, gently, on the lips. His mouth was soft and still, his breath barely brushing against her own mouth. She couldn't help but think of the last time they'd kissed: how alive she'd felt, how vibrant he'd been, how she'd refused to see it. And now it was all gone. Her tears rained down on his dark skin, sparkling like dewdrops where they landed.

Pulling her knees up to her chest, DE lay down next to Xander and closed her eyes. A yawn took hold of her, her whole body shuddering with a deep, heavy weariness she'd never felt before. Whatever was next, she was ready.

CHAPTER 50

XANDER

Tranquil. That's mainly what Xander felt when he woke up. He felt refreshed, like the debris of life had been washed off his soul or something. Whatever, he wasn't a poet. The feeling, though, was quickly overshadowed by confusion.

First, he was in all his clothes, and he always showered and undressed before turning in for the night. Second, and this was the bigger thing—DE was in his bed.

He stared down at her still form, wondering whether he was dreaming. The last thing he remembered was . . . Xander's eyebrows knitted together. Weird. He couldn't actually remember too much from the night before. Just a fuzzy, hazy sense that he'd been really, really tired.

His eyes caught on something on the bed, something that didn't belong. The change doll. It was lying a foot away from him, and though it didn't have eyes, he could've sworn he felt watched. He picked it up, turning it over, noticing the speck of blood where DE had pricked her finger and the other bead of dried blood that belonged to Emma Rose. It was weird. DE had told him before that the doll had made her feel a deep, vast sadness when they first found it. But now all he felt was . . . a sense of peace. A sense of *rightness* in the world.

He set the doll down and turned his attention back to DE, touching a finger to her cheek. It was cool, and she was very, very still. "DE?" he whispered, smoothing a strand of hair off her forehead. "Hey."

For a long minute, he watched her. Nothing happened. She didn't stir.

Xander's heart began to thud. The sleeping sickness. It came back to him in a flash. Everyone had been falling asleep, even the teachers. It had been accelerating, hadn't it? The psychic had said someone would die. . . . His mouth suddenly dry, Xander touched DE's shoulder and shook her. "DE. DE!"

And then—a small, soft sigh. Fluttering eyelashes. The next moment, she was looking up at him with those wild green eyes. "Xander?"

He exhaled in a rush, his eyes closing in sheer, blissful relief. Then he smiled, touched the tip of her nose. "Yeah. Yeah. It's me."

Her hand floated up to his face, an answering smile at her lips. "It's you. It's really you."

DE

Ten minutes after she woke up, DE and Xander were sitting up in his bed. He looked like she felt—a bit tired and slightly rumpled but mostly refreshed. As if she'd just had a really nice two-hour nap.

DE rested her back against the headboard and looked at him,

where he sat cross-legged across from her. They didn't touch, but she was painfully aware that she was on his *bed* and that he was mere inches away from her. And that she'd admitted she loved him. "How much do you remember?" she asked him, playing with the edge of the pillowcase. "I mean, from before you fell asleep . . . and after?"

Xander, who'd been smiling at her for the last ten minutes in a mysterious way she couldn't decipher, frowned at her question. "Hmm, let's see. I remember feeling really tired. Like, *really* tired. I wanted to go . . . somewhere, I can't remember where, but I couldn't. I fell into my bed and then . . ." He blew out a breath. "It felt a lot like falling asleep when you have a fever or something."

DE nodded; that's what she remembered about being overcome by the sickness too. "And, um . . ." She licked her suddenly dry lips. "You don't have any memories of anything after that?" Looking up at him through her eyelashes, she asked, "Specifically to do with me?"

Her heart thudded as she waited what felt like ten million years for Xander's response. His golden eyes searched the space above her head, that full mouth pursed. He shook his head. "I don't—" But then he stopped, his gaze snapping back to meet hers.

Oh god, oh god, oh god.

"DE." His voice was low, controlled. "I remember. I remember everything."

"Everything?" DE was not proud of the way her voice squeaked, but there it was. She was a squeaker in times of romantic stress, apparently.

Xander's eyes, burning an intense gold, didn't waver from hers. "I thought it was a dream, but it wasn't, was it? You said you weren't broken. That you were willing to open your heart to me. And you said . . ." He paused, still gazing steadily at her, and DE felt something warm puddling in her stomach. "You said you loved me."

She forced herself not to look away. "Yes," she said (squeaked). "I did." She swallowed. "I do."

A muscle in his jaw ticked. "You do? You're sure? You're sure I'm what you want?"

DE nodded before he was done speaking. "I've never been more sure. Xander, I—"

In the next moment he moved forward on the bed, kneeling before her. He scooped her up in his arms and kissed her, each breath, each press of his tongue, each pounding heartbeat against her own chest saying what she'd wanted, needed to hear all this time: *You're what I want too, DE. You're all I need.*

He pulled back from her a moment later, cheeks flushed, eyes overbright, a grin on his face that made her heart ache and want to explode into a thousand points of light at the same time. "I love you, McKinley. I love you, I love you, I love you."

She pressed her forehead against his, eyes closing, a tear dripping past her eyelashes down her cheek. This was what pure happiness felt like. This was belonging. This was home.

CHAPTER 51

DE

DE looked around at her friends disbelievingly. "So none of you remember *any*thing? The big storm, being closed off from the outside world, people falling asleep . . . ?"

They were all sitting at their usual table in the chaotic senior dining hall. The musical sound of cutlery clinking and bouncing off the high ceilings, the swell of laughter and chatter around them, someone spilling their coffee on the floor and yelling out a very creative expletive, the absolute, human *mess* of it all—DE let herself revel in it just a little bit. She never thought she'd hear it all again.

And then there were her friends. Her beautiful, glowing, *healthy* friends. Jaya and Grey were ensconced together, as usual, Caterina had her head on Rahul's shoulder, and Leo was whispering something into Will's ear and making him chuckle. Xander sat beside DE, holding her hand in his lap.

Jaya tossed her waterfall braid over her shoulder. "I remember feeling tired," she said, frowning a little. "And when I woke up, I felt . . . really, really refreshed. Content about everything. But that's it."

Grey rubbed her back absently with one hand, tucking into his sandwich with the other. "Pretty much my experience."

"Yeah, me too," Leo called out, looking up from Will for a second.

DE was completely flummoxed. Ms. Blackmoor had told her that people wouldn't really remember it, but this was unreal. It was like she'd lived a completely different previous week than everyone around her.

"My theory is that this was all a gas leak," Rahul said. "It would explain people falling asleep, the amnesia, all of it."

A gas leak. For the first time, DE wondered if that really was what they were all experiencing. Just a gas leak. But she'd seen what Ms. Blackmoor had done; how she'd changed. *But*, a tiny voice whispered in her mind, *couldn't that have been a result of hallucinations caused by a gas leak?* She shook her head. She could spend the rest of her life trying to figure it all out.

"I'm glad our memories are intact," Xander said quietly, a beautiful, private smile on his face, one reserved just for her.

She looked into those golden sand-dune eyes and felt an immense wave of gratitude wash over her. God, she was so *lucky*. After their moment on Xander's bed, she'd asked if he'd consider coming to New Hampshire with her in the fall, since she'd be attending Dartmouth and he had no plans as of yet. And he'd said yes. Without hesitation, without preamble, he'd said yes.

Well, what he'd *actually* said was, *I'd follow you to the ends of the earth, DE.* And then he'd kissed her again, making her melt against him.

Just thinking about it made her grin so hard, her cheeks hurt.

"Hey," Jaya said, tapping the back of her hand, bringing DE back to reality. "Want to get another coffee?"

DE smiled at her and scraped her chair back. "Yeah, sure." Turning to Xander, she said, "Be right back."

When they were waiting in line at the marble counter (the storm had blown over last night, and Dr. Waverly had assured them that staffing would resume to previous standards so students wouldn't have to wait in line, but that was still days in the future), Jaya turned to DE. Her big brown eyes shiny, she grabbed DE in a tight, almost painful hug that DE returned, her own eyes closed, tears threatening at the corners.

"I can't believe this," Jaya said a moment later when they pulled apart, shaking her head. "I was really in a *coma*."

DE nodded, swallowing against the lump in her throat. A group of seniors passed by them, shouting and laughing, and she waited till they were gone to respond. "Yeah. It was . . . it was terrifying, J. I thought I was going to lose you. And I realized— you're my sister. I don't know what I'd do if you ever . . ." She couldn't finish her thought, so she just nibbled her lower lip. "I don't *want* to know."

Jaya gathered her in a hug again, and DE relished the feeling of her warmth, of DE's chin pressing into the top of her head. "You won't have to," Jaya said firmly, pulling back again. They moved forward with the rest of the line, their hands grasped tightly together. "We're going to video chat all the time and visit each other as often as we can. Right?"

DE nodded vigorously. "Hell yeah, we are. Even after you and Grey get married."

Jaya rolled her eyes. "We've talked about that. That's eons away." She tossed a sly look over her shoulder at their dining table. "Although . . . maybe that's not true for you and Xander, hmm?" She waggled her eyebrows suggestively.

DE laughed and shook her head. "Stop it." She met her friend's eye and bit her bottom lip. "I *do* love him, though," she said quietly, afraid of saying it out loud, afraid things were too fragile, too dreamlike, liable to pop like an iridescent, fleeting soap bubble. "And he loves me too."

"As he should," Jaya said, beaming. "You're a catch and a half, Daphne Elizabeth McKinley. And I'm so fucking happy for you that you can finally see it."

DE gasped and clutched at her imaginary pearls. "Is that language befitting a princess, Jaya Rao?"

Laughing, they slung their arms around each other's shoulders, knowing this friendship would last a lifetime.

When DE and Jaya took their seats back at the table, the others were talking about Xander's family.

"I'm just so glad we found Atticus's journal," Xander said, threading his fingers with DE's as soon as she sat down. Man, she could get used to that. "I think it's going to help my family a lot."

DE sat up straighter and gestured to the rest of the table. "Oh, speaking of, tell them what you got Rosetta Academy to do."

It had only been a full day since everyone woke up, but Xander hadn't wasted any time talking to Dr. Waverly. Now, smiling, he looked around at their friends. "Oh, I just showed them Atticus's journal, what he'd said about Tobias Huntley and how Emma Rose had died. They were able to put two and two together. I mean, it was pretty obvious what had happened."

DE looked around the table, her face glowing. "And because of Xander, they're renaming Huntley Hall to Wakefield Hall. And they're going to rename the hill as well."

"Wow." Leo looked impressed. "That's about the happiest ending you could get from all this, huh?"

"Yep." Xander lifted DE's hand and kissed her knuckles. "It's a happy ending, all right."

Later, as they walked together out of the dining room, Xander grabbed her wrist gently.

"Hey." He spun her around, and she put her arms around his neck, smiling. "I'm glad I found you, McKinley."

DE grinned. "I'm glad I found *you*, Murthy. And you know what?" She tipped her head back, letting the sounds of Rosetta Academy—students laughing, greeting, teasing, talking to friends who'd become family to them—warm her skin through to her bones. "I'm so glad I found me too."

DE

After lunch that day, DE dragged Xander through the walkway to the teachers' quarters. She couldn't help but think back to her last walk through here: the bitter cold, the feeling that she'd never emerge from the darkness. And now it was all sunshine and warmth, bright colors and a literal bounce in her step. There were birds twittering in the trees outside, and their song lifted her soul, made her want to believe in magic.

Xander asked, "Where are we going?"

"I need to speak to Ms. Blackmoor." DE hadn't seen the teacher since everyone had woken up, and she needed to visit her, to ask her why DE hadn't died, why it had all worked out in the end. And maybe that'd help her figure out if this all *had* just been a toxic-fume-induced waking nightmare as well.

They climbed the turret, and DE knocked on the door. There was a shuffling inside, and then the door opened. A small Asian woman in her sixties with cropped silver hair and brown eyes stood before them. She smiled. "Hi, DE. Xander. To what do I owe this pleasure?"

DE stared at this woman she'd never seen before. "Uh . . . Ms. Blackmoor?"

The woman's smile got a little confused. "Yes? DE, are you all right?"

DE looked from the strange woman to Xander, who was watching DE with curiosity. "This is Ms. Blackmoor?"

Xander nodded slowly, as if he thought this was a trick of some kind. "Yeah?"

DE turned back to the woman, forced a smile. "I'm sorry to have bothered you. I forgot what I was going to ask."

The woman laughed. "Well, that's all right. Happens to me several times a day. Getting old is no fun, I tell you. I'll see you in class?"

DE and Xander nodded. As DE turned away, Ms. Blackmoor— the new Ms. Blackmoor—winked at her and, with a smile full of secrets, shut the door with a firm click.

When they were back in the walkway, Xander looked at her. "What was that all about?"

But DE just shook her head. How could she explain? "Nothing," she said, gnawing on her lower lip. "Nothing at all."

XANDER

That night, he stood in the middle of the cool attic, under the single dim light bulb, looking at DE in her oversized sweater, leggings, and boots. It had been so recently—and also eons ago—that they'd stood just like this, with her accusing him of being a creep. He smiled a little at the memory.

"Thinking of how I fell on my ass when we first met?" she asked, cocking one eyebrow.

Grinning now, he pulled her into his arms, his hands cinching her waist. He was lost in a sea of green. "Thinking about how I fell in love with you right then and there. I was just too stuck in my own head to see it."

Her cheeks were stained that pretty pink that drove him mad, visible to him even in the muted light. He was learning every bit of her, and the thought made him delirious with joy. "Mmm. Nice save, Murthy."

They kissed, Xander reveling in the velvet softness of her mouth, the delicate curve of her jaw. When they pulled apart, he murmured, "You sure about this?"

With a creak of the wooden floorboards, DE stepped out of

the circle of his arms and looked around the attic—*their* attic. "You know, I am." She sighed. "I'm not going to hide up here anymore. There's no need for me to hide anywhere. It doesn't matter who else thought I *should* be kept hidden—my parents . . . Alaric. Well, fuck them. I'm giving all that a big middle finger and I'm going to live my life in full color, in the spotlight or not, as I see fit. My life, my rules."

Xander couldn't help the beaming smile that crossed his face. "I love you."

"And I love you."

Xander took a breath. From his pocket, he pulled out the square piece of paper with the silver snowflake on one side. "I brought something to leave up here. As a goodbye to Atticus and Emma Rose, to the storm, to your psychic, whoever she was."

He walked over to one of the wooden trunks on the far side of the attic, where he'd rummaged around for blueprints once. Opening the trunk carefully, he slipped the paper inside and then let it close with a satisfying click. Turning to DE, he dusted off his hands. "There. Atticus's story is done. This chapter in my life is closed. And I hope it'll give some closure to my family, too. We don't have to keep going down old rabbit holes, and we don't have to stay lost in the sea of grief. We can move on. We can heal, if we choose to."

DE smiled a little, something like pride and understanding lighting her eyes. "Yes, we can."

She stuffed her hands into the pockets of her long sweater and then paused, her face contorting into a funny expression. When she pulled her right hand back out, it was holding the change doll.

Xander blinked, wondering if he was seeing things in the dim light. "Is that . . . ?"

DE looked at the doll, and it appeared to be studying her right back. "It's you," she said quietly. "Well, hello again." Huffing a small laugh, she shook her head. "Told you. This thing has a mind of its own."

"Maybe it just wants to be put to rest too. Now that it's done what it was intended to."

"Yeah. Maybe." DE walked over to the steamer trunk by the small diamond-shaped window, the one she used as a window seat. "I'll set you right here. So you can keep an eye out for other storms. Warn other people who may need it." Propping the doll against the corner, she ran a finger down its head. "Thanks for everything."

Then she turned to Xander. "Ready?"

He nodded. "Ready."

Once they picked their way down the ancient wooden stairs to the other side of the trapdoor, DE hoisted the padlock and chains they'd brought with them and set on the floor in preparation. She grinned. "Let's do this."

The new chains and padlock hung from the trapdoor, jangling lightly as DE and Xander made their way down the servants' quarter stairs for the last time, shoes clicking along the dull gray cement. At the bottom of the stairway was a door with the word EXIT above it.

DE paused for a minute, turning to Xander. He was already watching her, a faint smile at those lips, eyes locked on hers.

Taking a deep breath, DE pushed the door open, and they stepped outside together, into the sunshine, their fingers intertwining as the door behind them shut with a final *thunk*.

The world was alive today. The sun had bloomed to a happy

ball of glowing heat, and the evergreen trees were blooming with birds and squirrels, creatures blinking and yawning and coming back from hibernation. Much like DE and Xander and everyone else at Rosetta. The vast grounds of the Academy sprawled beyond, green grass covered under sparkling snow that was rapidly melting now that the storm had passed.

DE squeezed Xander's fingers and gazed at him. "Where do we go from here?"

Dipping his head to brush his lips against hers, he replied, "Anywhere we want."

ACKNOWLEDGMENTS

I am so happy that the third book in the Rosetta Academy series is now done and in the hands of my wonderful readers! I hope I've done DE justice and that you fall in love with her and the rest of the Rosetta crew just as much as I have over the course of three books.

As always, I'm so thankful to my agent Thao Le, my editor Kendra Levin, and the rest of the team at S&S BFYR for being such stalwart champions and cheerleaders.

Big hugs to my family (especially my daughter), who kept asking questions about the Rosetta Academy universe and made me extra eager to write DE's story. I hope I've done you proud!

And lastly, gratitude as ever to my sweet, lovely readers—especially the Sandhya's Sweethearts street team members—who are my why. I would not be living the life I'd dreamed of as an elementary school kid without you guys. Thanks for letting me spend my days telling stories!

ABOUT THE AUTHOR

Sandhya Menon is the *New York Times* bestselling author of *When Dimple Met Rishi*, *Of Curses and Kisses*, and many other novels that also feature lots of kissing, girl power, and swoony boys. Her books have been included in several cool places, including *Today*, *Teen Vogue*, NPR, *BuzzFeed*, and *Seventeen*. A full-time dog servant and writer, she makes her home in the foggy mountains of Colorado. Visit her online at SandhyaMenon.com.